Fallen Eagle: Alaska Front

Published by John J. Rust at Createspace

Copyright © 2016 John J. Rust

Other books by John J. Rust

Sea Raptor (Published by Severed Press)

Dark Wings

Arizona's All-Time Baseball Team

The Best Phillies Team Ever

Chip,

Enjoy this Epic
Battle,

Praise for John J. Rust's novels

FALLEN EAGLE: ALASKA FRONT

"An action adventure with spine-tingling realism. You won't be able to put this book down."
Brenda Whiteside, author of the Love and Murder Series

SEA RAPTOR

"Three-dimensional characters, lots of fast action-adventure in a complex who-can-you-trust plot, some fun gadgets, and a good knowledge of the military and the area it's set in help give this novel a sound foundation. Rust can definitely write well."
Matt Bille, author of "Shadows of Existence: Discoveries and Speculations in Zoology"

"This is a fast-paced thriller with lots of action, high tension, and a romantic interest. It's a 'man's book', with accompanying 'language', but I enjoyed it. Rust is a good writer and his stories do not disappoint."
Heidi Thomas, author of "Cowgirl Up: A History of Rodeo Women."

ALASKA FRONT

Book One of the Fallen Eagle trilogy

ONE

The rifle burst struck Lieutenant Colonel Jan-Erik Ruud in the chest.

He grunted, bringing up his rifle as the Venezuelan marine stared at him wide-eyed. The suppressed M4 chattered. So did the rifle of the armored figure to his left. Patches of blood exploded across the Venezuelan's torso. He fell through the hatchway.

"Sir. You okay?" Gunnery Sergeant Archie Corcoran stepped over to Ruud.

"Yeah, I'm fine." He tapped the advanced carbon polymer ballistic armor of his exoskeleton. "Chest stings a little."

"Better than the alternative."

"Hey, at least we know these things work as advertised," said Sergeant Nick Baldelli, who also wore a dark, boxy exoskeleton with a motocross-style helmet.

"Let's hope it stays that way." Ruud looked around the offshore oil rig, his smart visor's night vision turning the platform and steel structures around him phosphorescent green. Spears of dread dug into his stomach. He gritted his teeth, biting back a curse. Someone had to have heard the Venezuelan's AK-103 go off. How long before –

Klaxons wailed throughout the rig.

"Aw shit," Baldelli uttered.

"Let's move, Marines," said Ruud, "and forget about stealth."

Ruud slung his M4 over his shoulder and went for his other weapon, a long-barreled rifle with a rectangular magazine. The M107A1.

He raced around pipes, tanks, a crane, and a missile launcher, checking the feed from the ScanEagle drone overhead. A few sentries hurried around the main deck. Ruud figured they only had a couple of minutes before the oil rig's full security contingent got organized.

"Two to the front." Ruud brought up his big rifle. Two loud crashes erupted from the barrel. The .50 caliber rounds threw both Venezuelans backwards.

"One coming up on the rear," called out the fourth member of the unit, Sergeant Phil Kosco.

Ruud glanced at the feed from Kosco's shoulder camera. A Venezuelan fired from behind some piping. He heard two rounds thud against Kosco's armor. The sergeant returned fire with his M107. Metal splinters jumped up from the piping. The Venezuelan stumbled and dropped out of sight.

"Hostile down."

The four dashed around another missile launcher. Ruud checked the ScanEagle feed, then the images from Corcoran's, Baldelli's, and Kosco's cameras. He winced when he thought of all the other eyes watching these feeds hundreds of miles away. Not only his superiors at Marine Corps Special Operations Command, but officials with the Defense Advanced Research Projects Agency – or DARPA -- the Joint Chiefs of Staff, maybe even the President.

Ruud hated it, hated the thought of these men and women in their nice air-conditioned offices looking over his shoulder, judging him and his unit. Would they butt in and tell them how to proceed with the rest of this op?

Yeah, because micromanagement works so well.

He shoved aside the thoughts. He had a job to do.

A rectangular trailer lay twenty-five yards away, near the base of the observation tower. They were almost to their target.

Something moved near the edge of the platform.

A Venezuelan swung a 20mm Oerlikon cannon toward them.

"Take cover!" Ruud cut left, toward one of the block-shaped generators. He dove behind it just as the Venezuelan fired. Yellow tracers zipped and cracked around them. A few rounds punched through the steel housing.

Corcoran crawled behind the generator. Kosco let out a strangled cry and stumbled.

"Kosco!" Ruud shouted.

"I got 'im." Baldelli pulled the other Marine behind the generator. The four lay on their stomachs as more rounds zipped overhead and ripped through the metal.

"Talk to me, Marine!" Fear gripped Ruud's soul. *Don't be dead, damn you.*

"I'm fine." Kosco coughed. "They were right. This armor can take hits from twenty mil rounds."

"Up to a point," Ruud reminded him.

Another burst from the Oerlikon. All the rounds went high.

Ruud caught movement in his ScanEagle feed. Venezuelans poured out of a hatch on the other side of the platform. At least twenty-five, all armed.

No time to screw around. He switched on the M107's camera sight, crouched, and held the rifle over his head. A new window opened in his smart visor. It showed the Oerlikon and the Venezuelan behind it. He fired another burst. Two rounds clipped the side of the generator.

Lower . . . lower. Ruud brought down the rifle an inch, until the red death dot settled on the slit between the cannon's splinter shield. He fired.

The Venezuelan spun and collapsed.

"Baldelli. Kosco. Take out the control trailer." Ruud noticed a catwalk along the lower half of the oil rig's observation tower. "Gunny. Up there. Top cover. I'll use the Oerlikon. Go."

The Marine commandos sprinted to their assignments. Ruud slung the M107 over his shoulder as he reached the cannon. He glanced down at its former operator. The Venezuelan lay on his back, the .50 caliber round striking him in the neck, nearly decapitating him.

Ruud leaned into the C-shaped shoulder rests, then checked on Corcoran. The gunnery sergeant made his way up the ladder to the catwalk. He then looked at the ScanEagle feed. The Venezuelans were getting closer.

We should have had more men. Lord knew he'd made that argument during the planning stages of this operation, multiple times. General Dobson, the commander of MARSOC, even agreed. Both of them, however, were overruled by the idiots at Fort Fumble, a.k.a the Pentagon. The brass wanted to prove the effectiveness of their newest toy, the INDAS – Individual Armor System. The DARPA geniuses proclaimed the suit was like, "An infantry fighting vehicle with legs." The generals and admirals swallowed the stupid pitch, made by people who probably played *HALO* way too much growing up and thought a handful of soldiers in armored battlesuits could take on a hundred bad guys.

And our asses are on the line because of it.

The Venezuelans stopped behind metal structures, scanned ahead of them, then moved forward a couple of squads at a time. No charging ahead blindly. These guys were well trained. Then again, Venezuela's marines were some of the best troops that country had.

Not that their training and skill would save them.

Ruud watched one squad dash forward, the others covering their advance. Seconds later, another squad darted out.

Ruud thumbed the trigger. The Oerlikon shuddered. The big 20mm shells ripped through the enemy marines. The ones behind cover opened fire. A couple of rounds pinged off the Oerlikon's splinter shield.

A small, round object fell among the Venezuelans. Ruud looked up at the observation tower. Corcoran stood on the catwalk, dropping another grenade.

An explosion kicked up a small storm of orange sparks. A second one followed. Men screamed in agony. Ruud fired the Oerlikon again.

"Aw dammit!" The curse burst through Ruud's earpiece.

"Talk to me, Kosco."

"My smart visor just went tits up. No night vision, no video feeds. I'm blind."

"Bullshit you're blind. Go Mark One Eyeball."

A snort, then, "Yes, sir."

Ruud shook his head and fired again. Kosco was definitely one of those Marines who seemed too dependent on technology.

He fired another burst at the Venezuelans. Corcoran joined in with his big M240 machine gun, firing down on the enemy. Ruud checked the feeds from his men. Despite his visor being down, Kosco's shoulder cam still came through. He and Baldelli continued to set charges on the missile control trailer.

The ScanEagle picked up two Venezuelan sentries approaching from the left. Ruud swung around the Oerlikon and fired. Both men spun and dropped to the ground.

"Charges in place," radioed Baldelli. He and Kosco hurried away from the trailer and squatted behind a steel tank. "Fire in the hole!"

A fireball sprang up next to the tower. A loud *crump* followed an instant later.

"I've got another group of marines on the move," Corcoran reported. "Ten strong."

Ruud glanced at the ScanEagle feed. More Venezuelans rounded the far corner of the platform and charged them.

"Relax," said Baldelli. "I got this."

He broke cover. A couple of surviving marines from the first wave opened fire. Rounds sparked harmlessly off Baldelli's armor. He raised a stubby M25 and fired two grenades. Both exploded in mid-air, showering the second wave of Venezuelans with steel flechette darts. All ten crumpled to the deck.

"Colonel!" Corcoran yelled. "Behind you!"

Ruud swung around. A mustached man in fatigues leveled a pistol at him. He started to duck on instinct.

The pistol cracked once, twice, three times. One round struck Ruud's helmet. His head jerked back. The Venezuelan kept firing, lowering his arm as he did. Another round struck Ruud's shoulder. His leg muscles tensed. He pushed off. Ruud soared ten feet through the air and landed in front of the Venezuelan. He put a round into Ruud's chest at point blank range. It didn't even dent the armor.

Ruud threw a right hook. The armored gauntlet hit the Venezuelan's temple with a sickening *thud*. He collapsed. An ugly, bloody indentation marred the side of his head. Ruud spotted the insignia on the Venezuelan's collar, a gold square with two thin white lines and a circle on top. He was a *capitán de fragata,* a navy commander, maybe the CO of this oil rig turned sea fortress.

Now these guys have no leader, and no way to fire their missiles.

"Gunny, with me. We'll sweep belowdeck for any more Venezuelans. Baldelli, Kosco, take out all the deck guns. I don't want someone we missed to pop up and use one of them on our guys."

The three Marine commandos acknowledged their orders.

Ruud and Corcoran met minimal resistance as they made their way within the rig's interior. They'd eliminated most of the marine security contingent. What remained were navy support personnel. Technicians, cooks, quartermasters, men who probably hadn't even held a rifle or pistol since basic training. One look at their big guns and sci-fi exoskeletons and they surrendered without trouble. Ruud and Corcoran locked the prisoners, numbering over seventy, in the mess hall, after collecting all utensils, pots, pans and anything else they might use for weapons.

Ruud climbed a metal ladder to the main deck, activating the INDAS's satellite communications system. A new screen appeared to his left. Staring back at him was a lean, angular-faced man with a shaved head and glasses.

"Sand Castle, Devil One."

"This is Sand Castle," replied Major General Phil Dobson. "Go, Devil One."

"Troy has fallen. I say again, Troy has fallen."

Dobson nodded upon hearing the code that the oil rig had been secured. "Copy that. I'll contact the *Bataan* and have them dispatch the rifle company to your position. Good work."

"Thank you, sir."

"Sand Castle out."

General Dobson's image vanished.

Ruud sent Baldelli to guard the prisoners. He then removed his helmet, feeling the cool sea breeze sweep over his sweaty face. He extended a nozzle from the INDAS's shoulder and stuck it in his mouth, taking a long pull from the built-in water container.

Ruud stared out at the darkened ocean. With the oil rig's SAMs and anti-ship missiles no longer threatening American planes and warships, Operation: Tropic Fire could commence. For three months, Trinidad and Tobago had been under Venezuelan occupation, the culmination of months of allegations by leaders of the South American country that the little Caribbean island nation had conducted illegal oil drilling in their territorial waters. It seemed like a matter that could be solved by diplomacy, not war. Then again, Venezuelan President Arocha wasn't known for being reasonable, or sane.

Now U.S. troops, planes, and ships were on their way to Trinidad and Tobago, ready to kick some ass.

He scanned the night sky for any sign of the V-22 Ospreys carrying the rifle company when Corcoran came over to him. He had his helmet off, revealing an angular, cocoa-skinned face.

"Well, the folks back at Fort Fumble must be happy. We just showed them their latest toys work."

"More importantly, their guinea pigs survived." Ruud tapped his chest.

"That's always an added bonus, isn't it?" Corcoran smiled.

"Honestly, it would have been simpler to just drop a few JDAMs on this thing."

"I agree. Too bad the politicians think differently."

Ruud nodded. Washington wanted to limit the amount of damage to Trinidad and Tobago's infrastructure. He did agree, to a point. If blowing up a building saved American lives, he had no problem with it. Structures could be rebuilt. You couldn't do that with human beings.

"We still need to find out what happened with Kosco's smart visor," Ruud said. "Next time something like that happens, it could mean the difference between us completing our objective or going home in a box."

"Yup," Corcoran replied.

"That and see about adding an air conditioner to this thing. I must have sweated off ten pounds since I put it on."

"We're Marines, sir. We don't need to be comfortable."

"Speak for yourself, Gunny," said Ruud.

Corcoran chuckled softly, then stopped. His brow furrowed.

"What?" asked Ruud.

"I thought I saw something in the water."

Ruud turned around, putting on his helmet. The night vision revealed a knife-shaped object gliding through the water a couple of miles out.

"That can't be one of ours," said Corcoran. "We're not supposed to have a ship within fifty miles of here."

"Magnification times five." The smart visor responded to Ruud's voice command. He could make out the ship clearly. It had a long, slender hull with a jagged island, an antenna behind it, and a helicopter deck in the rear. It also had two forward gun turrets and missile launchers near the island.

A computer-generated box formed around the ship. Lines of data appeared.

Contact ID: Udaloy-class destroyer
Country of origin: Russia
Speed: 35 knots
Complement: 300

Armament: Missiles: SS-N-22 ASM, SA-N-9 & SA-N-11 SAM
Guns: 2 130mm, 4 30mm CIWS
2 quad-barrel torpedo tubes
2 RBU-6000 ASW rocket launchers

Ruud clenched his jaw. It couldn't be the Russians. They didn't have any ships in the Caribbean.

But the Venezuelans had three Udaloys. Hell, they bought most of their weapons from Russia.

"This isn't good."

"Definitely not." Corcoran shook his head. "That thing's got more than enough firepower to blow our Ospreys out of the sky."

"Well we're not going to let that happen." Ruud switched frequencies on his comm unit. "Devil One, Green Knight Four."

"Green Knight Four, go," came the reply from the pilot of one of two Marine Corps F-35 Lightning IIs circling nearby.

"We've got a Venezuelan Navy Udaloy-class destroyer two miles southeast of Troy. Please do us a favor and get rid of it."

"Acknowledged, Devil One. Green Knight Four and Five inbound."

Ruud kept his eyes glued to the approaching Udaloy as he contacted the V-22s to warn them about the threat. He'd just signed off when he heard jet engines overhead.

"Green Knight Four," radioed the pilot. "I have a visual on the target."

Several seconds passed before the pilot spoke again. "Green Knight Four, JDAM lock . . . JDAM away."

"Green Knight Five, JDAM lock . . . JDAM away."

The roar of jet engines grew louder by the second. Ruud saw a dark, oblong shape streak overhead, followed by another. He looked back at the Udaloy.

Two bright orange balls lit up the darkened sea. A crash and rumble followed. The fireballs merged and rose into the air.

"Direct hit," reported Green Knight Four. "Scratch one destroyer. Repeat, scratch one destroyer."

"Good shooting, Green Knight," said Ruud.

"Thank you, Devil One."

Ruud drew a breath and stared at the burning wreckage of the Udaloy. "Well, that's one less thing to worry about."

Fifteen minutes later, the first V-22 touched down on the helicopter platform. The rear ramp came down and thirty Marines emerged. They approached Ruud, Corcoran, and Kosco, many gawking at their exoskeletons. A few uttered, "Whoa" or "Cool."

"Hey. Where can I get me one of those?" One Marine nodded to them.

"Area Fifty-One," joked Corcoran. "The aliens gave them to us."

"Ha. Funny." The Marine grinned and continued on with the rest of his platoon.

"Why, Gunny." Ruud turned to him. "You actually have a sense of humor."

"Yeah, that's my one joke for the year. Gotta wait till next year for my next funny."

Ruud chuckled.

"Devil One, Sand Castle," General Dobson radioed from Camp Lejeune in North Carolina.

"Devil One, go."

A pause. "We just got confirmation on that Udaloy you ordered the air strike on." Dobson spoke in a subdued tone.

Ruud felt the hairs rise on the back of his neck. "What about it, sir?"

Another pause, longer than the last. Something definitely was wrong.

"I just got word from Southern Command. It didn't belong to Venezuela."

Ruud stiffened. "What do you mean it wasn't Venezuelan?"

"It was the *UNS Klaipeda*, from the Directorate of Peace Enforcement fleet. Devil One, you just sank a United Nations ship."

TWO

"There were only sixteen survivors from that ship. Sixteen out of a crew of almost three hundred." Secretary General Ohmara Saihi maintained a straight posture as he sat at his desk. He stared across his spacious, brightly lit office at United Nations headquarters in New York. The large HD monitor on the wall showed an image of a slender, middle-aged woman with brown hair. He couldn't deny that U.S. President Emily Moore was very attractive. That beauty won over many of the unenlightened in her image-obsessed nation. They never would have elected her had they realized her stunning looks concealed the darkest of souls, along with a complete lack of intelligence.

"I'm aware of how many sailors were lost on your ship, Mister Secretary General," replied Moore. "I have already stated that we regret this accident and are willing to give compensation to the United Nations and the families of the dead crew members."

"The gesture is appreciated, but money cannot be a substitute for justice. It cannot erase what your Marines have done. Accident or not, nearly three hundred men and women who served the cause of peace perished on that ship. The Marines responsible for their deaths must be tried before the International Criminal Court."

"Our Defense Department is conducting an investigation into the sinking of the *Klaipeda*. They're fully capable of determining if criminal charges should be brought against those Marines."

Saihi gave a slight shake of his head. "Our fellow global citizens will not believe that. Certainly the families of our deceased sailors will not believe that. Your military will never punish their own. They will protect them. That is what the powerful do. They protect those who serve them.

But you, Madam President, can deviate from this trend. You can demonstrate that you are truly part of the global community, that you desire justice for the victims of American bombs, by handing over those Marines to the International Criminal Court. It is the only way to guarantee a fair trial."

Moore looked away for a moment. Was she actually considering his offer?

"If you're concerned about fairness, I am willing to let UN legal representatives work with our DoD investigators in gathering evidence to determine if a court martial is warranted."

A flicker of surprise went through Saihi. He'd expected Moore to be unwavering in her sense of nationalism. *But how far is she willing to go with UN involvement?*

"I assume any trial of these Marines will be overseen by American military officials," said Saihi.

"Correct."

"Will you allow a member of the Directorate of Peace Enforcement to sit on the judicial panel of this court martial?"

"I'm sorry." Moore shook her head. "There are no provisions in the Manual for Courts-Martial to allow a member of a foreign military to sit on the panel. You are, however, welcome to send observers."

"Your proposal is unacceptable," said Saihi.

"It's my best offer, Mister Secretary General. I'm going to get criticism from my supporters for allowing anyone from the United Nations within the same zip code as this investigation, but since it was your ship that was sunk, it's only right that you're involved in some way in this process."

"If you want our involvement, have these Marines tried before International Criminal Court, not by the same military they serve."

"The United States is not a signatory to the ICC," said Moore. "It has no jurisdiction over our citizens."

"That is not true, Madam President." Saihi raised a finger for emphasis. "When the Directorate of Peace Enforcement was established, amendments were made to the Rome Statute of the International Criminal Court. Hostile action taken against members of the DPE does fall under the court's jurisdiction, even if committed by a citizen of a nation that is not a signatory to the statute."

"Only if the government of that nation agrees to hand over that citizen, or in this case, citizens, to the ICC. We will not do that. I have complete faith in the U.S. military system of justice."

"The rest of the world does not. Many believe the sinking of the *Klaipeda* was deliberate."

"That's ridiculous."

"Not when you consider your hostile rhetoric toward the United Nations over the years," said Saihi. "You have accused us of supporting terrorists, enabling mass murderers, infringing on individual liberties and calling the Directorate of Peace Enforcement a private army accountable to no government. Your less stable surrogates have accused us of wanting to conquer the world, and gone as far as to label me the antichrist. Is it any wonder why so many global citizens feel you and your military would purposefully destroy a United Nations ship?"

"People are entitled to their opinions, even if they happen to be wrong."

Saihi stiffened, anger flaring within him. The arrogance of this woman, to think that simply being American automatically made you right.

"As I've said," Moore continued. "The sinking of the *Klaipeda* was a tragic accident. That, unfortunately, happens in war. But I think you and your DPE commanders have to accept some responsibility."

Saihi tilted his head. "How can you justify such a statement?"

"You had to have known Trinidad and Tobago was an area of potential conflict."

"That is why we dispatched the *Klaipeda* there, to monitor the situation."

"And you didn't think to alert us to the presence of a United Nations warship --"

"Peace support vessel," he interrupted.

Moore gave a noticeable roll of the eyes. Saihi knew the woman despised what Americans called "political correctness," but what he considered enlightened speech.

"As I was saying," an annoyed Moore continued. "You didn't think to alert us to the fact one of your . . . *peace support vessels* was operating in an area where the United States was conducting military operations?"

"The Directorate of Peace Enforcement does not answer to the United States."

"Surely your admirals alerted you to the risk, especially sending a ship similar in class to what the Venezuelan navy operates."

"Risk is nothing new to the DPE, as demonstrated in the past when they pacified the Somali pirates and the rebels in the Central African Republic. As for *Klaipeda* being of a similar class to the ships Venezuela operates, it was a coincidence. It was the closest vessel we had in the area. Perhaps if your Marines were not so eager to drop their bombs, they would have taken more time to properly identify the *Klaipeda.*"

"The Marines were engaged in an operation to re-take an oil rig that had been turned into an armed platform by the Venezuelans. A squadron of V-22s was en route with a rifle company when your ship appeared. They only had seconds to decide if it was a potential threat and act."

"That is no comfort to the families of those dead sailors." Saihi drew a slow breath. "This incident could have been avoided if you had not rushed toward a violent resolution and allowed the United Nations to resolve the conflict between Trinidad and Venezuela."

"We did go to the United Nations," said Moore. "All you did was push the matter onto the backburner. Meanwhile, hundreds of thousands of Trinidadians were living under the heel of a dictator. How long would you have talked and talked and denied them freedom?"

Saihi inwardly cringed. How he detested that word, "freedom." "How many Trinidadian civilians have died, and will die, because of the bombs dropped by your planes?"

"The U.S. military does everything possible to avoid civilian casualties. If you are so worried about civilian casualties, what about those inflicted by Venezuela during their invasion? How many others have suffered during this occupation? We had to act."

"That is why so many global citizens distrust your country, even despise it. You believe you are the only ones who know what is right and what is wrong, when it is appropriate to use force and when it is not." Saihi leaned forward. "Madam President, I am giving you the opportunity to show your country does respect the feelings and concerns of the global community, that you truly care about justice for those without power and influence. Turn those Marines over to the International Criminal Court. In addition, withdraw your forces from Trinidad and Tobago, as a sign you reject imperialist desires. I will even invite you to speak before the General Assembly to air your concerns and work with us to resolve this situation peacefully."

"We are already resolving the situation without the United Nations," said Moore. "In all likelihood, we won't have to deal with your organization on any issue. Congress is scheduled to debate the UN Membership Termination Bill after their summer recess. All indications are it will pass."

"If that bill passes, and you approve it, you risk becoming a pariah nation. We live in a global community. All nations are interdependent on each other. You cannot abandon the rest of the world."

"The United States will always be part of the world community, but we do not need to be in the UN for that."

"Madam President." Saihi held out both hands. "I urge you to reconsider."

"My mind is made up. The Marines involved in the *Klaipeda* sinking will be investigated by the Department of Defense, who will determine if criminal charges are warranted. We will make accommodations if you wish to send representatives to aid in the investigation. Now, if there is no more, Mister Secretary, I have a war to oversee. Good day."

Saihi said nothing, just nodded.

The screen blacked out.

Fingertips pressed together, Saihi leaned back in his padded, ergonomic chair, drawing a deep breath. A spark of anger grew within him, as it always did when an unenlightened cretin refused to accept his wisdom.

He quickly buried that anger. His dialogue with Moore had gone exactly the way he wanted. A smile spread across his face.

"History will show you gave President Moore a way to avoid what must come."

Saihi looked over at the source of those words. Seated in a leather chair in the corner of the office was a tall, hawk-faced man with sagging skin and gray-brown hair wearing a powder blue tunic and trousers, the dress uniform of the Directorate of Peace Enforcement.

"Did you expect the outcome of this exchange to be different?" Saihi asked General Martin McCullum.

"Of course not," McCullum replied in a thick New Zealander accent. "People like President Moore can't see beyond their own sense of patriotism."

"Correct." Saihi rose from his chair, stretching out his tall frame. He walked around the desk, scratching his white beard. Sunlight shining through the large, bullet-resistant window warmed his balding pate.

McCullum got to his feet as Saihi approached. The Secretary General beamed. "It's finally happened, my friend. This is what we've planned for, what we've wanted since we formed the Directorate of Peace Enforcement. The *Klaipeda's* sinking is only the beginning. Soon we shall have all the justification we need to carry out our most ambitious operation."

He clutched McCullum's shoulder. "When we have finished, we shall have what we always desired . . . the human race of one mind, one voice, one world."

"One mind, one voice, one world," McCullum repeated in a reverent tone.

"Now, go to our base in the Kuril Islands and implement Exercise Copper Blue."

"Yes, Mister Secretary General. Our peace enforcers will be glad to hear that. They've been cooped up on those rock piles for over a year."

Saihi nodded. "This is something we could not rush. We had to wait until the time was right to make our move."

"The time couldn't be any more right," noted McCullum. "I've heard rumblings that if the Americans pass their bill to withdraw from the UN, other nations might do the same." The veins in his neck stuck out. "This whole place could unravel if that happens."

"We cannot, *must not,* allow that to happen. The fate of the world rests in our hands. Now go see to our forces in the Pacific. I will tell the Special Action Unit to alert our operatives in America to prepare for the next phase. With the strength of Gaia, mother spirit of the Earth, we will triumph."

McCullum saluted and left the office.

Saihi walked over to the window, staring down at the East River. His mind drifted back nearly forty years, when his father worked in this very building, serving as Morocco's ambassador. At the time, he thought the man dedicated to the cause of peace. It wasn't long before he learned the truth. His father had been like all the other ambassadors. They only talked about how much they desired peace, but lacked the courage to turn those words into action.

The world would soon learn Ohmara Saihi did not lack that courage.

THREE

Ruud stepped out of the Pentagon in his olive Class A uniform, his men behind him. The suffocating July heat and humidity wrapped around him, not that it bothered him much. He'd operated in environments much hotter than this.

What did bother him was the mass of people in front of the five-sided center of power for the U.S. Armed Forces. He scowled as he put on his cap. Hundreds of signs and banners bobbed and waved among the demonstrators.

Justice for the Klaipeda . . . Arrest Marine Butchers . . . USMC, United States Murder Corps.

Ruud clenched a fist when he saw images of President Moore and a Marine in Dress Blues, both with Hitler mustaches and swastika armbands painted on. Another placard showed an American flag with the field of fifty stars replaced by a swastika.

"Lousy, ungrateful fuckfaces," Baldelli growled.

"Easy, Baldelli." Corcoran put a hand on his shoulder.

"Yeah, I'd be able to rest easier if I could pound on one of those America-hatin' pricks."

Ruud walked down the steps, still glaring at the protestors. The sight sickened him. Yes, people had a right to protest, but how could anyone direct such hate toward their own country? A country that let everyone have their say without fear of arrest, where you could worship whatever religion you wanted, or not worship at all, where even if you grew up dirt poor, you could make something of yourself if you worked hard. The many opportunities and freedoms were the reasons his parents emigrated here from Sweden when he was a child. They worked hard and now owned a feed store in Rapid City, South Dakota. Ruud was given the opportunity to serve his adopted country for fifteen years in the Marine Corps.

Will I be able to keep serving?

Lips pressed in a tight line, he led the other three members of the Advanced Marine Reaction Team, a.k.a The Iron Devils, toward the parking lot. They'd spent the entire morning telling everyone from the Judge Advocate General's office to the Marine Commandant himself about their actions on the oil rig. Ruud had no idea how this would shake out. Would they be recommended for court martial? Even if they wriggled out of that, would they remain in MARSOC after such a monumental fuck up?

He strode up to a green sedan, still eyeing the protestors. One of them held up a pole with an effigy of a Marine. Others hit it with bats and rocks. Ruud glanced at Baldelli. The stocky, dark-haired Marine shook with rage.

Better get him in the car before he charges those assholes.

The four piled in the sedan, Ruud driving. He pulled up to the entrance of the cloverleaf. Several dozen protestors lined the roadway.

Two of them rushed the car.

"Fucking murderers!" one shouted. "Someone should drop a bomb on your fucking asses!"

A squad of Pentagon police officers intercepted them. Ruud noticed one protestor wore a light blue armband. It bore the dove and shield symbol of the Directorate of Peace Enforcement. Bordering it were the words, UN FRIEND OF PEACE.

Ruud drove on as the officers wrestled the two men to the ground.

"Yeah, use the taser," cheered Baldelli. "And mace . . . and batons . . . aw hell, just kick the shit out of 'em."

Ruud glanced at the protestors along the cloverleaf. Many wore similar blue armbands. He grunted and shook his head. The UN Friends of Peace was advertised as an independent group to help promote the United Nations' ideals of peace and global unity. To Ruud, it was nothing but an Ohmara Saihi fan club, one that had way too many Americans as members.

They left the protestors behind and got on I-95, stopping in Richmond for lunch. They didn't utter a word about the *Klaipeda* sinking. So far their identities had been kept under wraps. All it would take was one diner to overhear them and post it on Facebook or Twitter, then the press would be all over it.

It was early evening when the four Marines returned to Camp Lejeune.

"Make sure you get plenty of rest," Ruud told them after exiting the sedan. "We've got a busy day tomorrow. Firing range, hand-to-hand combat, and time at the MOUT facility." He used the acronym for Military Operations in Urban Terrain.

"Do we even need it?" grumbled Baldelli. "After today, I get the feeling the brass wouldn't want us standing next to a Toys for Tots box, forget about actual combat."

"There's still fighting going on in Trinidad and Tobago, and there are still plenty of bad guys around the world raping, killing, pillaging and what have you. Until they kick us out of The Corps or throw us in Leavenworth, we carry on like we could be deployed at any moment."

"Yes, sir," Baldelli replied.

Ruud's face stiffened, trying to maintain a confident expression. He had to admit, however, Baldelli was right. After what happened with the *Klaipeda,* the Iron Devils were on the sidelines for the immediate future.

Maybe permanently.

Better to stay busy than just sit around and think about this shit.

Ruud walked back to his BOQ - Bachelor Officer Quarters – got a frozen dinner from the freezer and threw it in the microwave. He went into the small, sparsely decorated living room and picked up the remote. Did he dare put on the news? He knew what they'd be talking about.

Maybe some celebrity did something stupid. Maybe that's trumped the Klaipeda.

Here's hoping.

Ruud turned on FOX News. A male reporter decked out in a Kevlar helmet and vest stood on a hotel balcony. Distant gunfire crackled behind him.

Nope. Trinidad and Tobago is still in the news.

". . . Venezuelan troops have surrendered in many parts of Trinidad and Tobago, there is still heavy resistance here in the capital. U.S. military commanders are confident it won't be long until that resistance crumbles. The Navy and Air Force are in complete control of the skies and seas, making it impossible for Venezuelan forces to be re-supplied from their country."

Ruud gave a quick, satisfactory nod. Operation: Tropic Fire was little over a week old. He figured, hoped, all combat operations would be over within another week.

We should be down there. How much quicker could they end the fighting with their INDAS suits? How many American and Trinidadian deaths could they prevent?

When the reporter in Port of Spain finished, new footage appeared. Hordes of people crowding a street, shouting and holding up signs.

"From Washington to Los Angeles," the anchor began, "protests continue over the accidental sinking of the UN vessel *Klaipeda* by U.S. military forces in the opening hours of Operation: Tropic Fire."

Ruud's grip on the remote tightened as he watched the report.

"The Los Angeles chapter of UN Friends of Peace posted on its Facebook page that protests will not stop until the Marines responsible are behind bars. United Nations Secretary General Ohmara Saihi again called on President Moore to have the Marines tried before the International Criminal Court. In Washington, House Minority Leader Ismael Villarreal took part in a protest outside the Pentagon, where he leveled harsh criticism toward the President and the Marine Corps."

A chubby, mustached man appeared on the screen. "The deaths of the men and women aboard the *Klaipeda* can be laid directly at President Moore's feet. For years, she has played on the hatred her supporters have for the United Nations, accusing the men and women who work there in the name of peace as being anti-American, anti-Semitic, and anti-freedom. Her United States Murder Corps has translated that to mean they can wantonly destroy United Nations ships and slaughter their crews. Words have consequences, and President Moore must be held accountable for hers."

"Go fuck yourself." Ruud crushed the off button with his thumb. He flung the remote against the sofa.

Ruud stomped into the kitchen as the microwave beeped. He ignored it, pressing his fists on the circular table. He shut his eyes, a storm of guilt, regret, and anger welling up. His mind pulled up the image of the fireballs consuming the *Klaipeda,* killing nearly three hundred men and women.

Dead because of me.

It wasn't the first time he'd killed. That came with the territory. But everyone he'd killed over the past fifteen years had been legitimate targets. Enemy soldiers, terrorists, pirates, international criminals. Threats to his country, its allies, and innocent people in general.

The crew of the *Klaipeda* weren't a threat to anyone. They just had the misfortune of being in the wrong place at the wrong time.

What could I have done differently? Ruud clenched his fists. Maybe he should have contacted Southern Command to see if they had intel about any non-Venezuelan ships in the area. Maybe he shouldn't have assumed the Udaloy was Venezuelan.

Ruud walked out of the kitchenette, letting his meal sit in the microwave. He didn't feel like eating. He gazed at the handful of framed photos hanging on the wall. Most showed him with other Marines. One photo in particular drew his eye, him with a woman and three other young men, all in their early twenties. His younger self didn't smile, trying to look intimidating as he clutched a bass guitar. Damn, but he'd been skinny back then. He'd added about twenty pounds of muscle to his 5'10 frame since, bringing him up to 175 pounds. Not that big when compared to the muscular, 6'2 Gunny Corcoran, but at least he was no longer a stick.

Ruud then looked at the woman who stood next to him in the photo. She was slim and wore a black dress, stockings and high-heeled boots. Shoulder-length, ebony hair framed a face more oval than round with high cheekbones, cream-colored skin, and dark green eyes that were beautiful and mysterious.

What could have been.

It wasn't the first time he'd thought that when staring at this photo. He and Krista Brandt had been together for much of their time in Icefire. Three years. But when he graduated from ROTC at the University of Alaska-Anchorage, he had to leave her and the band to fulfill his commitment to the Marine Corps, to the country that gave him and his parents so many opportunities.

Icefire had gone on to become a very successful metal band, with Grammy nominations and platinum records to their credit. Much as he loved being in The Corps, Ruud couldn't help but wonder what life would have been like with the band.

Right now, more than anything, he wished he had gone down that other path, where the most dangerous things were dumbass fans jumping onto the stage or getting too close to the pyro, where he and Krista might still be together.

Where he didn't give an order that killed nearly three hundred UN sailors.

Someone knocked on the door. Ruud let out a slow breath, walked over and opened it. Corcoran stood in front of him, holding up a six-pack of beer. "I figured you could use this."

"It can't hurt." Ruud nodded for him to come in. They sat at the table, each opening a bottle.

"You offer any to Baldelli and Kosco?" Ruud held up his beer before taking a swig.

"They're my next stops."

Ruud nodded. "I think Kosco is holding up well, all things considered. Baldelli . . . I'm tempted to restrict him to base. I have a bad feeling if he sees anyone with a Friend of Peace armband he'll pound their head through their ass."

"That wouldn't break my heart." Corcoran took a pull from his beer. "Unfortunately, it'd be a PR black eye for The Corps. Maybe two black eyes the way things are going."

Ruud snorted, staring down at the floor. "I fucked up big time, Gunny."

"I would've made the same call, sir. We thought that ship was a threat."

"Well, we thought wrong, and now look. The America haters are out in full force, we have members of our own government wanting to turn us over to the UN. What's worse . . ." Ruud's jaw clenched for a moment. "What's worse is I fucked up your career, and Baldelli's, and Kosco's, and those pilots, and probably General Dobson's career, too."

"You gotta stop beating yourself up, sir."

"It's hard not to when you killed nearly three hundred people who didn't deserve it."

"I'm not saying it's easy. I'm not saying I don't think about those sailors. But letting guilt eat you up won't bring them back, and it won't change what's happening." Corcoran gulped his beer. "Hell, what were those dumbasses doing there in the first place? Sailing into a war zone, in the same kind of ship the Venezuelan navy has, or I guess had, since we put all their ships on the bottom of the ocean. Point is, they had to've known they could get caught in the crossfire."

Ruud put his beer bottle on the table. "Gunny, you remember last year in Albania?"

"I always remember countries where people tried to shoot my ass off."

Ruud grinned briefly. Shortly before being assigned to the Iron Devils, he and Corcoran took part in the Albanian Intervention, where they stopped rebel soldiers and police from overthrowing the government. "When we got back, I remember reading about a UN frigate poking around the Adriatic Sea near one of our carrier groups. We came close to firing on it."

"And now the UN sends another ship near where our forces are operating in the Caribbean, only this time we do sink it."

Ruud slowly rotated the bottle back and forth in his hand.

Corcoran's brow furrowed. "Something on your mind, sir?"

"Just thinking, Gunny. This is going to sound crazy, but what if the UN --"

Another knock at the door interrupted him.

"Looks like this place is becoming party central," said Corcoran.

Ruud chuckled and went over to the door. When he opened it, General Dobson stood in front of him.

"General?"

"Colonel."

Ruud stepped aside, letting Dobson in. The head of MARSOC stared at the kitchen table. "You have beer? Good. I could use one."

"Help yourself, sir." Corcoran got up as Dobson went over and plucked out a bottle.

"I'm probably going to need a lot more of these tomorrow." The general twisted off the cap and took a slug.

"Something wrong, sir?" asked Ruud.

"Wrong? Colonel, we are well beyond something being *wrong.*"

"I don't like the sound of that," said Corcoran.

Dobson took another swig of beer. "House Minority Leader Villarreal is coming here tomorrow."

"What?" Ruud blinked in surprise.

"What the hell for?" blurted Corcoran.

"He and some of his America-hating buddies are coming to Lejeune on what they're calling a fact-finding trip," explained Dobson. "He's also bringing a bunch of reporters with him. No matter what we say, Villarreal and the press are going to twist our words, smear The Corps, try to turn more people against us, maybe even sway the board of inquiry to recommend you all for court martial."

Ruud's jaw clenched, fury burning within him. Men – *Not men, slimebags* – like Villarreal pissed him off to no end. They didn't care about the facts. They just hated the military, and jumped on any chance to embarrass it, to destroy the careers and reputations of good men and women.

"Does he know it was my unit involved in the *Klaipeda* sinking?" asked Ruud.

"I don't know." Dobson shrugged. "Hell, it wouldn't surprise me. No one can keep a damn secret in Washington. But I'm not going to give that son-of-a-bitch the chance to use you and your men to further his agenda. I'm getting you out of here, tonight."

"What'll you tell Villarreal if he asks for us?" asked Corcoran.

"I'll sell him a bullshit story that you're in the middle of some forest or desert thousands of miles from here doing survival training. Actually, it'll be a half-truth. You will be thousands of miles from here, but not for survival training. I have a friend, a retired three-star, who has a cabin in the woods. He and his new girlfriend are going on a month-long cruise, says you can hide out in his cabin until the board of inquiry convenes."

"So where is this cabin?" Ruud asked Dobson.

"Alaska."

FOUR

Ruud flicked his fishing rod. The line soared out, the lure hitting the water with a soft splash. He leaned back, taking in the stream and surrounding trees, noting the cool of the air, trying to do anything he could to forget about the *Klaipeda* and the upcoming board of inquiry.

He found it hard to do with Corcoran, Baldelli and Kosco around him. Just one look at any of them hurled his mind back to that night on the oil rig.

"So how long do we have to wait to catch a fish?" moaned Baldelli.

"We won't catch shit if you keep talkin'," Corcoran scolded him. "You're scaring the damn fish away."

"Hey, I got something." Kosco pulled back his rod and cranked the reel.

"Ha!" Baldelli wore a smug grin. "I ain't scarin' nothin' away."

In less than a minute, Kosco reeled in his catch. The fish looked about half-a-foot long, olive and black with a diamond-shaped tail. A burbot, one of Alaska's most common fish.

"Great job," Baldelli said in a slow, sarcastic tone. "Tonight we eat like kings."

Kosco snorted at him. "At least I caught something."

They spent much of the afternoon at the stream, catching more fish and having a few beers. Then they hiked a mile through the woods to the general's cabin. A jeep and pick-up sat in the driveway. Both belonged to General Harris, who had left them the keys. To the west, Ruud saw the urban sprawl of Anchorage, Alaska's biggest city, the place he'd spent his college years. All sorts of memories spooled through his mind. Field maneuvers with his ROTC unit, playing bass with Icefire, and spending time with Krista.

For dinner, they ate the fish they caught. His meal wouldn't make the menu of any five-star restaurant, but it still tasted pretty good. Afterwards, Kosco grabbed his Kindle and went to one of the bedrooms, happy to use the downtime to catch up on his reading. Corcoran and Baldelli sat in the living room watching *Sportscenter*. Ruud went online to check the news. Their names hadn't been released in connection with the *Klaipeda* sinking . . . yet.

At least there was good news from Trinidad and Tobago. The last pockets of Venezuelan resistance had surrendered. He also saw that a sizeable Directorate of Peace Enforcement fleet force was due to sortie from their Kuril Islands base for a large-scale exercise in the Pacific.

"Perfect timing," Ruud muttered to himself. The DPE's Exercise Copper Blue was the reason General Dobson wanted them to bring along their INDAS suits and weapons.

"I seriously doubt the UN would actually attack us," his CO had said. "But the way tensions are between us, one misunderstanding, one accident, could escalate into a full-blown shooting war. I want you ready in case that happens."

Ruud found a video of Secretary General Saihi's address to the General Assembly from earlier today. He hesitated before playing it.

"Every day that passes without President Moore handing over those Marines to the International Criminal Court is another day that proves she does not care about justice for our sailors and their families." Saihi spoke in a voice not loud, yet not soft. But something about his cadence made it almost impossible to tune out, like he was about to make a profound statement at any moment.

"To my fellow global citizens in America," Saihi continued. "I urge you to do everything in your power to make your president see reason, to make her do what is right. Do not think you have no power. You do. I know there are millions of my Friends of Peace in America, you who see beyond your artificial borders, who seek peace and justice for everyone in the world, not just for a single country. Join your voices together. Let President Moore know that you will not rest until those who killed our sailors are brought to trial before the International Criminal Court. Alone, you may feel powerless. But together, you have the power to force change, change for the better. Change for what is right. Remember, when you are of one mind, one voice, one world, nothing can stop you."

The words made Ruud shudder. There was something almost cult-like about Saihi. Even worse, a lot of people seemed to be drinking his Kool-Aid. Massive protests were still going on in Washington, New York, Los Angeles, and twenty other major cities. Not all the protests were peaceful. A Marine recruiting office in Seattle had been firebombed. Police cars were vandalized in LA. A clash between protestors and counter-protestors in Dallas left forty injured. Hundreds had been arrested across the country.

For the leader of an organization dedicated to peace, Saihi had done more to heighten the tension between the U.S. and the UN than decrease it.

Would any of this be happening if I hadn't ordered those planes to bomb the Klaipeda? Ruud banged a fist on the kitchen table, causing Corcoran and Baldelli to look his way.

"You okay, sir?" asked the gunnery sergeant.

"I'm fine. The news just pisses me off. I'm going outside for some air."

Ruud shoved open the front door. He went over to a hand-carved wooden bench on the porch and sat down. He looked through the trees at Anchorage. No lights blazed in the city, even though it was after eight. At this time of year, the sun still hung far above the horizon.

He leaned against the bench's back, pulled the phone from his pocket, then plugged in his headphones. He tapped his music library, calling up the list of Icefire albums. It took him about a second to make his choice. *Eclipse of the Soul,* his favorite album.

An ethereal, orchestral sound emanated from his earbuds, the opening of the first track, "Enchantment of Night." A hard, driving guitar followed, as well as the crash of drums and the thumping of the bass. Next came a woman singing in a powerful, operatic voice. It all blended into the incredible, epic form of music known as symphonic metal.

Ruud slowly breathed in the cool, pine-scented air of the Alaskan forest, mesmerized by Krista's singing. *My God, she had such a beautiful voice.*

He closed his eyes, carried away by the music. On the second song, "Whispering Shadows," Ruud focused on the bass part. He held up his left fist and plucked at the air with his right middle and index fingers, hitting the notes perfectly.

At least they found a damn good bass player to replace me.

Ruud continued to play "air bass." He maintained the rhythm even as he flashed back to his time with Icefire, playing in bars and nightclubs, at school dances and campus events. Crammed into their drummer's van with all their equipment to head for gigs in places like Palmer, Seward, and Kenai. Sleeping by the side of the road in said van. Dealing with sketch bar owners who tried to shortchange them, including the one in Wasilla Ruud threatened to throw through a window if he didn't pay them, "Every fucking cent you fucking owe us."

Then came that day, just a couple of months before graduation. Anchorage's indoor football team booked Icefire as the halftime entertainment. The arena had been half-full, but they killed it. The crowd cheered louder for them than the football team. After the show, Krista had said, "Holy shit, guys. I think we can actually go big time."

They did, all without him. Ruud had made a commitment to the Marine Corps. He had to leave Icefire, leave Krista. The break-up had been amicable, but no less heartbreaking. But what could they do? She would be going all over the world singing before thousands of screaming metalheads, while he would be going all over the world to kill bad guys. How could they maintain any sort of relationship?

Someone tapped him on the shoulder. He opened his eyes and looked up at Corcoran.

"What's up, Gunny?" Ruud removed his earbuds.

Corcoran shook his head. "Never could understand your kind of music. How the hell do you combine opera and heavy metal and don't make it sound like shit?"

"You need to broaden your horizons."

"I'll stick to what my parents raised me on. Stevie Wonder, Bob Seger. You know, real music."

Ruud chuckled.

"Lemme guess," said Corcoran. "Icefire."

"You guess right."

"What a surprise. Taking a stroll down memory lane?"

"Yeah," replied Ruud. "I wouldn't mind staying on memory lane, but, no point in wishing for the impossible. You have to face what's in front of you, even if it's a Category Three shitstorm."

"Mm." Corcoran nodded and stared out at Anchorage. "Didn't you tell me Krista Brandt still lives in Alaska?"

"Yeah. She has a place in Talkeetna, a little town about a hundred miles north of here."

"Uh-huh." Corcoran nodded again. "Why don't you go up there and see her?"

"Are you serious?"

"Hell yeah, I'm serious. You need to get far away from anything having to do with The Corps, including us. You gonna tell me you don't think about the *Klaipeda* every time you look at one of us?"

Ruud sighed. "No, I can't."

Corcoran took a seat beside him on the bench. "You're never gonna forget what happened, never gonna forget about those UN sailors who died. But if you don't find some way to cope with it, that guilt's gonna eat up your soul, drive you to depression, to the point you might eat your gun. I've seen it happen to other friends of mine. I don't want it happening to you."

"You think a few days with my former girlfriend will make everything right?"

"Maybe not everything, but it could be a start. Spend some time with someone who's not in The Corps. Go on a nature hike or jump into a freezing lake or whatever the hell people in Alaska do for fun."

Ruud chuckled as Corcoran continued. "Heck, rekindle what you two had. Maybe it'll help you see you can do normal things even after everything that happened in the Caribbean."

"What about you guys?"

"Shit, sir." Corcoran gave him a dismissive wave. "We're adults. We can find ways to entertain ourselves. Hell, Anchorage is right over there. General Dobson didn't say we can't go into the city. We just have to keep a low profile. It certainly helps that it's tourist season. I may not even stick out too much. There's gotta be a few black folks that come to Alaska for vacation."

Ruud chewed on his lip for a second. "Are you sure about this, Gunny?"

"I give you my permission to live every man's fantasy and hang out with a smokin' hot rock star."

"Since when do officers need a gunnery sergeant's permission to do anything?"

"Since the day God invented gunnery sergeants." Corcoran gave him a wry grin.

Ruud grinned back. He took a deep breath, shut off the music and called up Krista's number. It rang once, twice.

She picked up before the third ring. "Jan-Erik?"

His heart skipped a beat. "Hey, Krista."

FIVE

Ruud woke up early, getting in some PT before taking the general's jeep into Anchorage. After having breakfast at a local diner, he walked across the street to a convenience store. Ruud bought a blue ballcap with an image of Alaska on it. That, his sunglasses, and his four-day old beard gave him a decent, improvised disguise in the event his name was leaked to the press.

I'm surprised it hasn't happened yet.

Ruud got onto the Seward Highway going north. When he came to the intersection with 36th Avenue, he glanced right. A wave of nostalgia hit him.

What the hell. He turned off the highway. In a few minutes, he drove past a series of square buildings and parking lots surrounded by pine trees. Ruud grinned. He hadn't laid eyes on UA-Anchorage since his graduation fifteen years ago. *Has it really been fifteen years?*

He drove around the campus. With the exception of a couple of new buildings, it looked pretty much the same. His eyes lingered on the student union and the sports complex where Icefire had put on several concerts. He drove by the dorms, remembering Monty Python and *Die Hard* movie marathons he and his friends had during really bad snowstorms.

Ruud wound his way around Mosquito Lake, where students played pick-up hockey games during winter, and where he and Krista had several picnics during the warmer months. He took a staggered breath, recalling the times they lay together on the blanket, kissing and holding each other.

Then he remembered that day at the airport, following graduation, hugging a sobbing Krista, not wanting to let go of her, not wanting to accept the fact their chosen careers meant they had to go their separate ways.

Now . . .

A quiver swept through his chest as he headed back to the Seward Highway. Traffic had stopped about a half-mile from the intersection. Ruud sat there, not moving, for five minutes. Ten minutes. He tapped on the steering wheel, listening to a classic rock station, wondering when the hell they were going to move.

A couple of young men walked down the sidewalk. Ruud guessed their ages at nineteen or twenty. Probably students taking summer classes at UAA.

He rolled down the passenger window. "Hey, guys." He spoke with a neutral inflection, covering up his natural Swedish accent.

"Yeah?" The taller of the two turned to him.

"What's going on up there?"

"Fucking protestors," the kid snorted. "Calling our soldiers murderers and shit."

Ruud thanked him, and continued to sit in the jeep. Twenty minutes later, traffic finally moved. When Ruud made it to the intersection, he saw several protestors sitting on the sidewalk, arms behind their backs, police officers around them. A handful of men and women stood by a small copse of trees across the street. One held a large photo of President Moore with prison bars painted over her. Every one of them wore a blue UN Friends of Peace armband.

Ruud continued up the Seward Highway. The urban sprawl of Anchorage gave way to forests. He drove for another hour-and-a-half before reaching the exit for Talkeetna. That's when he spotted two men by the side of the road. One was squat and held a video camera. The other had a tall, lean build and hacked at a tree with a knife. He ripped away a piece of bark and ate it.

Bet they'll put that up on YouTube. Ruud chuckled and drove on. He learned during his four years in Alaska that the state had many colorful characters.

Ruud drove through the center of Talkeetna with its wooden buildings surrounded by pine forests. A couple of miles outside of town, he turned onto a dirt road that led to a large cabin overlooking the river.

I'm here. He just stared at the cabin, his heartbeat picking up. It'd been five years since he'd last seen Krista in person, when she gave a special concert at Camp Lejeune. They'd only been able to talk for a few minutes before she and the band had to leave for their next gig.

Now they'd have a lot more time to catch up. Maybe do more than just catch up.

Ruud slid out of the jeep, breathing in the cool, fresh air. He took in the pine trees around him. In the distance, a mass of clouds blotted out Mount McKinley. He strode up to the door, hesitated for a moment, then knocked.

The door opened. Ruud's chest tightened when he saw Krista. A black t-shirt showing Alaskan wildlife and blue jeans hugged her slender frame. Her black hair, streaked with purple, flowed past her shoulders.

She looked as beautiful as ever.

"Jan-Erik!" Her face lit up. She threw her arms around him.

An electric jolt went through Ruud as he hugged her back.

"Oh, it's so good to see you again." She gave him a quick peck on the cheek.

His insides shuddered. "You too. How have you been?"

"Nice and relaxed." Krista broke the hug, much to Ruud's disappointment. "We just finished our tour last month. Come on in, I'll tell you about it."

"Thanks." He grabbed his duffelbag and entered the cabin. The spacious living room sported a brown bear pelt near the fireplace and a few caribou antlers on the wall. Several framed photos caught his eye, especially one with Krista and rocker Ted Nugent, both dressed in hunting jackets and carrying bows.

And, of course, there were the glass cases showing off Icefire's platinum records.

"And everyone thinks rock stars live in mansions," Ruud said.

Krista wrinkled her face in a distasteful look. "Yeah, like I really want some seventy room monstrosity in Los Angeles or Miami and deal with all that big city shit. Nope. After months on the road, I love the peace and quiet of the wilderness."

"Well you certainly couldn't ask for better scenery. This place is great."

"Thanks." Krista smiled, then led him to the guest room. After hitting the bathroom, Ruud joined her in the living room. She offered him a vitamin water before they both sat on the sofa.

"I still can't believe you're in Alaska," Krista said. "I thought you'd be down on Trinidad and Tobago."

"Mm." Ruud's jaw tightened. He focused on the bottle of orange liquid in his hand. So much for trying to forget about all that crap.

Krista shifted on the cushion. "Um, were you down there?"

Ruud let out a slow breath. "Yeah. Yeah I was."

"Jan-Erik?" Krista gently touched his forearm. "Are you okay?"

He turned to her, noting the concern on her face. He chewed on his lip. Should he tell her? Would she view him in a different light?

"Um, is this about what happened with that UN ship?" asked Krista. "I know you guys have taken a lot of shit for it. Kinda unfair, I think. It was an accident, right?"

"I . . . we still killed nearly three hundred UN sailors." Ruud felt his jaw tighten, wondering if Krista noticed his slip.

Her eyes widened. She put a hand on her chest. "Oh my God. It wasn't . . . you weren't involved in that."

Ruud looked to the floor. He set his bottle on the coffee table and clasped his hands together. He dared a glance at Krista. She still looked shocked.

No point in hiding it now. Ruud turned to her, his tongue feeling thick. "I was the one who gave the order to bomb that ship."

Krista's mouth opened, but she didn't speak. Just stared at him. Ruud scanned her eyes, her face, looking for disappointment, maybe even disgust.

All he found was sympathy.

"I'm so sorry." She leaned over and hugged him. "How . . . I mean . . ."

Ruud took hold of her hand. "It's pretty much like they've been saying on the news, minus the 'Marines are murderers' crap guys like Saihi are spouting. We secured an oil rig the Venezuelans were using as a sea fortress, then that destroyer showed up. We thought it was Venezuelan, and we had some Ospreys with a rifle company en route. I needed to protect them, so I ordered our F-35s to take out the ship. Didn't know until later it was DPE."

They sat in silence, Krista looking down, slowly rubbing her fingers back and forth on her knees, as though wondering what to say next.

"So . . . So what's going to happen to you?" she finally spoke. "They're not gonna turn you over to the International Criminal Court like the UN wants."

"I doubt it," Ruud replied. "President Moore seems adamant about that. Plus, she's always been a big supporter of the military, unlike the dumbass before her."

"Does that mean you're not gonna get in trouble?"

"No. The Marine Corps will convene a board of inquiry. They'll determine if my men and I should be court martialed."

"I'm sure you won't," said Krista. "I'm sure they'll understand it was an accident."

"Even if you're right, it still goes on my record," Ruud explained. "Whenever I come up for promotion or another assignment, people will look at it and think there must be something wrong if I had to go before a board of inquiry. Basically, that's it for my career."

"What a load of horseshit."

"True, but that's how it is in the military."

Krista closed her eyes. "Jan-Erik, I'm so sorry. You probably came up here to forget about all that, and here I am dredging it all up."

"It's okay. Not your fault."

She hugged him again, then exhaled loudly, placing a hand on Ruud's shoulder. "Look, you came here to get away from that . . . that shit, right?"

"That was my plan. So far it doesn't seem to be working." He grimaced and looked Krista in the eyes. "Sorry."

"Forget it." She straightened up, taking his right hand in both of hers. "Look, you said you wanted to come here and forget about what happened, right?"

"Yeah?"

"So that's what we're gonna do. You and me. Fishing, hunting, hiking, camping, all the stuff normal people do in Alaska. What do you say?"

Ruud focused on the feel of Krista's hands over his. A smile formed on his face. "That sounds good to me."

SIX

General McCullum moaned with delight as he bit into his cucumber sandwich, savoring its sweet taste. Just a couple of days ago, the sight of any food made him nauseous. A soldier by trade, he wasn't used to the constant motion on a ship. But until the operation commenced, he had to use the big aircraft carrier for his headquarters.

Thankfully, some meditation and crystal therapy sessions helped him overcome his sea sickness.

May Gaia bless you, Fawn. You never cease to help me.

McCullum looked at the digital photo frame on the left corner of his desk. It showed him with his arm around a petite, younger woman with long dark hair and glasses. His second wife, Fawn.

He reached out and ran a finger over her. *Where would I be were it not for you?*

McCullum clenched his teeth, remembering those dark days with the New Zealand contingent of UNMIS, the United Nations Mission In Sudan. He grimaced at the images of starving children and people slaughtered by rebels and criminal gangs in the most horrific ways. All the while, his fellow peacekeepers stood by and did nothing, handcuffed by leaders in New York too afraid to make a decision.

His experiences in Sudan had haunted him, turned him into an alcoholic. His first wife left him as a result.

Good riddance. She didn't understand what I went through.

Fawn did. This gentle woman, so wise beyond her 29 years, had peered into his broken soul and found a way to repair it. She taught him how to meditate, to use crystals to heal his body and spirit. He learned from her how Earth was not just a planet, but a living organism which reacted to the pain and suffering caused by humans. The Indian Ocean Tsunami, the 2010 Chilean Earthquake, the 2011 Japan Quake. Those disasters had been the planet's way of lashing out at the Americans for all the bombs they dropped in their imperialistic wars.

She also introduced him to someone else who would change his life before ever meeting him face-to-face. Fawn had played for him numerous speeches of Ohmara Saihi. Never had he heard someone speak with such assuredness, such intelligence. The man had such a perfect vision for the planet. Saihi spoke about rising above the outdated notions of nationalism and patriotism, how concepts like freedom, individualism, and materialism stood in the way of serving the planet. He also envisioned a time when there would be no countries, no borders, just a single, united world.

McCullum wanted to be part of that world.

He resigned his commission with the New Zealand Defence Force and joined the Directorate of Peace Enforcement. He had led the mission that purged the Central African Republic of its murderous rebels. Now he was in charge of the most important operation in the name of peace, an operation that would bring about Secretary General Saihi's vision of one mind, one voice, one world.

McCullum finished his sandwich, washing it down with a herbal tea, then checked the secure files on his tablet. The only new item of relevance was the first batch of American troops had returned to the States from Trinidad and Tobago. Most remained on the islands to provide security and humanitarian aid.

That will work to our advantage.

He lowered the tablet, staring past his desk at the two chairs in the "living room," the single bed, and the bathroom of his VIP quarters on the *Boutros Boutros-Ghali.* Most would consider the space small, but for an aircraft carrier with five thousand sailors, it was damn luxurious.

McCullum breathed deep and tapped a finger on his desk. The men and women throughout the fleet were conducting all manner of drills to maintain the illusion of Copper Blue being nothing more than a simple exercise. Until the real operation began, he didn't have a lot to do.

He read over another update on the current positions of U.S. Navy ships when he caught the time in the corner of his tablet's screen. McCullum grinned. In just a few minutes, there would be something he'd thoroughly enjoy.

At precisely 1200 hours, a series of high-pitched whistles emitted from the carrier's 1-MC speaker system.

"Attention all crew. Attention all crew. Standby for a message from the Secretary General of the United Nations, Ohmara Saihi."

McCullum leaned back in his chair, hands folded across his chest. Anticipation rippled throughout his body, as it always did before he heard a speech from Saihi.

"Loyal members of the Directorate of Peace Enforcement," Saihi's pre-recorded voice filled McCullum's cabin, and his very soul. "I trust you are all well, and working hard toward our ultimate goal of a world where peace, harmony, and enlightenment reign. There are many obstacles we must overcome to achieve our dream, but which of these obstacles impede our efforts the most?"

"It must be war," McCullum said to himself.

"It is the concept of freedom," Saihi answered his own question.

A half-grin formed on McCullum's face. *I was off. That's what you get trying to out-think a brilliant mind like Ohmara Saihi.*

"Countries such as the United States like to espouse the supposed benefits of freedom," said Saihi. "They believe that it is the divine right of all humans to choose their own path in life. But is that truly what is best for us as a race? Is that truly what is best for the planet? When people are allowed to live their lives in any manner they desire, the choices they make are inevitably the wrong ones. They choose to live only for themselves. To acquire wealth only for themselves, to live in houses with more space than any person needs, to own vehicles that pollute our air. They care nothing for the resources they steal from those most in need. They care nothing for the damage they cause our planet. When freedom is bestowed upon people, it gives birth to chaos."

McCullum nodded as Saihi went on. "What is more beneficial to the planet and all the species that live upon her? Is it billions of people following their own, narrow path of individualism, or billions of people following the same path of global responsibility? A path that will ensure all are clothed, fed, and sheltered. A path where all will achieve enlightenment. A path where all are of one mind, one voice, one world."

"One mind, one voice, one world," McCullum repeated. Energy rushed through him. He felt reinvigorated. All doubt, all negative thoughts, removed. Guided by the wisdom of Ohmara Saihi, there was no way they could fail.

He picked up his tablet and opened another secure file, this one titled, *The Way to an Enlightened World by Ohmara Saihi.*

You can never have enough inspiration from this man.

McCullum read through the first two pages when an alert flashed in his secure email. It was from his Chief of Security Information.

Scylla trip to resort confirmed. Arrival in two days.

He sat straighter in his chair. "Scylla," a hideous sea monster from Greek mythology, was the codename for President Moore. "Resort" was the codename for her home state of Alaska.

McCullum forwarded the email to Secretary General Saihi. The reply came back a couple of minutes later. It sent a shudder of joy through him.

Initiate next phase of Operation: New Dawn.

SEVEN

Ruud stared at the tall pines around him. The only sound, other than his and Krista's footsteps, came from the water of the Talkeetna River lapping against the shore. He gazed beyond the river, to the large, jagged form of Mount McKinley in the distance, wishing the clouds around it would go away. That gleaming white peak was a thing of beauty.

He closed his eyes and breathed deep. A place like this made it easy to forget one's troubles.

Almost. Memories of *Klaipeda's* destruction and worries over the board of inquiry still floated across the back of his mind.

Ruud looked over his shoulder at Krista, dressed in a green-black-brown splotched ballcap and jacket, blue jeans and hiking boots. She also had a Smith & Wesson M&P40 pistol strapped to her side. In Alaska, you didn't go into the wilderness unless you were armed. You never knew when you might encounter either a two-legged or four-legged predator.

Ruud also carried a pistol, Krista's Ruger SR9.

"You want to take a break already?" She teased him.

He responded with a brief laugh. "Please. I've marched up to twelve miles, in full gear, without taking a break. I can manage a little nature hike. What about you?"

Krista's mouth hung open, pretending to look offended. "Are you kidding? Running back and forth on stage two hours a night is a great way to stay in shape. We keep going."

"Yes, ma'am." He threw her a salute, making her laugh.

They continued hiking, Ruud glancing back at her. Krista wasn't kidding about staying in shape. Her body appeared much more toned than it had during their college days.

They stopped a few times to take pictures of some of the wildlife they came across, like river otters, a red fox, even a bald eagle. At one point, Ruud held up his left fist, the military gesture for "halt" and pointed down the trail.

"What?" asked Krista.

He held a finger to his lips and pointed again.

"Oh," Krista whispered. "I see him."

A lynx stood off to the side of the trail, its face buried in a brown and red lump, maybe a squirrel or rabbit. The brown-furred cat snapped its head toward them, held them in its gaze for a few moments, then sprinted into the brush.

"Got 'im." Krista waggled her phone in front of her. "Been a while since I've seen a lynx around here. This is why I love going on these hikes." She sidled up to Ruud and nudged him with her elbow. "Just like old times, huh?"

"Yeah," he smiled at her, thinking of all the nature hikes they did back at UAA. A rush of heat went through him. If this really had been like old times, they would have stopped, put down a blanket, and made love in the middle of the woods.

She stepped in front of him, her eyes darting to the side. "So, um, are you with anyone?"

"I was. She was an Osprey pilot. We were together almost a year, then she got transferred to Okinawa. It's sort of hard to maintain a relationship when you're seven thousand miles apart."

"I'm sorry," said Krista.

Ruud shrugged. "That's what happens when Marines date one another. One day things are going really well, the next, one of you is shipped off to the other side of the world." He held his breath for a moment before speaking. "Um, what about you?"

"Single again. You know that band Shattered Sky?"

"Yeah. I love their song 'Fallen Icon.'"

"Well, they opened for us during our *Cosmic Tapestry* tour. Their guitar player and I just hit it off."

Ruud tensed, not wanting to think about Krista being with another guy. He tried to be logical. *What, you expected her to be celibate the last fifteen years? You sure as hell haven't.*

That still didn't make him comfortable to hear her talk about her love life.

"Then," Krista continued, "after the tour, well, we both went to separate studios with our bands to work on our next albums, then we went on tour, playing in different cities, sometimes even different countries, on the same night."

She walked over to the edge of the trail, staring out at the Talkeetna River. "We sure as hell didn't choose careers that are conducive to relationships, did we?"

"You're right about that." He moved next to her.

Krista turned to him. "Well, I may be thirty-seven and not married, but I sure as shit love what I'm doing. How about you?" She winced. "Oh, um, sorry."

"No, that's fine." Ruud gently squeezed her arm, feeling a brief shudder go through her. "I love what I do. Or maybe it's more accurate to say I find my job satisfying, important. Much as some people what to bury their heads in the sand about it, there are a lot of evil people in this world, and the only thing they want to do is kill. Americans, Europeans, anyone who doesn't go along with whatever twisted philosophy they're peddling. I make sure they don't hurt any more innocent people, ever. Whether I get to do that again, well, that's up in the air."

"What . . . what do you think'll happen to you?"

"It depends. If the board recommends court martial and I'm found guilty, you're going to have yourself a prison pen pal. If the board decides not to recommend court martial, or if they do and I'm found innocent, two things. One, they *persuade* me to leave The Corps, or two, they turn me into a REMF."

"REMF?" Krista's brow furrowed.

"Rear-Echelon Mother Fucker. Basically, someone who never gets within a hundred miles of an actual battlefield." Ruud scowled. "I didn't join up to spend all my time sitting at a fucking desk typing up reports and recommendations that no one will read. If that happens, then you can bet your ass my time in The Corps will be over sooner rather than later."

"Then what will you do?"

Ruud looked out at the river. "I have no idea."

Krista rubbed his arm. Ruud felt a hitch in his breath before she spoke. "I'm sure there are plenty of bands in the market for a new bass player. You still play, right?"

"On occasion. Probably not enough to get hooked up with even a halfway decent band."

"Bullshit," said Krista. "You were a kick ass bass player."

"Yeah, fifteen years ago."

"That sort of talent is in the blood. It doesn't go away." Krista paused. "Hell, if that doesn't pan out, you can come to work for our security staff."

"Thanks, but I don't want any charity."

"What fucking charity? Shit, you're a Marine commando. You've, like, fought terrorists. Some drunken asshole rushing the stage shouldn't be a problem."

Ruud grinned. "Thanks. I guess I just want to see how this all plays out before I make any decisions."

They hiked for another hour before heading back to Krista's cabin. After washing up, she headed for the kitchen. "What do you think of caribou steaks for dinner?"

"Caribou steaks?" Ruud's mouth watered. "You know how long it's been since I've had that?"

"Probably not since you left Alaska. I doubt there are a lot of places in the Lower Forty-Eight that serve 'em. Go chill out while I get 'em ready."

Ruud flopped down on the sofa, anticipation rising as he thought of his first taste of caribou meat in fifteen years. He picked up the remote and turned on the large, wall-mounted plasma screen TV.

"Wait a minute." Krista marched out of the kitchen and snatched the remote from his hand.

"What the hell?"

"I don't want you watching any news. You're supposed to forget about the real world." Krista went over to a shelf next to the TV and pulled out a DVD. "Here. Watch this. It's our set from Wacken Open Air last year."

She put the disc in the player, turned it on, and went back to the kitchen.

Ruud settled into the large cushions as the program opened with an overhead shot the huge crowd. There had to be tens of thousands. Icefire started off with a hard, powerful orchestral sound, followed by thrashing guitars. Then Krista bounded onto the stage, hand raised, index finger and pinky extended in the heavy metal salute. Ruud stiffened when he saw her outfit, a black leather top and mini-skirt that showed off her firm, shapely legs.

My God, she is so beautiful.

"Wacken!" Krista hollered. "Are you ready to bang your fucking heads?"

Ruud swallowed. That turned him on even more.

He watched the concert, enjoying the music, especially Krista's operatic voice. He also enjoyed watching her run and jump around the stage, doing some very good karate kicks, and whipping her black-purple hair up and down as she banged her head to guitar solos.

He prayed no one told him to stand anytime soon.

The concert was three-quarters over when Krista called to him, "All right. It's caribou time."

The meal was delicious. The rich, tender taste made him realize how much he missed caribou meat. He also realized Krista was a damn good cook. She hadn't shown off skills like this when they dated. Then again, beyond making oatmeal or Raman Noodles in their dorms, most college students rarely cooked for themselves.

They kept the dinner conversation light, mainly about Icefire's performance at Wacken Open Air. More than once, Ruud imagined himself standing side-by-side with Krista, rocking the bass at one of Europe's largest metal festivals.

After dinner, he finished watching the rest of Icefire's Wacken performance. He looked over the rest of Krista's concert DVDs, trying to decide between Iron Maiden or Nightwish when she called out, "Jan-Erik. Could you come down here?"

He walked out of the living room, past the kitchen, and down to the basement. To his right, boxes and storage containers lined the walls. To the left was a small studio. Krista stood inside, holding up a black bass guitar, a Squire Vintage Modified Jaguar by the look of it.

"What's this all about?"

"I've been working on a new song the past couple of weeks and want to hear how the bass sounds in it."

"And you want me to play?"

"Duh. You were our original bass player. Come on, show me what you got . . . that is, if you still got anything."

Ruud shot her a faux scowl. "Give me that."

She grinned and handed him the Jaguar. He put the strap around his neck, feeling that familiar tingle going through his body, the one he always felt right before he was about to play.

Krista showed him sheets of paper with hand-written lyrics and musical notes. The title was "Slave to the Screen." It looked like a pretty intense song.

Cool.

Ruud's middle and index fingers worked the strings, producing a deep, driving beat, while Krista sang, the lyrics telling the story of a young girl trying to free herself from her generation's enslavement by cell phones and social media. A few times, Ruud added his own licks when he felt the emotion of the song called for it.

When she finished singing, she turned to him with a smile. "Shit a fucking brick, you fucking rocked!"

"Well, maybe I do play more than occasionally."

"How about you just have it in you?" Krista gently poked Ruud's chest. The touch sent a quiver through his body. "You're a natural. You always have been."

"Thanks. And I think you've come up with a kick ass song for your next album."

"I'm glad you think so. It's just, sometimes it drives me nuts to see kids with their noses buried in their phones every minute of the day. My God, there's more to this world than staring at a fucking screen and telling everyone what mood you're in."

A jolt of energy went through Ruud. That was another quality of Krista's he loved. Her passion. She never held back about things that pissed her off.

They continued to work on the song, adding and deleting lyrics, figuring out which words to emphasize, where the best place was for a guitar solo, how the synthesizers should generate an orchestral swell toward the end as the girl comes to her decision to throw away her cell phone and explore the world around her.

"Look at us," Ruud said. "Sitting around, working on new songs. Just like old times, huh?"

"Yeah, just like old times." Krista bit her lip. "Well, not quite."

She stared at him, not saying a word. He met her gaze, taking in those dark green eyes, those milky, flawless features.

"You know how many times I've kicked myself for leaving you?" Ruud said.

"You know how many times I've wondered what life would have been like if we stayed together?" Krista responded.

"That would have been tough, considering what we do for a living."

"Yeah. Still . . ." Krista stared at the floor, then looked back up at him. "C'mon."

She walked out of the studio without waiting for a response.

Ruud set the bass on its stand and followed her upstairs to the living room. She gave him a seductive smile and lay on the bearskin rug next to the fireplace.

"What are you doing?" he asked.

"Do I have to draw you a picture?"

"It might help get me more aroused."

Krista laughed. "You mean you're not aroused enough? I'm insulted."

Ruud smiled and lowered himself beside her. He took her in his arms and kissed her.

EIGHT

Ruud's eyes flickered open. Sunlight streamed through the blinds over the bedroom window. He stretched under the covers.

Krista lay beside him, arms around her pillow.

Grinning, he played with strands of her black and purple hair. Heat gripped his body as he recalled last night. They had made love on the bearskin rug, then on the sofa before moving to the bedroom. In all their time together at UAA, he couldn't remember a night so intense, so passionate. It was like they tried to make up for spending the last fifteen years apart.

Ruud continued stroking Krista's hair, staring at her smooth, clear face. His heartbeat picked up. It felt so good to be back with her.

But for how much longer?

He closed his eyes, not wanting to think about the *Klaipeda* or the board of inquiry. Krista was the only thing he wanted to think about.

Ruud moved his hand down her bare back, then along her side. He kissed her shoulder, then the back of her neck. She purred and opened her eyes.

"Good morning," he whispered in her ear, before kissing it.

"Mm, you're damn right it's a good morning." Krista ran her fingers through Ruud's beard.

"How about we make it a great morning?"

Krista smiled and slid against him, pressing her breasts against Ruud's chest and running her leg up and down his. Electric tingles surged through his body as they kissed, then made love.

After showering and dressing, they drove into what passed for Talkeetna's downtown, pulling into a gravel parking lot next to a wine-red wooden building with a white slanted roof. A hand-crafted sign out front read MILLIE'S CAFÉ. The diner was three-quarters full, most of the crowd locals, Ruud assumed.

"Mornin', Krista," several people greeted her. She responded in kind, then turned to the tall, lean Eskimo Ruud had seen eating tree bark on the side of the road the other day. "Why, Miles. You're actually eating real food today."

"One can't live on crickets alone, you know," said Miles Koonooka.

Ruud softly chuckled. Krista had told him over dinner last night that Koonooka did his own survival web series.

"Good morning, Krista." An overweight woman with blond-gray hair called out from behind the counter, which she thumped with her pudgy hand. "Have a seat right here."

"Thanks, Millie."

They headed over, Ruud noticing a wall-mounted TV tuned to what looked like a local morning show out of Anchorage. He forced himself to ignore it.

No news, remember.

Millie handed them menus after they sat down, her eyes darting to Ruud. She looked him up and down, smiled wide, and looked back at Krista. "So who's your friend?" Millie waggled her eyebrows.

"This is an old college friend of mine. J . . . John Erikson."

Ruud relaxed as Krista remembered to use his alias.

"Wonderful to meet you." Millie shook his hand. "Welcome to Talkeetna."

"Thank you, ma'am."

"Ooh, so formal. Just call me Millie, willya?"

"Okay, ma . . . Millie." Ruud stifled a groan. He had to remember to dial back his Marine bearing. He wanted to blend in as much as possible.

Millie took their drink orders, orange juice for him and English Breakfast Tea for Krista. She came back a couple of minutes later with their beverages, then took their breakfast orders. Millie headed to the kitchen as a paunchy man in a light blue shirt, navy blue pants and Smoky Bear entered the cafe.

"Hey, Ed," Krista greeted him.

"Miss Brandt," the Alaska state trooper muttered, then sat at the counter. A slim, blond teenage waitress poured him a cup of coffee when a man with a scraggily gray beard and worn flannel shirt came up to him. The trooper groaned. "What is it this time, Deke?"

"It's that Tracey kid. I keep tellin' you, Sergeant Harlow, he's always driving by my trailer, blarin' that damn noise he calls music, wakin' me up. When are you gonna throw his ass in the clink?"

"I already talked to Will Tracey. He says he's keeping his stereo down."

"Well he's lyin'. Kids today, they got no respect for anyone. Selfish little creeps, all of them."

"Oh just chill, Deke," said a woman with long brown hair and a flowery, ankle-length skirt sitting at a nearby table. "Kids need to express themselves. We can't put limitations on them and stifle their creativity."

"Bah! Express themselves. You know what that is, Solstice? Another way of saying let 'em act like a bunch of animals. And it's no wonder they do, listening to a bunch of drugged out idiots screaming about screwing everything in sight and shooting cops." Deke fixed his gaze on Krista.

"C'mon, Deke. I don't do drugs and I've never sung about killing cops."

"So you say." Deke turned back to Sergeant Harlow. "Just do something about Tracey already."

Deke tromped back to his seat.

Harlow grumbled something and sipped his coffee.

Ruud leaned closer to Krista and whispered, "Well that was entertaining."

"Oh, it's just Deke being Deke. He bitches to Ed Harlow about everything. But every little town needs their resident grumpy old man."

"He looks happy about that." Ruud nodded to Harlow.

"Ed's not happy in general. Story is, he was transporting a prisoner to Juneau. They stopped for a pee break and the guy escaped. Took two days to find him."

"So they exiled him here." Ruud knew little towns like Talkeetna didn't have their own police force and relied on the Alaska State Troopers for their law enforcement needs.

"Yeah. And for him, Talkeetna has to be the ass end of nowhere. Not that living in the ass end of nowhere is all that bad."

A few minutes later, Millie came out with their breakfasts. Ruud had scrambled eggs, hash browns, and toast. Krista had oatmeal and a bowl of fruit.

"So what plans do you two have?" Millie asked.

"Oh, maybe go hunting, head up to Mount McKinley, and some . . . other activities." A wry grin formed on Krista's face.

"You naughty girl." Millie giggled. She then patted Ruud's hand. "I'm sure you'll have a wonderful time. Hopefully a *very* wonderful time."

With an ear-to-ear grin, Millie headed off to other end of the counter.

"She's . . . something," Ruud said.

"Millie's a sweetheart. She always looks out for me when I'm up here."

They ate their breakfasts, Krista chatting with some of the other patrons. The hippie chick, Solstice, talked about the latest earthenware pottery she'd created. Harlow groused about how his son, who lived with his ex-wife in Juneau, would rather play video games all day instead of getting a summer job. A distinguished-looking man named Clyde Lasher, a former network news reporter, discussed the topic for his community radio show - photo radar in Anchorage - an idea he considered idiotic. The teenage waitress named Ginny explained in an excited tone how the same Will Tracey that Deke bitched about invited her to go off-roading with him this weekend.

It amused Ruud. A successful rock star sat in this little café and folks talked to her about everyday things, like she was a neighbor instead of a celebrity.

He loved the fact that, despite her wealth and fame, Krista remained as down to earth as she had been during their college days.

"Aw, man. It's happening. It's happening."

Ruud turned to a bearded man with a paunch sitting farther down the counter, who pointed at the TV. A male news anchor was on the screen, the shield and dove symbol of the DPE displayed in the top right hand corner.

"Secretary General Saihi said the deployment of DPE personnel to Cuba is in response to that government's request for additional security forces to deter what they call, quote, 'Potential American aggression in the wake of their recent illegal war with Venezuela,' end quote. UN officials say they will send additional peace enforcers to the DPE base in Nicaragua. A State Department spokesman said these moves only heighten tensions in the Caribbean."

Ruud gritted his teeth, trying to fight off the memories of the *Klaipeda* blowing up.

"See?" The man looked at the other patrons. "Cuba, Nicaragua, that fleet sailing around the Pacific. They're surrounding us. It won't be long before UN troops are in every city, making us bow down to that SOB Saihi."

Ruud furrowed his brow. *Is this guy for real?* He'd trust a man selling him a Rolex on a New York street corner more than he ever would Saihi and the UN, but to think they'd really invade the United States? That was serious conspiracy theory paranoia.

"Protests and acts of violence stemming from the *Klaipeda* sinking continue throughout the country," the anchor continued. "Thousands demonstrated outside the naval base in San Diego yesterday. Authorities say two hundred were arrested, with hundreds of thousands of dollars in property damage reported. In Bremerton, Washington, three Navy sailors were hospitalized after being assaulted by a group of self-described Saihi supporters. The UN Friends of Peace is urging its supporters through Facebook and Twitter to go to Alaska, where President Moore is due to arrive tomorrow for her summer vacation."

"Unbelievable." The man threw up his hands. "Saihi's got our own people doing his dirty work. He's already got an army of collaborators for when the DPE comes."

"Yeah, sure, Andy," muttered Harlow.

"Hey, this is what the UN's been planning all along. This whole Directorate of Peace Enforcement is a bunch of crap. It's an army, an army big enough to take us on. That's what they want to do. Take over the U.S., then the world. Then everyone gets told what to do, what to say, and you can kiss your guns good-bye."

"That's fine with me," said Solstice. "The world would be a better place without guns."

"Yeah, for wanna-be dictators like Saihi. An unarmed populace is easier to control than an armed one."

"Saihi's not a dictator," Solstice countered. "He just wants what's best for the world."

"What's best for the world is letting people live their own lives." Andy scowled at the TV. "I tell you, if any DPE jackboots try to take my guns, they're in for a fight."

Ruud stared at Andy for a few more moments before turning back to Krista. "What's that guy's story?"

"Andy Dempster? He's been going on for years about the UN taking over the world. But they're not doing it by themselves. They're actually controlled by the Trilateral Commission, or the Illuminati, or maybe aliens. Sometimes it's hard to keep track of all his crazy-ass conspiracy theories."

When they finished eating, Krista paid for their breakfasts, leaving a very generous tip.

"Quite a few colorful characters for such a small town," Ruud said as they walked across the parking lot.

"I love 'em. I'd rather be around people like this than the brain dead, self-important dipshits those manufactured pop stars always hang with."

Ruud couldn't help but smile as he got into the jeep.

"So what shall it be today?" Krista started the engine. "Hunting, fishing, or spending the rest of the day in bed?"

Ruud squeezed her hand. "As long as it involves being with you, and not watching any news, I'm fine with anything."

Krista tilted her head and raised her thin eyebrows. "Then spending the rest of the day in bed it is."

NINE

I wonder what my father would think of what I am about to do.

The thought came to Saihi as he sat at his desk, staring at the wall monitor that displayed the feeds from several security cameras in front of UN Headquarters.

He probably would not approve. Or maybe he would be jealous that I had the courage to act while he did not.

Saihi swung his chair toward the window in his office. He stared at the overcast sky, memories of his younger years spent in America surfacing. Streets jammed with vehicles polluting the air. Garbage strewn everywhere. Corporations forcing people to buy useless products or stuff themselves with disgusting, unhealthy food. Every time he turned on the news, there had been something about the Cold War. Saihi snorted. How long had the U.S. kept the nations of the world pitted against one another in order to sell weapons and steal oil?

What had his father done about it? He complained, every damn night.

"Why can't you do anything to change their minds?" Saihi had asked on more than one occasion.

Most times, his father answered, "There are too many egos, too many agendas, too many self-serving individuals."

Saihi shook his head. Even back then, he knew that creating a better world was impossible so long as selfish people held positions of power.

He thought his father was different. He thought as Morocco's UN ambassador he would keep working to bring peace and enlightenment to the world.

Then came that day. Saihi had been twenty, home for the weekend from Fordham. His father had come home, looking depressed. When Saihi asked what was wrong, his father muttered his usual complaints. What hadn't been usual was the way he ended it.

"World peace is impossible, a delusion. No one can ever bring it about."

On that day, he'd lost all respect for his father. He saw the man for what he truly was. Weak. He opted to do what the vast majority of people did. Just stand by and let all the suffering in the world continue.

Saihi vowed he would never be like his father. He took more communications classes at Fordham, joined the school's debate club. He learned techniques on how to persuade people, and put it to good use.

Marching and holding up signs had accomplished nothing. Instead, Saihi convinced several classmates to take more direct action in bringing about change. They wrecked the university's ROTC office and vandalized vehicles and buildings at Fort Hamilton. If an article appeared in the Fordham student newspaper they disagreed with, they snatched up every copy and destroyed them. Billboards, businesses, fast food restaurants, churches. He and his followers targeted them all. Many had been arrested. Since his father's diplomatic immunity extended to Saihi, the American police couldn't touch him.

He turned back to the monitor. One feed showed a line of taxis across the street, ready to take UN employees home, or wherever else they needed to go. Maybe to a bar or restaurant to fill their bodies with poison. Maybe to some meaningless sporting event, or an art gallery, or a theater, or a whorehouse. Someplace to pursue their selfish needs instead of doing something to serve the planet.

Saihi glanced at the time display in the corner of one of the feeds. 4:50. It should happen in about ten minutes.

He passed the time posting on his Facebook page and Twitter account. *American Friends of Peace. I will speak to you live tomorrow at 9 p U.S. EDT.*

In a couple of minutes, he'd received hundreds of likes. The number climbed by the second.

Saihi looked up at the security feeds. He pressed his palms down on the desk. His heartbeat increased, fueled by anticipation.

Men and women filed out of the building. Regular employees, mostly. Tour guides, food servers, maintenance workers, administrative assistants. A few minutes passed before he picked out the faces of some of the ambassadors. Russia. The Netherlands. Kenya. Thailand.

Perhaps now?

Then he saw the American and Israeli ambassadors.

As much as he wished it, it couldn't happen now.

The American ambassador stopped to talk with reporters near the front entrance.

No, dammit. Keep moving. Saihi's breaths quickened as he watched more people stream out of the building. This could not happen with the American ambassador in the vicinity.

The man finally gave a short wave and went on his way. Saihi exhaled in relief.

The line of people continued. Saihi's eyes flickered between the crowd and the cabs across the street. A few drove off. He noticed one UN employee standing beside a taxi, jabbing his hands out to the side as if arguing. After a few more seconds, he stomped away.

Saihi felt a bead of nervous sweat trickle down his left temple. How much longer?

The driver's side door of a taxi opened. The driver shoved his hands in his pockets and walked away at a quick pace.

A couple of minutes passed. The mass of UN employees thinned. Saihi recognized four ambassadors exiting the building. Finland, Paraguay, Botswana and Malaysia. All four he counted among his loyal supporters.

Such a shame.

Saihi tensed. He sensed it happening any second . . . any second . . .

The abandoned cab disappeared in a fireball. The blast washed over the other taxis. Saihi heard a deep rumble from the street below. A vibration went through the building. The images on all the cameras shook. All the people in front of the building, well over a hundred, collapsed. Many were soaked with blood.

Saihi shut off the monitors, got up and hurried to the window. He was only a few feet away when two of his bodyguards burst into his office.

"Mister Secretary," one of them, a burly tan-skinned man, shouted, "We must go!"

"What, what happened?" Saihi did his best to sound stunned.

The bodyguards took him by the arms and hustled him out of the office. Other tough-looking, dark-suited men formed a human wall around him, leading him to the nearest stairwell. He knew they wouldn't use the elevator. If the power went out, he'd be trapped inside, an easy target.

One of the bodyguards shoved open the door. They all rushed down the stairs. Saihi maintained his shocked, confused look for the benefit of his bodyguards. None of them knew the truth about what just happened.

Inside, Saihi felt nothing but satisfaction.

TEN

It was just before five in the morning when Ruud and Krista left the cabin. He paused on the porch, looking at the sunlight filtering through the trees.

"I think I'm starting to get used to this again."

"What?" Krista looked over her shoulder as she descended the stairs.

"The sun being out this early," Ruud answered, "and not going down until nearly midnight."

"One of the perks of living in this state." Krista grinned.

"Yeah, but trade off is sixteen or eighteen-hour nights in the winter."

"That just means spending more time indoors, for other activities." She waggled her eyebrows at him.

Ruud chuckled as he got into Krista's jeep. They drove south to Seward for a day of whale watching. Worry scratched the back of his mind as he approached the boat. He glanced at the other people around him. He hadn't watched or read any news since breakfast at Millie's yesterday. Had the press identified him and the other Iron Devils as the Marines who sank the *Klaipeda?*

General Dobson would have contacted me if that happened. Even so, his beard, sunglasses, and ballcap should be an adequate enough disguise. That and covering up his Swedish accent.

He looked over at Krista, who wore a UAA ballcap and sunglasses, and had her hair in a bun. No one appeared to recognize her. If anyone did, Ruud had no doubt they'd take a picture and post it on some social media site. That would bring the paparazzi here in no time.

Or maybe not. Paparazzi and tabloids concentrated more on pop stars and asinine celebrities than on heavy metal singers, even ones as successful as Krista.

They cruised down the Kenai Fjords. Ruud stood along the starboard observation deck, his arm around Krista. They spotted seals, stellar sea lions, a pod of orcas, and the capper, a pair of humpback whales. He marveled at the creatures. So immense and powerful, yet so peaceful.

He breathed in the salty air, his eyes flickering between the humpbacks and the mountains around them. Where else but in Alaska could he witness a gorgeous scene like this?

Where else but in Alaska could he be with Krista?

The boat returned to the pier early in the afternoon. Ruud followed the flow of the crowd, holding hands with Krista. He felt . . . normal. He wasn't a Marine, just a guy spending the day with a beautiful, wonderful woman.

Ruud squeezed Krista's hand as they returned to the jeep and drove north. When they reached Anchorage, Krista said, "You in the mood for an early dinner?"

"That sounds good to me. Where do you want to go?"

"I'm gonna surprise you."

She exited Route One onto Northern Lights Boulevard. The houses on the left, the businesses on the right, and the trees lining the road were all familiar to him. As they approached one intersection, Ruud's brow furrowed. He leaned forward, catching sight of a white wood building on the corner with a slanted roof. His eyes widened when he recognized it.

"Are you going where I think you're going?"

Krista smiled and nodded. "You bet your sexy ass I am."

Ruud felt a rush of elation as he gazed at the white sign with red trim near the parking lot entrance. "Hank's Meats N' Eats: Home of Alaska's Best Moose Burger."

They aren't kidding. The restaurant had been a favorite hangout for Ruud, Krista, and their friends at college.

After they pulled into the parking lot, Ruud turned to Krista. "You are the most awesome woman that ever lived." He kissed her.

"Thanks. I figured you haven't had a moose burger since you graduated."

"Not just any moose burger, but . . ."

"The best moose burger in Alaska," they said at the same time, then laughed.

They entered the restaurant. Less than a quarter of the tables were full. It was just a little after four. Business would probably pick up soon.

A portly, dark-haired waitress seated them by one of the windows and took their drink orders. Ruud checked the menu, settling on his choice quickly, BBQ moose burger with fries. He looked out the window at the middle school on the other side of the intersection. His eyebrows knitted together when he noticed something beyond the main building. A large video screen poked up from the athletic field. Hundreds of people gathered around it.

The waitress, Rachel according to her nametag, returned with their drinks and took their orders.

"Do you know what's going on over there?" Ruud pointed down the street.

Rachel snorted. "Them? They're fans of that UN guy, the one calling the President and our Marines murderers."

"Secretary General Saihi."

"Yeah. Him. They've been flying in from the Lower Forty-Eight the past couple'a days."

Ruud nodded, remembering the newscast from yesterday about the UN Friends of Peace coming to Alaska to protest President Moore during her vacation.

"So why are they all over there?" asked Krista.

"They're gonna watch some speech by Saihi," answered Rachel. "I guess he's gonna talk about that car bomb."

Ruud sat up straighter. "What car bomb?"

"You didn't hear?"

"No." Ruud shook his head. "We've been out of the loop the last couple of days."

"Oh, it was horrible." Rachel put a hand over her chest. "This car blew up right in front of the UN building. Killed a hundred people, I think."

"Oh my God," stammered Krista.

"I know. Times like this, I'm glad I'm in Alaska, far away from all that craziness."

Rachel left to put in their orders. Ruud looked across the table. "Um, Krista. I know you said --"

"Oh forget it. I think this is something we need to look at."

They both took out their phones. Ruud pressed the news app. His grip on the cell phone tightened when he saw the headline.

"Four Ambassadors Among 86 Dead in UN Bombing."

According to the article, the bomb had been hidden in a taxi and exploded after five in the afternoon, when many UN ambassadors and employees were leaving. Investigators found evidence the device had been homemade with fertilizer, gasoline, and nails. Along with the eighty-six dead, over a hundred-fifty had been injured. A group calling itself the Sword of Freedom took credit for the attack.

"This is the last thing we need," Ruud said in a hushed tone.

"Saihi can't blame the President for this." Krista looked up from her phone. "This was just some group of crazies who killed all those people."

"Don't bet on it. People like Saihi always find a way to blame the U.S. for everything."

Their food arrived a few minutes later. The moose burger tasted good, great actually, but Ruud found it hard to enjoy after reading about the UN bombing. His eyes kept drifting to the large screen down the street. The crowd had grown over the past ten minutes. He guessed they had to number over a thousand. A few police officers had also shown up, standing around the intersection.

When he and Krista finished eating, they exited the restaurant. Krista headed toward the parking lot.

Ruud headed down the street.

"Where are you going?" asked Krista.

"I want to see what Saihi says."

"What?" Krista's voice went up an octave.

"What can I say? I'm curious, especially since whatever comes out of that shithead's mouth could have an impact on my life, and the lives of my men."

Krista folded her arms and tilted her head. "You do know you're going into the lion's den. What if they find out you were involved in the *Klaipeda's* sinking?"

"They haven't released my name yet, and anyway, I'm in disguise." He rubbed his beard. "Come on."

Krista emitted a heavy sigh, then threw out her arms. "Aw, what the hell. This wouldn't be the first stupid-ass thing I've ever done."

They crossed the street, passing the cops, and walked toward the athletic field. A thick mass of humanity stood around the screen. More people packed the sidewalk along the fence. Many wore the blue UN Friends of Peace armbands. A bearded, stringy-haired man with a bullhorn stood on a bench, punching the air with a fist as he spoke.

"President Moore and the white power structure she serves are no longer keeping their true intentions secret. They are now murdering non-Americans and non-Caucasians in full view of the world. Anyone who doesn't look like them or talk like them or think like them is an enemy, an enemy they want to exterminate!"

The crowd booed. Some shouted, "Down with the U.S.A.!" or "Exterminate President Moore!"

"Assholes." Ruud hissed through clenched teeth.

He and Krista crossed the street. More Friends of Peace stood along the sidewalk. Ruud spotted a few police officers and news crews along the periphery of the crowd. Beyond them stood a group of about two hundred, several holding American flags. Counter-protestors. That sent a rush of pride through him, followed by disappointment that more hadn't shown up.

Ruud started to turn back to the screen when movement nearby caught his attention. A girl with long brown hair and a rainbow-colored Rasta beret waved her arms as she spoke with two lanky young men, one with a beard, one without shoes.

"You know Moore ordered that bombing, just like she told those butchers in the military to blow up that ship."

"I read this blog that said it was the CIA that bombed the UN," the bearded kid said. "They just pretended to be domestic terrorists."

"Yeah, well wait till you hear this." Shoeless held up a finger. "A bunch of people are saying when Congress passes that bill to get us out of the UN, Moore's gonna start bombing DPE bases all over the world."

"I believe it," the girl declared. "The DPE's a threat to American imperialism."

A groan bubbled in Ruud's throat. He didn't know whether to be angry at their comments or astounded by their sheer stupidity.

The screen flickered to life, showing a couple of news talking heads sitting in a studio. They spent about two minutes giving their thoughts on what Saihi might say in his speech when one of them said, "We've just received word that Secretary General Saihi is stepping to the podium, so we now go live to United Nations Headquarters in New York."

The scene cut to Saihi standing at a lectern with a large blue and white UN flag in the background. He looked directly at the camera.

"My fellow global citizens, before I begin, I ask that you take a moment to remember all those who perished so horribly in yesterday's attack on this very building."

Silence fell over the crowd. Ruud counted to ten in his head before Saihi resumed.

"These are dark times for the United Nations, for all those who embrace peace and enlightenment. Over the past two weeks, this organization has been the victim of two deadly, unprovoked attacks. First, our peace support vessel *Klaipeda* was sunk by the U.S. military, costing the lives of over two hundred and eighty men and women. As heinous as that attack was, the people on that ship knew the risks that came with trying to accomplish their desire of ridding the world of the scourge of war. It was a risk they accepted. But yesterday's attack . . ."

Saihi paused, biting his lower lip. Ruud wondered if all the deaths truly affected him or if it was an act for the camera.

"Yesterday's attack on United Nations Headquarters was one of the most depraved acts of evil I have ever encountered. The men and women who were slaughtered just outside this building of peace were unarmed, a threat to no one. They were translators, cooks, maintenance workers. Ordinary people playing a part, no matter how small, in trying to make this world better for all. Yet what was their reward? A brutal, agonizing death."

Ruud noticed some of the people in the crowd weeping or putting comforting arms around each other.

"It would be easy to lay the blame on these two attacks at the feet of the American Marines and this group calling itself the Sword of Freedom," Saihi went on. "But blame must also be placed on the woman who has slandered the United Nations, claiming we cater to dictators and terrorists, making baseless accusations that we want to rule the world. Such words planted seeds of hatred in the Marines and the members of the Sword of Freedom, seeds that culminated in horrific acts of violence."

Saihi straightened. "The woman I am referring to is, of course, American President Emily Moore."

Many in the crowd booed or shouted things like, "Murdering bitch" and "Nazi cunt!" It caused Ruud to miss part of Saihi's speech.

". . . must learn that such rhetoric has consequences. Consequences that lead to tragedies such as this."

The screen dissolved from Saihi to a photo of a young, pretty black girl with smooth, angular features and her hair in a bun.

"This is Alimata Riner," said Saihi. "A twenty year old woman from France, studying social sciences at New York University. She was on a summer internship here at the United Nations. A bright young woman whose heart was filled with compassion for this planet and all that inhabit it. Her goal after graduation was to join a humanitarian organization and help those affected by war, famine, and disease. Now, Alimata will never have that opportunity. She was one of the eighty-six innocents murdered in yesterday's attack."

More people in the crowd cried. Krista lowered her head. Ruud felt a wave of sympathy toward this poor girl. He also felt disgust at Saihi for using her to further his agenda against President Moore.

"Poor Alimata would still be alive were it not for President Moore's irresponsible and hateful words toward the United Nations and those who serve this great organization," Saihi continued. "Many of you, no doubt, will demand she apologize for her comments that inspired this violence. But mere words of remorse cannot undo the damage that has been done. Only action can. I call upon President Moore to turn over the Marines who sank the *Klaipeda* to the International Criminal Court, along with any members of the Sword of Freedom responsible for the attack on United Nations Headquarters. Once she has done that, President Moore must do the honorable thing and resign from office, along with her entire cabinet."

Screams of joy erupted from the crowd, rivaling the volume Ruud had heard at packed stadiums and arenas by fans cheering their sports teams. It drowned out what Sahai was saying for a full minute.

". . . up to you, my Friends of Peace. You must unite your voices. You must take to the streets and let the world hear your demands. You must not stop, you must not waver, until everyone responsible for these reprehensible actions is brought to justice. Rest assured, I will join with your voices. Together, *we will have justice*. Nothing can stop us when we are of one mind, one voice, one world."

"One mind, one voice, one world," the crowd chanted.

A chill went up Ruud's spine. He'd been under fire countless times during his life, but what he witnessed here was just as scary. These people weren't merely supporters of Saihi. They were followers, or maybe worshippers would be a better word. He also found the way Saihi spoke unsettling. He never yelled like a madman. His voice had a soothing, hypnotic quality. No matter what he said, you felt compelled to listen.

Ruud could only think of one way to describe Saihi. Cult leader.

"That is one crazy-ass mother fucker," Krista said to him, keeping her voice low.

"What did you say?" came a shrill voice nearby.

Ruud's head snapped to the right. The young woman with the beret stared at them, trembling with fury.

That girl must have rabbit ears.

"Aw hell." Krista sighed, then gave a resigned shrug. "I said, that is one crazy-ass mother fucker."

"How dare you?" the girl stomped toward them, followed by her male friends. Ruud tensed, bracing himself for trouble.

"Secretary General Saihi is dedicated to the cause of peace. How dare you say that about him?"

"You probably loved it when the UN got bombed," said the bearded kid. "Fewer minorities and foreigners in the world, huh?"

"You are so full of shit," Krista snapped back.

"I bet you're spies for that psycho bitch Moore." Shoeless stabbed a finger at them. "What, you gonna send your drones here to blow us all up?" He whirled around. "Hey! President Moore sent her spies her. She wants to kill us for not supporting her corporate war machine."

Ruud's heart pounded as twenty more Friends of Peace moved toward him.

ELEVEN

"Okay, everybody." Ruud held up his hands. "Calm down. Everyone has the right to their opinion, whether you agree with it or not."

"Fuck you and your freedom of speech crap!" Beret Girl shouted. "That's just code for blocking everything we do in the name of peace."

The small crowd cheered her. Several pointed at Ruud and Krista, shouting, "Nazis!" "Murderers!" "Racists!"

Ruud held his breath. He doubted he could talk his way out of this, and special ops Marine or not, no way was he going to win a twenty-on-one fight.

"What's the problem here?"

Ruud looked over the heads of the mob. Two cops walked toward them. Just two. He would have felt better if it had been thirty.

"Fuck off, pig!" yelled one young man.

"Try beating us, you shitheads." A girl held up her phone. "I'm recording you."

"Everyone calm down," ordered one officer.

The mob responded with more vulgarities.

Ruud grabbed Krista's arm and backed away. Every hair on his body tingled. This was going to get very ugly, very fast.

Shoeless reached into his backpack and pulled out a metal water bottle. "I got something for you jackboots!" He reared back his arm.

Ruud released Krista and rushed forward. Shoeless's arm started to come forward when Ruud lowered his shoulder. He slammed into the young man's back. Shoeless fell into two of his friends. The trio collapsed on the sidewalk in a tangle of arms and legs.

A dozen other Friends of Peace glared at him.

This isn't going to end well. Ruud crouched in a fighting stance. He knew he was going down, but he'd make damn sure he took some of these assholes with him.

"What the fuck?" He heard Krista yell behind him.

He turned. Beret Girl grabbed Krista's arm.

"I'm gonna show you what happens to --"

Beret Girl got interrupted by Krista's fist, which smashed into her mouth. The young woman spun and sank to her knees, blood spilling from her lips.

The rest of her friends started forward. Ruud brought up both fists.

Two streams of liquid splattered against the mob. Many coughed and pressed their hands against their faces. Ruud caught a whiff of a harsh, burning stench.

Pepperspray.

He twisted away, catching a glimpse through the mob of the cops with their spray canisters. He hurried over to Krista.

"Time to go." Ruud clutched her hand.

"I'm not gonna argue."

They ran a few yards when Ruud heard a crazed yell to his right. A tall black man rushed at him.

"I'm gonna kill you, mother fucker!"

Ruud shoved Krista aside, leaned to the left and stuck out his leg. The man tripped over it. His face cracked against the pavement. He lay there, groaning in pain. Ruud stared at him for a moment. He'd received some of the best hand-to-hand combat training in the Marine Corps, and what did he use to take down this dumbass? A tactic he'd learned on the playground when he was seven.

The air filled with angry shouts. Hundreds charged the police and counter-protestors. Fists went up and down. Objects flew through the air. A dark white cloud billowed up among the rioters. Tear gas.

Ruud reached out for Krista.

"Look out!" she screamed.

He spun around. Another rioter charged him, arms stretched out, ready to grab him.

Ruud grabbed the young man's left arm, pivoted and flung him over his shoulder. He landed on his back, face twisted in pain. Ruud dropped to one knee and punched him in the face for good measure.

"You! Don't move!"

Ruud looked up. A police officer hurried toward him, followed by two more.

"Oh for piss sake," he growled. General Dobson would love it if he got arrested in the middle of a riot.

"Krista! The fence!" Ruud jerked his head toward the wooden fence along the sidewalk.

Krista nodded. She ran at it, jumped and hauled herself over.

"I said stop, dammit!" The lead cop drew his taser.

Ruud grabbed the top of the fence and pulled himself up.

The cop fired his taser. The prongs clattered against the wood panels. Ruud threw one leg over, then the other, and landed in a backyard. Krista stood a couple of feet away. They ran out of the yard and down the little suburban street. Ruud checked over his shoulder. No sign of the police. Maybe they got held up by some rioters. He led Krista up a driveway and between a pair of cream-colored houses. Again he looked over his shoulder.

One cop appeared down the street. Then another.

"Shit." They didn't slow down as they neared another wooden fence. He and Krista scaled it with ease and found themselves behind a large rectangular building. The sounds of nearly a thousand voices raised in anger blanketed the neighborhood. Sirens blared in the distance.

Ruud ran along the alley between the building and the fence, Krista keeping up. They didn't have much time before the riot expanded to the surrounding blocks, or before the police caught up with them.

They reached the edge of the building. Ruud checked behind him. He couldn't see the cops. They couldn't be that far from the fence.

He and Krista raced around the corner. The parking lot for Hanks Meats N' Eats lay about a fifty yards away. Ruud took a couple of gulps of air. Invisible hands squeezed his lungs and legs. He looked at Krista. She was sucking down oxygen.

"Just a little farther." He squeezed her shoulder. "You can do it."

"Damn right I can do it. I ain't going to jail tonight."

After a final, deep breath, they took off running. Ruud's lungs felt like something was crushing them by the time they reached their jeep. Krista jammed the keys into the ignition. Ruud checked out the back window. No sign of the cops, yet.

"Go, go, go," he urged.

"I'm fucking going." Krista started the engine. The jeep shot out of the parking lot. A car horn blared behind them. The light at the intersection turned yellow. Krista sped up and jammed the wheel left. The jeep tore down Lake Otis Parkway.

When they reached 15th Avenue near the small airport, Krista turned left, picked up AK-1, and headed north. Ruud kept looking behind them for any police cars. He saw none.

"Don't stop until we're back in Talkeetna," he told Krista.

"I wasn't planning to."

Ruud allowed himself to relax when they left Anchorage behind them. He sagged in his seat.

Stupid, stupid, stupid. He turned to Krista. She could have beaten to a pulp, or worse, all because he wanted to see Saihi's speech.

"I'm sorry. I should have known better. You . . . you could have gotten hurt, and it would have been my fault."

"Hey, you weren't the one who mouthed off to the dumb hippie bitch and kicked off a riot. How about we say we were both stupid?"

"Deal."

Krista almost bounced in her seat. Ruud figured she was going through adrenaline overload.

"I probably shouldn't say this, but running from the cops like that . . ." She pounded on the steering wheel with her palm. "That was some serious fucking rebel rock star shit right there."

Ruud stared at her for several seconds . . . and broke out laughing. Part of him knew he shouldn't be laughing with a riot they caused going on back in Anchorage. But what the hell? He'd come this close to either being pummeled by nearly two dozen hardcore Saihi zombies or thrown in jail by the police. He'd escaped with both his body and freedom intact. He needed some kind of release, even if some might think it inappropriate.

Besides, what Krista said was damn funny.

Once he stopped laughing, he thought about Saihi's followers, how little it took to set them off. They'd probably cause a shitload of problems in Anchorage for the rest of the day, maybe for days to come.

And that's just a thousand of them. Worry gripped him when he realized Saihi had a few million followers across the United States.

TWELVE

When Ruud awoke the next morning, he stared at the ceiling, replaying the riot in his mind. As he had several times the previous night, he offered up a quick prayer of thanks to God for getting them out of there in one piece. When they got back to Talkeetna, he turned on one of the Anchorage channels. The riot had lasted a few hours. Several homes and businesses were damaged, hundreds had been arrested and several dozen people suffered injuries, none life threatening, thankfully.

It could have been a hell of a lot worse.

He pressed his head deeper into the pillow, thinking about Saihi's speech, thinking about the *Klaipeda,* thinking about something he'd said to Gunny Corcoran before they left for Alaska.

Ruud slid out of bed, glancing over at Krista. She was still asleep. He hit the bathroom, put on a fresh t-shirt and shorts, and went to the kitchen. After starting the coffee maker, he grabbed his tablet and sat on the sofa. The headlines on his news feed concerned massive protests in Washington, Los Angeles, New York, San Francisco, Denver and Seattle, all beginning hours after Saihi's speech. There had been arrests, acts of vandalism, and a few injuries, but no Anchorage-type riots.

Ruud searched various news sources, reading numerous articles. After nearly an hour, a pattern began to develop.

"Hey."

Ruud looked up. He felt a rush of heat below his waist. Krista stood in the living room entrance, clad in just a black Within Temptation t-shirt. He found it impossible to keep his eyes off her legs.

"Um, morning."

"What're you up to?" She glided over to him.

Ruud forced himself to look up at Krista's face. "Research."

"On what?" She plopped down next to him, folding her legs underneath her. Krista's knees brushed against his leg, fueling Ruud's desire.

He took a staggered breath, trying to refocus. "Um . . . I've been doing some thinking. "Before they sent us to Alaska, I mentioned to Gunny --"

"Who?"

"Sorry. Archie Corcoran, my gunnery sergeant. Anyway, I was telling him about a story I heard about the Albanian Intervention last year. The DPE had a frigate in the Adriatic that got close to one of our carriers. Too close, in fact."

"Did anything happen?" asked Krista.

"No." Ruud shook his head. "We had a missile lock on it, but we kept warning them to turn around. After about ten minutes, they did."

"Well that's good."

"You'd think so, but I dug a little deeper, and . . ." His jaw tightened. "I swear, I'm going to sound like your conspiracy theory friend Andy Dempster."

"Don't worry. I'm sure I can make you a decent tin foil hat." Krista grinned.

Ruud smiled back. "Right after we announced we were going to lead a NATO intervention into Albania, the DPE started moving a large number of troops, ships, and planes to their base in the Kuril Islands. They said it was part of an exercise called Copper Blue. But just when they had everything in place, they cancelled it."

"Why?"

"The UN never explained. But it takes a lot of time, effort, and money to put together a force like that for an exercise. You don't just cancel it without a reason. But here's what's weird. Everyone and everything that was supposed to be involved in Exercise Copper Blue stayed in the Kurils, at least until a few days ago when they sortied."

"So they wanted to keep them there until they were ready to do the exercise again," suggested Krista.

"No. When you cancel an exercise, you send your troops back to their original bases. I did some checking." Ruud held up his tablet. "The DPE has a good-sized base in the Kurils. Still, with about two divisions of soldiers, and all the extra pilots, groundcrew, and sailors, the place would be overcrowded. That's going to tax the base's resources, not to mention the mental strain it puts on the troops. You hardly have any elbow room, you're probably living in a tent, the weather is miserable, there's not much in the way of recreation, and it'd be tough to maintain their training. That's a recipe for low morale, discipline problems, even sickness, all of which equals ineffective soldiers."

"Then why keep 'em cooped up on that big bowl of suck?"

"I'm getting to that." Ruud shifted on the sofa. "I told you about the frigate the DPE sent out during the Albanian Intervention. Well, I found a few other interesting articles. Two months after we completed operations in Albania, a couple of DPE Rafale fighters from the Kurils penetrated U.S. air space. They flew over the Aleutians before some of our F-22s escorted them out. The UN claimed they strayed off-course. Then last November, we tracked a DPE submarine shadowing one of our carrier groups in the Mediterranean. Then in March, a DPE destroyer entered U.S. territorial waters off Virginia, about twenty miles from Norfolk, one of our largest naval bases."

"Did anything happen?" asked Krista.

"We sent out some planes and a Coast Guard cutter. They warned them off, several times. Eventually, they turned around. The DPE claimed the ship had a faulty GPS."

"So why are they doing all this?" Krista slid closer to Ruud. "It's almost like they want to provoke a fight with us."

Ruud said nothing. His face stiffened.

Krista tilted her head. "You really think that's what they want?"

"These are all provocative acts by a foreign power. Any one of them could have ended in shots being fired. They didn't . . . until the *Klaipeda.*"

"You think the *Klaipeda* was a part of this?"

"I do." Ruud nodded. "It's like for the past year Saihi's been goading us into taking a shot at his forces, and at Trinidad and Tobago, we took the bait."

"So why did he need five chances before that happened?" Krista brushed a strand of hair from her face. "Why didn't those guys do something before to get you to shoot at them?"

"They couldn't do anything obvious to provoke us, like paint our ships and planes with radar or ping our carrier with sonar. Then they'd look like the aggressor. They also couldn't linger in our waters or air space too long. A few minutes can be explained away as a plane or ship being off-course. Any longer and most people will assume you're up to no good. When too much time passed and we didn't open fire, they probably had to turn back."

"So you think the UN actually wants to start a war with us?"

"Maybe." Ruud rested the tablet on his leg. "I mean, along with those ships and planes trying to provoke us, look at Saihi's speeches of late. He's not trying to defuse the situation. If anything, he's making it worse."

Krista tensed before she spoke. "So what happens if we have a war?"

"The DPE has sizeable ground, sea, and air forces. They have good equipment, their personnel are well trained. In a straight up fight, we'd win, I don't doubt that. But we'd suffer a lot of losses."

Krista rubbed her forehead and exhaled slowly. "I don't understand. Why would Saihi start a war he can't win?"

"Maybe he's hoping for a pyrrhic victory. We decimate the DPE, but take a lot of casualties doing it. Our forces would be severely degraded, and Saihi can claim the DPE sacrificed itself to further the cause of peace and enlightenment. That's where Exercise Copper Blue comes in. A force that big could hit all our bases in the Pacific, the West Coast and right here in Alaska, and they put to sea just a few days ago."

Krista clenched one of the sofa cushions.

Ruud continued. "The DPE also has a base in Nicaragua. The planes there can strike our bases in the Southwest. Then they deploy subs along the East Coast and Gulf Coast. Their cruise missiles can hit our major bases from Louisiana to Virginia, as well as Washington."

"That's some pretty scary shit, Jan-Erik."

"I know. Of course, I might be completely off. You said it yourself, Ohmara Saihi is a crazy-ass mother fucker. Who the hell knows what's going on in that twisted mind of his."

"Why don't you tell your general about this?" suggested Krista.

Ruud sighed and shook his head. "It's only a theory, and it sounds like the same kind of theory the conspiracy wackos come up with. Take a bunch of seemingly random events and connect them together to create some nefarious plan to take over the world. I have no actual proof. General Dobson's a good man, but if I tell him what I told you, he'll order a psych eval for me."

He dropped his tablet on the sofa and let out a soft chuckle. "Maybe that's what I should do if I leave The Corps. I can get my own conspiracy theory radio show, talk about how Ohmara Saihi is really an alien in disguise, paving the way for an invasion of Earth."

"And also that he's married to Bigfoot and keeps the Loch Ness Monster as a pet." Krista grinned.

Ruud turned to her, chuckling again.

A quick beep sounded from his tablet, signaling he had an email. He opened it.

It was from General Dobson.

Ruud scanned it. A knot formed in his chest. "Oh shit."

"What?" asked Krista.

He turned his tablet so they could both see the message.

Article appeared on Washington Post website ten minutes ago naming you and the Iron Devils as the ones responsible for sinking the Klaipeda.

THIRTEEN

Saihi leaned back in his chair, steepled hands under his chin. Sheer delight swept through him as he stared at the wall monitor in the conference room onboard a United Nations 767. It showed images of tens of thousands of demonstrators in Washington, New York, and Los Angeles.

"At last count, there are protests in nearly forty American cities" said Emre Irtegun, a stocky, mustachioed Turk who served as the DPE's security information chief.

"Have any of them turned violent?" asked a tall, oval-faced man with graying temples.

"Yes," Irtegun answered Agustin Palacio, a former Argentine general who headed the Directorate of Peace Enforcement. "Most of it is the usual vandalism associated with riots. Broken windows, overturned cars, rocks, bottles, and other things hurled at police. Several dozen injuries have been reported, but none life threatening."

"I don't see any let up in the protests," stated Claude Dupray, head of the Cyber Security Section. "I've seen Facebook and Instagram posts and tweets from Friends of Peace chapters in America calling for more protests. They're also reporting a large increase in new members over the past week."

"It is as I hoped." Saihi smiled, looking around at the DPE leaders. "More and more Americans are opening their eyes to the corrupt and murderous nature of their government."

Palacio nodded. "The more supporters we gain, the better for us when Operation: New Dawn commences."

Saihi shifted his gaze to Irtegun. "Is there any new information on the whereabouts of Lieutenant Colonel Jan-Erik Ruud and the other Marines who sank the *Klaipeda?* "

"Unfortunately, no." The former chief of police for Izmir shook his head. "According to our supporters in the American government, the head of the Marines' special operations forces has said Ruud and his men are on some sort of sensitive mission and are incommunicado."

"A lie." Palacio spat out the words. "The man is protecting those murderers."

"I have no doubt," said Irtegun. "But our American Friends of Peace chapters are helping in our search for them. They used photographs of the Marines to create wanted posters and posted them on numerous social media sites. They also have members watching all U.S. Navy and Marine Corps bases, as well as the homes of their families."

"I assigned some of my people to monitor the Marines' social media accounts." Dupray folded his hands on top of his computer. "In case they try to make contact with relatives or friends. But all their accounts have been deactivated."

"These are men who are trained operate behind enemy lines," said Palacio. "They are experts at staying hidden. They are not going to risk exposure with a Facebook post."

"Likewise, they will not go to the homes of family members or friends," Irtegun added.

"They cannot stay hidden forever." Saihi slid forward in his seat. "We will find Lieutenant Colonel Ruud and his men either before or after Operation: New Dawn commences."

"Ha!" Dupray blurted, bouncing in his seat.

"What is it?" Palacio's face tightened in a stern look.

A slight grin formed on Saihi's lips, thinking of his DPE chief's low opinion of Dupray. Whereas Palacio was immaculate in his appearance with a pressed beige suit and short, neatly trimmed hair, Dupray couldn't be more of a polar opposite. He wore an untucked, bland shirt, piercings in his ears and eyebrows, and had brown hair flowing past his shoulders.

Saihi did not care about the thirty-five year old Belgian's appearance. The man was a computer genius, which he demonstrated as leader of a hacktavist group before joining the DPE.

"I just got a message from one of my people." Dupray beamed at the others. "A hacker just crashed the U.S. Department of Defense website. Mark my words, this is only the beginning. When this gets out, there'll be more attempts on other government websites."

"Let us hope so." Saihi's gaze settled on Irtegun. "Speaking of the U.S. Government, do we still have the current locations of all their cabinet secretaries?"

"Yes, Mister Secretary General. All Special Action Unit teams are in place, ready to move when the time is right."

"Good." Saihi swung his chair toward Palacio. "What is the current disposition of the American military?"

"Their alert status is higher than normal, likely a cautionary measure due to the tension between us."

"But they are not acting like they expect to be attacked any moment, correct?"

"Yes, Mister Secretary General."

Saihi's shoulders rose as he drew an energizing breath. *They have no idea what is about to come.*

Whispers of doubt, of fear, floated through the back of his mind. What if something went wrong? What if the American CIA or NSA came across something to alert them to his plan?

No. That will not happen. Saihi's jaw stiffened. He would succeed. He would bring peace and save the Earth. He would not be a failure like his father.

"The Americans are keeping a sizeable force in and around Trinidad and Tobago," said Palacio. "They have one carrier group in the area centered on the *George Washington.* The Eighty-Second Airborne and the Marine Second Division have three of their brigades on the islands in order to maintain security until the Trinidadian police and defense forces are reconstituted."

"What of our forces in the area?" asked Saihi.

"They should all be in place by this evening."

A thrilling jolt shot through Saihi. That was more good news.

He looked at Dupray. "Is our special message ready?"

"Yes, Mister Secretary General. It will be sent out simultaneously via Facebook, Twitter, email, and text five minutes after Operation: New Dawn has begun."

Saihi nodded. By collecting data from social media, voter registrations, YouTube videos, and news articles and soundbites, Dupray and his people complied a list of politicians, government and law enforcement officials, civic leaders, members of the media, academics, even college and high school students, whose views were in line with his. The "special message" they'd receive would spell out the reasons for his actions and his future intentions. Judging from their posts, comments, and likes over the years, he had no doubt they would support him.

Dupray also used those same sources of information to identify those who might threaten Saihi's vision of an enlightened world. They would be dealt with.

"There is one aspect of our next phase that greatly concerns me," said Irtegun.

Saihi's forehead wrinkled. "What might that be?"

"The escalation we are hoping for in its wake. What if it prompts President Moore to return to Washington instead of remaining in Alaska?"

"I wouldn't worry," Palacio reassured Irtegun. "We have SAU teams in position for that contingency."

"She is much more vulnerable in Alaska than in the White House, quite possibly the most heavily fortified government building on the planet."

"The SAU has developed numerous strategies to breach the White House, or capture President Moore should she be evacuated from the grounds." Palacio spoke in an even tone, without a hint of worry. "You are correct that Alaska is more ideal than Washington, but whatever the case, our forces will accomplish their task."

"Indeed." Saihi nodded to the DPE director. "All thoughts, all words, from this point on must be positive. Negative thoughts, negative words, will only produce negative energy, which will flow from you and affect all living beings around you, then all living beings around them, and so on. Therefore, we must extinguish all negativity within ourselves. We must be of one mind, one voice, one world."

"One mind, one voice, one world," his three directors repeated.

They continued their meeting as the plane flew east over the Atlantic, discussing logistics, positions to give prominent Americans who embrace the cause of enlightenment, and where to set up UN "special facilities." A few times, Saihi caught himself looking at the digital clock in the corner of the monitor, set for Greenwich Mean Time. Anticipation, even impatience, grew as he counted the minutes until the next phase of his plan began.

With five minutes remaining, he called a halt to the meeting and turned to Dupray. "Put the live stream from the Los Angeles protest on the main screen."

"Yes, Mister Secretary General." The Belgian poked his tablet with a finger. The wall monitor blinked, then showed a mass of people crowding a city street, shouting, raising fists or holding signs. In the corner was the web address for the Friends of Peace Los Angeles Chapter. The camera shifted from the protestors to a line of police in riot gear further down the street.

"Yeah, try something, pigs!" the camera operator shouted. "I'll blast it all over the web. Fucking Nazi pieces of shit."

Saihi folded his hands, his stomach and chest quivering, anxious for what was coming. He scanned the loud, angry crowd, picking out blacks, whites, Latinos, Asians, Arabs. A diverse gathering, just as he'd hoped for.

A round woman with short dark hair and brown skin shoved her face in the camera. "It's time for the United States Murder Corps to pay for what they've done." She turned to the crowd. "Fuck Pearl Harbor! Fuck Nine-Eleven! Remember the *Klaipeda!* Remember the *Klaipeda!*"

Many in the crowd cheered and shouted the phrase.

"Yeah! You go, Jazmin!" The man holding the camera yelled his support to the female protester.

Jazmin swung her head back to the camera. "Yeah, there's a shitload of people down here, but we need more. So get your asses down here. Show our imperialist, racist government we won't stop until those Marines are strung up. If you're not here with us, that means you support that cunt tyrant Emily Moore, and that means you can fucking rot in hell! You're the reason --"

Saihi gave a slight jerk when he heard a muffled *pop* off screen.

"What the fuck?" said the camera operator. Jazmin just looked around, mouth agape.

Screams went up. The image whipped around, then steadied. Someone lay on the ground, a Latino woman. Blood pooled around her head.

Saihi heard another shot. Blood gushed from the head of a black man. He dropped face first onto the street.

Jazmin screamed.

"Shit! Shit!" The camera operator ran, the image shaking. It steadied as he crouched behind a lamppost.

Two more shots punctuated the air.

"They're shooting at us!" Jazmin hollered. "Up there! Up there!"

The camera rose. Saihi held his breath, sliding to the edge of his seat.

A man in a dark blue uniform stood on a nearby rooftop. POLICE was emblazoned across his vest in big yellow letters. He raised his rifle and fired. Then he stood there for a couple of seconds, in full view of everyone, before turning and disappearing from sight.

The camera swept over the crowd. People ran or knelt behind whatever cover they could find. Several laid on the asphalt. Saihi counted four that did not move.

"The fucking cops," the camera operator raged. "The fucking cops just shot at us!"

"Mother fuckers!" Jazmin hurried over to the other protestors. "No more of this shit. They kill us, we kill them. Kill the fucking pigs!"

Saihi watched as some of the crowd ran away, while others charged the police. A human wave slammed into officers' riot shields. Fists and batons flailed. Bottles, rocks, and other objects flew through the air.

A shudder of elation went through Saihi. He took a deep, satisfied breath as rioters and police battled. He thought of the four bodies he'd seen before the clash. All had been non-Caucasians. A flash of sympathy went through him. Those people had no doubt been subjected to oppression and abuse by America's racist power structure. But their deaths would serve a greater purpose.

Saihi monitored various newscasts for the duration of the flight. An hour after the shooting, whole sections of Los Angeles were burning.

After another hour, riots had broken out in Washington and San Francisco. By the time the 767 touched down at the DPE's base in Mauritania, a dozen more American cities experienced violent protests.

Saihi stared out the window, taking in the line of transport planes. Beyond them was a sea of tents for DPE paratroopers. He looked back at the monitor, watching the riots throughout the United States with a sense of triumph.

He now had the justification to implement Operation: New Dawn.

FOURTEEN

Emily Moore wished she could delete the Presidential Daily Brief, and all the troubles that came with it.

If it were only that easy.

She sat at the oak table in the kitchen of her vacation cabin in Kenai, reading from her tablet. Her coffee cup sat on a placemat, untouched since she sat down.

The rioting had not let up. If anything, it had gotten worse overnight. There were ten deaths and over two hundred injuries reported just in Los Angeles. Dozens more had died in other riots across the country, with over a thousand injured and many more arrested. Property damage had reached into the tens of millions of dollars.

Moore scanned the photos attached to her PDB. Los Angeles. Washington. New York. San Francisco. Oakland. Seattle. Miami. St. Louis. Newark. Detroit. They all had the same images. Enraged protesters looting and fighting with police, store windows smashed, cars overturned or on fire, and buildings burning.

Her stomach turned into a cold ball of lead. A tsunami of emotions battered her. She didn't know whether to scream in anger or cry as the country she loved tore itself apart.

Moore continued reading. The chief of the LAPD denied that any of his officers killed anyone at the demonstration that sparked this chaos, suggesting it had been an imposter. His theory, however, fell on deaf ears. Mere words could do nothing to counter the image of that man in the POLICE vest shooting unarmed protestors.

It makes me wonder if anything I say will make a difference.

"You holding up okay?"

Moore looked up to see her husband Dave walk into the kitchen. She forced a grin as he gently grasped her shoulder and kissed her forehead.

She patted Dave's hand. "We're going to have to cut this vacation short. With everything going on, I need to be back in Washington. Though what good that'll do, I don't know. Making a speech from the Oval Office won't end these riots."

"It's all image, hon, and you know it." Dave walked over to the coffee maker. "If you're here in Kenai, people'll think you're lounging around while the country goes to hell."

Moore grunted. "Amazing how people think a president can only look like they're in charge if they're at the White House." She leaned her head back, closing her eyes. "Oh, what I wouldn't give to be back in the National Guard. Just me, my MPs, and one city street of rioters to worry about, instead of every street in the country."

She sighed, placed the tablet on the table and finally took a sip of her coffee, grimacing. It was lukewarm. "This is all Ohmara Saihi's doing. Every time he speaks, he encourages this behavior. Just last night on the news he said these riots are the expected outcome of decades of marginalizing," she held up her fingers to make quotation marks, "'those who do not resemble the men and women who hold power in the United States.' That really helps calm things down, doesn't it? And all I can do is counter him with soundbites and official statements because he refuses to take my calls or see our ambassador."

"What about going through a third party?" Dave returned to the table with two steaming coffee mugs. He handed one to Moore.

"Thanks." She took a sip. Nice and hot. "I thought about that. I know Saihi isn't fond of the British, Polish, or Israeli ambassadors, so they're out. Maybe I could get the Japanese or Swiss ambassadors to do it. A lot of the others, however . . ." Her gaze dropped to the oak floorboards.

"What?" asked Dave.

Moore looked up. "A lot of the ambassadors at the UN, they just seem . . . devoted to Saihi. Our delegation has said there are several ambassadors who truly believe Ohmara Saihi is the only man who can save the world. He's not just running an organization that's supposed to promote peace, he used it to create a worldwide cult of personality, complete with his own army, or Directorate of Peace Enforcement or whatever the hell he wants to call it."

"Which means it's going to make it hard to convince him to tone down his rhetoric," said Dave. "Guys like that think they're the smartest people in the room, and if you don't believe it, just ask them."

Moore laughed softly. "I think it's more than that. I think Saihi believes anyone who doesn't think like him isn't just wrong, they're an enemy."

"Maybe he'll talk to you if you tell him you found enlightenment." A grin creased Dave's narrow face. "Isn't that Saihi's favorite word?"

Moore laughed again, then got to her feet. "I'm going for a run."

"Good. You do your best thinking when running. Maybe you'll come up with a way to settle things down."

"I damn well better."

Moore went to the bedroom and put on her jogging clothes. She was making her way to the door, with her Secret Service agents around her, when an aide brought her a satellite phone.

"It's the Secretary of Defense."

What now? Moore tensed before taking the phone. "Yes, Grant?"

"Madam President," replied Defense Secretary Grant Hegan. "We have a situation."

Of course, Moore stifled a sigh. *Because we don't have enough situations.* "What is it?"

"NORAD reports the DPE air fleet from Mauritania bound for Cuba has changed course."

"Where are they headed now?"

"Washington D.C."

Moore gripped her phone tighter. "Have they entered our air space?"

"No, but if they continue on their current course, they will soon. But that's not the only potential threat."

"What else is going on?"

"There's another DPE air fleet that took off from the Kurils," said Hegan. "They're heading for Alaska."

Dread shot through Moore. She imagined bombs falling on Washington and Anchorage. *No. Saihi couldn't be that crazy. He knows he couldn't win a war against us.*

"I've put all fighter wings on the East Coast and Alaska on alert," Hegan told her. "We need to intercept the DPE flights and divert them away from U.S. air space."

Moore opened her mouth to respond, then stopped. Maybe that's what Saihi wanted, to have her order American fighters into the air. Then at the last minute, he'd order his planes to turn around and scream to the world, "See how violent America is? We get too close to their precious border and they threaten to shoot us down."

"Grant, keep our fighters on alert. Send up just a few planes and keep them over land."

"But Madam President, there are combat aircraft in those air fleets, heading directly for our country."

"Even you can't believe the UN would actually attack us. I think this is a ploy by Secretary General Saihi to make us look like over-reactionary warmongers. He wants to embarrass us. If we send up all our fighters, it gives him ammunition that we are hostile to the UN. We're not going to fall for that. Just send up a few jets, but tell them they are not to approach either DPE squadron."

"What if those UN planes enter our air space?" asked Hegan.

"Then send up everything we've got and tell them to turn around or they'll be shot down."

"Yes, Madam President."

"Keep me posted."

"I will."

Moore ended the call and handed the phone back to the aide.

"Madam President," said Scott Sharp, the head of her Protection Detail. "We need to take you to a secure location. Joint Base Elmendorf-Richardson in Anchorage is the closest one."

"Absolutely not," she told the muscular black agent. "I do that and that SOB Saihi will paint me as paranoid and equate me with those conspiracy nuts who think the United Nations is trying to take over the world."

"It's for your own protection, Madam President."

"I appreciate your concern, Scott, but my answer is no and that's final."

An annoyed looked passed over Sharp's face. "Yes, Madam President."

With that settled, Moore exited the cabin, breathing in the cool morning air. She headed for the jogging path, staring out at the Kenai River and the trees along its banks. The beauty of the scenery was lost on her. What if this wasn't a bluff? What if those planes –

The water rippled. Moore stopped, eyebrows knitted together. She made out a dark, oblong shadow just below the surface. Could an orca have strayed into the river?

The object broke the surface. Another one appeared, then a third. Moore's eyes widened. They were definitely not orcas.

They were mini subs!

What are they --?

Moore never finished her thought. Secret Service agents swarmed the river bank, pistols and submachine guns drawn.

"Move! Move! Move!"

Strong arms grabbed her and hustled her back to the cabin. She glanced over her shoulder and glimpsed a circular device resembling a large loudspeaker behind the sail of each submarine. Dread grew within her. She'd seen such devices years ago, during a crowd control demonstration by the Alaska State Troopers.

Moore clenched her jaw, knowing what was co--

A piercing whine drilled into her ears. She cried out, pressing her hands over her ears. The world around her swirled. Moore swayed left, then right, then collapsed.

FIFTEEN

Concern built up in Ruud as he and Krista neared the door of Millie's Café. Every time he left the cabin and went into Talkeetna, he feared someone would recognize him, despite his beard, despite hiding his Swedish accent. Tension squeezed his shoulders and chest whenever he was around other people, expecting someone to shout, "There's the guy who sank that UN ship!"

Ruud thought about holing up in Krista's cabin for the remainder of his stay, but decided against it. Many of the townspeople knew they were an item and went into town regularly. Suddenly dropping off the face of the earth might make folks suspicious. Better to keep up appearances, make everything look normal.

As far as everyone knows, I'm John Erikson, a friend of Krista's from college.

Besides, how many people would really believe the Marine responsible for sinking the *Klaipeda* would be hiding out in a little town in Alaska?

Millie beamed as they entered the café. "Good morning, you two."

"Morning, Millie." Krista gave her a short wave and headed for the counter.

"Hi, Millie." Ruud's eyes flickered around the café as other customers greeted them. His gaze lingered on Clyde Lasher, the ex-reporter, and the hippie chick Solstice. What if they learned his true identity?

Both just said, "Hello," and went back to eating their breakfasts.

Ruud sat next to Krista. Millie handed them menus and said, "So, any big plans for today?"

"I don't know," Krista answered. "We might go up to Mount McKinley, or we might just stay indoors all day, and all night, and all tomorrow morning."

"Ooooh." Millie's mouth formed a perfect "O." "You naughty girl." She glanced over at Ruud and grinned. "Not that I can blame you."

"Get you own hot stud, Millie." Krista slid her arm around Ruud's elbow. "This one's taken."

The two women laughed. Ruud shrugged and smiled as Millie went to take care of another customer. He glanced up at the TV, jaw clenched as he watched rioters and police battle it out in Miami. A selfish feeling crept through him. While he worried about someone finding out his true identity, the entire country was tearing itself apart. Dozens had died and more than a thousand had been injured. Every hour, it seemed, riots broke out in some other city, and the casualty count soared.

How did things get so bad?

Millie returned a couple of minutes later to take their orders. After she left, Ruud started to look back up at the TV when Krista tugged at his shoulder.

"Hey," she said. "I don't know if you heard about this, but a couple of months ago this school district in Vermont voted to ban cheering at high school graduations."

Ruud's brow furrowed, wondering how Krista could talk about something like that with riots sweeping the country. *Maybe she's just trying to get our minds off it. It's not like we can do anything about it here in the middle of Alaska.*

"No, I haven't," he answered.

"The dumbshit school board voted for it, some bullcrap about it taking away attention from other students or disturbing other people in the audience. They said if any family members cheer or applaud, they'll not only be forced to leave the graduation, but the school will withhold the student's diploma until they do ten hours of community service."

"You gotta be kidding me? What do they think this is, the old Soviet Union?" Ruud leaned closer to Krista and lowered his voice. "Me and every other Marine fight to ensure everyone's freedoms in this country. I hear stuff like this, I start to wonder if soon there will be any freedoms left to fight for."

"I know what you mean. I've been boiling over this for weeks, and I think I'm finally ready to do a song about it. I wanna call it, 'A Lone Voice.' This is a song we need to play pissed off. I'm looking for a really hard beat. I mean, play like you're kicking someone's ass right through their damn skull."

Ruud's heart sped up as he stared at Krista. Her eyes blazed with a volatile mix of fury and passion. He had seen this reaction from her plenty of times in college when she came up with a song she felt strongly about.

Damn, if it didn't turn him on.

She started throwing out lyric ideas when Ruud saw two people enter the café. The man was dressed in a flannel shirt and jeans. The woman, however, stood out noticeably. She wore neatly pressed slacks and a fashionable beige trenchcoat that looked like it had been bought yesterday. She had a milky complexion and coiffed blonde hair. Andy Dempster, Lasher, Solstice, and some of the other regulars also gave the woman curious looks. She definitely wasn't a local or a tourist. Suspicion buzzed in the back of Ruud's mind.

The woman looked their way, her eyes widening. She turned to the man and jerked her head to the door. He exited the café.

Ruud's suspicious buzz turned into warning bells as the woman walked toward them, smiling wide. "Well, well, well, talk about a lucky break. Krista Brandt, as I live and breathe."

Krista eyed the woman warily. "Can I help you?"

"Theresa O'Neill, MSNBC."

Every muscle in Ruud's body tightened. A network reporter in a teeny-tiny Alaska town. This could not be good.

"Nice to meet you," Krista spoke in a flat tone. "As you can see, I'm about to eat. If you want an interview, you can get in touch with my publicist."

"Actually, I want to talk to you about something more important than your band." Theresa checked over her shoulder. Her companion returned, this time with a video camera.

"Now hang on just a minute." Millie pointed at the cameraman from behind the counter. "You can't come in here with that thing and disturb my costumers."

Theresa pretended like she hadn't heard Millie. Her focus remained on Krista. "You dated Lieutenant Colonel Jan-Erik Ruud in college, didn't you?"

Ruud closed his eyes. *Shit, shit, shit!* How stupid could he have been? He should have known once some puss-sucking maggot in Washington leaked his name, the press would dig into his past, talking to everyone in his life from his family to his old kindergarten teacher. It was only a matter of time before they learned of his relationship with Krista.

"It's none of your business," said Krista.

"I disagree. I think your fans would like to know about your association with the man accused of murdering nearly three hundred United Nations sailors."

Ruud's eyes narrowed. What happened to the *Klaipeda* had not been murder, just a tragic accident. Not that this damn reporter cared. "Murder" would get bigger ratings than an "accident."

"It was a mistake," said Krista.

"Nearly three hundred UN sailors died in that bombing," Theresa countered. "That's quite a mistake."

Krista said nothing. She clenched her mug and sipped her tea.

"Have you been in contact with Colonel Ruud since the sinking of the *Klaipeda?*" asked Theresa.

Again, Krista didn't answer.

"Do you still have feelings for Colonel Ruud? Have your feelings for him changed because of this?"

Krista held her mug so tight it shook. She turned to Ruud and frowned.

Theresa followed her gaze. "Could this be Colonel Ruud?"

He started to open his mouth, ready to deny it, but stopped. It would do no good. She'd fingered him.

"Hmm, let's see." She pulled out her phone and thumbed the screen. She held it up near him, her eyes shifting from the screen, which Ruud assumed showed his picture, to him.

"That's it." Millie slashed her arm across the air. "I want you two out of here."

"Sorry, but I'm here to do a job."

"No you're not. You're bugging my customers. Now leave before I call the police."

"And what can they do? Arrest us for exercising our First Amendment rights?"

"No, but they can arrest you for trespassing." Millie picked up the phone.

Theresa did not appear fazed. She continued looking from her phone to Ruud. "You know, take away the beard and the ballcap . . ." Now her eyes settled on him. "Lieutenant Colonel Ruud, I presume?"

His jaw tightened as he glared at Theresa. He cursed her. He cursed himself. *Stupid, selfish idiot.* Ruud balled his fist, restraining himself from pounding the counter in frustration. He'd been so anxious to see Krista again he hadn't considered this possibility. Worse still, he'd dragged Krista into this. What sort of impact might this have on her career?

"Colonel, do you regret what happened to the crew of the *Klaipeda?*"

More than you know. Ruud stared at the floor. He thought about his theory, that *Klaipeda* had been a set-up by Saihi to trigger a conflict between the U.S. and the UN. Not that he would tell that to Theresa. She'd probably have an orgasm if she could paint him as a murderer *and* a batshit crazy conspiracy theorist.

"Do you have anything to say to the families of those dead UN sailors?"

"Hey, bitch! Leave 'im alone!"

Everyone turned to Dempster.

"If that is Colonel Ruud, he's a damn hero. The DPE ain't about peace. The UN's gonna use 'em to take over the world. At least Colonel Ruud showed those bastards there are Americans who still know how to kick ass."

Theresa chuckled softly and turned back to Ruud. "No wonder you came here. You have a lot of people sympathetic to what you did."

"No, you're wrong." Solstice shook her head. "I'm not like him." She nodded at Dempster. "I abhor violence."

"Yeah," Dempster scoffed. "Like your precious UN never killed anyone."

Theresa ignored the argument. "As I said, Colonel, the men and women on *Klaipeda* had families. Don't you think they deserve an explanation for what happened that night?"

Ruud's shoulders sagged. He did think about that. Faceless men, women, and children floated through his mind, all related in some way to the *Klaipeda* crew. They would never see their loved ones again, all because of him.

Or maybe because Saihi wanted them to get killed.

"This is why I left network news," Lasher spoke up. "Too many of you have no respect for other people's privacy, rush to judgment, facts be damned, and try to ruin as many lives as you can."

Theresa tilted her head as she stared at him. "Hey, I've seen old videos of you. You're Clyde Lasher. My God, what are you doing here?"

"I got sick of being around people like you." He jerked his head toward her.

Ruud didn't catch Theresa's response. The secure satellite phone in his pocket buzzed.

That phone only rang when there was a crisis somewhere in the world.
He headed for the men's room.

"Colonel Ruud," Theresa called out. "I'm not finished talking to you."

"Well, he's finished with you." Krista leapt off her seat and blocked the reporter's path.

Ruud entered the small restroom, which was empty. He turned on the faucet of the lone sink to interfere with any listening devices that may have been planted. Not that he really thought there were any here, but one never assumed anything in his line of work. He leaned against the door to prevent anyone from entering.

"Devil One."

"Sand Castle," replied General Dobson.

"I've got bad news, sir. A reporter from MSNBC just showed up here."

"Colonel, that's the least of our concerns right now."

Ruud's forehead crinkled. "What's going on?"

"The President's been kidnapped."

"What?" The shock hit Ruud like a blow to the gut. He stood frozen, trying to accept what his CO had told him. "How the hell could that happen?"

"The President and her Secret Service detail were incapacitated by acoustic weapons. The bad guys made off with her in a mini sub in the Kenai River."

"Who took her?"

"We haven't confirmed it yet, but the safe money is on the Directorate of Peace Enforcement."

"Are they out of their damn minds?" Ruud blurted.

"Colonel, the President's kidnapping is just the tip of the iceberg."

"What could be worse than that?"

"We've lost contact with the entire cabinet," Dobson answered.

Cold, invisible fingers clamped around Ruud's stomach. This was turning into a damn nightmare.

Dobson continued, "The Veep, SECDEF, the AG, everyone down to the Secretary of Veterans Affairs. They also snagged the Speaker of the House and the President Pro Tem."

Ruud listened numbly. The Speaker and the President Pro Tem, the senior U.S. Senator of the majority party, were third and fourth in the line of succession.

He shook his head in disbelief. "How the hell did the DPE get all of them?"

"If the reports from the President's protection detail are any indication, it looks like the DPE infiltrated special ops teams into the country. Hell, most of the lower level secretaries don't even have bodyguards. A gang of middle schoolers could kidnap them. Luckily, the DPE didn't get any of the Joint Chiefs. They're mobilizing every asset they can to locate President Moore and her Cabinet, and to defend the homeland."

Ruud cranked an eyebrow. "Defend the homeland? It sounds like we're facing another threat."

"We are. All those DPE ships and planes from their base in the Kurils, they're heading for Alaska."

Ruud's heart hammered in his chest at the thought of thousands upon thousands of DPE personnel about to descend upon this state.

"And that DPE air fleet supposedly headed for Cuba," said Dobson. "That's bullshit. They're coming straight for Washington."

Tremors went up Ruud's legs. His throat clenched. *I was right.* Saihi did want a war with the U.S., and he started it by neutralizing the country's entire civilian leadership.

"NORAD's detected multiple cruise missile launches at the East Coast and Alaska. I think it's safe to assume they're targeting key military and government facilities."

Crazy fucking bastards. Ruud closed his eyes, ridding himself of shock. He had to accept what was happening and deal with it.

"What do you want me to do, sir?"

"Link up with the rest of the Iron Devils. I want you four to be my eyes and ears in Alaska. Gather whatever intel you can on the DPE and feed it to me."

"Yes, sir. I'll hit the road ASAP and contact Gunny Corcoran and the others en route."

"Very good. God's speed, Colonel."

"Thank you, sir. Devil One, out."

Ruud pocketed the phone, took a cleansing breath to gather himself, and exited the men's room.

"Colonel," Theresa called out. "I have to --"

"Shut up. I have no time for you." Ruud stopped in front of Krista. "I need to borrow your jeep."

"What for?"

"That was my CO. I have to go to Anchorage and link up with my unit."

"Colonel Ruud." Theresa's tone became insistent. "You need to come clean about your role in the *Klaipeda* sinking."

"Ma'am, pretty soon you're going to have a much bigger story than me."

"And what's that?"

"The United Nations is about to invade Alaska."

SIXTEEN

Gunnery Sergeant Archie Corcoran worked up a good sweat by the time he, Baldelli, and Kosco returned to the cabin.

Nothing like a five-mile run to get your morning started.

After a quick water break, they did push-ups, sit-ups, and burpees.

"All right, let's get some breakfast," Corcoran told the other two Marines. "When we're done eating, we'll work on tracking, then make improvised weapons with whatever we can find in the forest."

"You expect us to suddenly wind up in caveman days, Gunny?" Baldelli quipped.

"You never know when you might be stranded somewhere and need to turn a branch and a rock into a club. Now grab something to eat before we head out."

"Yes, Gunny." Baldelli walked back to the cabin, looking over his shoulder at Kosco. "Maybe I can learn how to make a slingshot or a blowgun. That'll come in handy next time I've got jihadis on my ass in the desert."

The young Marine kept his voice low, but Corcoran heard him. He folded his arms across his chest, debating whether or not to give Baldelli an ass-chewing. He decided to let it slide.

Can't blame him for bitching. They hadn't left the cabin since their names came out on the news. Even with their beards and sunglasses, Corcoran didn't want to take the chance someone in Anchorage might recognize them. He'd certainly draw attention. Tall, muscular black men couldn't be a very common sight in Anchorage. Plus, the riot a few days ago showed the Friends of Peace had a big presence in the city. They had wanted posters with their pictures on the websites and social media pages.

Corcoran didn't want to take the chance on some shitbag Saihi zombie spotting them.

"If anything, having to hole up here gives us a chance to maintain our edge," he had told Baldelli and Kosco the other day. The two probably thought that was bullshit. Both had brains in their heads, Kosco especially, since he'd been in National Honor Society in high school and did a semester at Brown University before joining The Corps. They knew the PT and training exercises were just ways to keep busy and not think about being stuck in the woods and the fallout from the *Klaipeda* sinking.

A low, sustained roar churned through the sky, penetrating Corcoran's thoughts. He looked up through the breaks in the trees. Two twin-tailed, arrow-shaped jet fighters streaked overhead. F-22 Raptors from Joint Base Elmendorf-Richardson. He'd heard them a few times during their run.

Must be some kinda exercise. He ground his teeth as he eyed the jets, thinking of their pilots. They could go on official training exercises. They could leave their base, go to a bar, find a hot piece of ass and get laid. They didn't have to worry about being court-martialed or kicked out of the Marine Corps.

The thought sent a nervous shudder through Corcoran. He'd been in The Corps since he was eighteen, following in his father and grandfather's footsteps. Being a Marine was in his blood, his soul. He felt proud every time he put on that uniform, knowing he was giving to a cause larger than himself. Even with twenty-five years of service under his belt, he wasn't ready to leave.

I may not have a choice. He felt his throat tighten. His father and grandfather left with honorable discharges. What sort of shame would he bring to his family if his career ended in a prison cell?

Corcoran thought of his parents in Tennessee, thought of the rioting across the country. Fear crept through him. What if some crazy shitbucket from the Friends of Peace tried to hurt them?

Then they'd be in for a hell of a surprise. Pop might be in his seventies, but he was a retired Marine and still tough as hell. The dozen rifles and handguns he owned would also make any dumbass America-hating puddle of worm puke think twice about messing with him.

Corcoran said a quick prayer for his parents, then started to the cabin.

The satellite phone clipped to his belt rang.

"Devil Two," he answered.

"Devil One." It was Colonel Ruud.

"Problem, sir?" The colonel wouldn't use the secure sat phone for a social call.

"Yeah, a problem twice the size of Mount Everest."

Tension coiled around Corcoran's insides. "What is it?"

"I just heard from Sand Castle." Ruud paused and took a breath. "You're not going to believe this. The DPE kidnapped the President."

"What?" Corcoran gave a slight shake of his head, shock battering him. He almost asked Ruud to repeat what he'd said. It just sounded too unbelievable.

"That's not all. They infiltrated special ops teams into the U.S. and captured the cabinet. Our entire civilian leadership is gone."

Corcoran stood frozen, ignoring the world around him. He fought to accept what Ruud had told him. Standing around in disbelief wouldn't solve anything. "So what are we gonna do about it?"

"Are Baldelli and Kosco with you?"

"Yes, sir."

"Get them and put me on speakerphone."

Corcoran went into the cabin. Baldelli and Kosco were just sitting down at the kitchen table.

"What is it, Gunny?" asked Kosco.

"Colonel's on the phone. The DPE just captured the President and her cabinet."

"Are you shittin' me?" Baldelli gaped at him.

Corcoran didn't answer. He thumbed the speaker button and laid the phone on the kitchen table. Ruud not only told them about the President's capture, but that UN air fleets were bearing down on Washington and Alaska.

Kosco stared at the phone, not blinking, like he was still struggling to accept the news. "Saihi's really gone over the edge. He's started a damn war."

"So we'll kick his batshit crazy ass," said Baldelli.

"What are our orders, sir?" asked Corcoran.

"Right now, Sand Castle wants us to observe DPE activity and transmit all intel back to him."

"Roger," replied Corcoran.

"I'm on my way to your pos." Ruud used the slang for position. "Stay safe."

"You too, sir."

When Ruud signed off, Corcoran looked over to Baldelli and Kosco. The former stood with his mouth agape, gaze locked on the phone, while the latter maintained a stoic expression, though shock and concern lit his eyes.

"First thing we do," said Corcoran, "is inventory our ammo and food. We have a good vantage point here to see all of Anchorage. This is the biggest city in Alaska, and with Joint Base Elmendorf-Richardson here, it's a prime target for the DPE. Now let's arm up."

"Yes, Gunny," the two Marines replied. They started toward the basement when a distant rumble filtered into the cabin. All three stared at the front door. Needles of dread plunged into Corcoran's stomach. He was all too familiar with that sound.

The trio hurried to the door. Corcoran threw it opened and ran onto the dirt driveway.

"Holy shit," blurted Baldelli.

Corcoran's chest tightened. He couldn't release the breath he was holding. A plume of ugly gray-black smoke rose to the north, in the direction of Elmendorf-Richardson. A contrail bore down on the base. Seconds later, a fireball sprang into the air. A third missile soon hit JBER.

"Kosco." Corcoran shook himself out of his stupor. "Get our tablets."

"Yes, Gunny." He rushed back to the cabin.

"There's another one." Baldelli pointed. A fourth fireball erupted from the base.

"My God," Corcoran said in a whisper, his stomach dropping into a black hole. He'd seen plenty of villages and cities under attack during his time in The Corps. But this, this was an American city being bombed. His mind still couldn't fully accept that fact.

Footsteps pounded behind him. Kosco ran toward them with their tablets.

"Kosco, record the attack," ordered Corcoran. "We'll upload the footage to General Dobson later. Baldelli, monitor local TV and radio. I'll try to ID the targets the DPE are hitting."

Kosco aimed his tablet to the northern part of the city, where all the explosions occurred. Corcoran called up a map of Anchorage and marked the target areas with red dots. Most of them were concentrated on JBER. A few were just south of the base. Going by the map, it appeared Anchorage City Hall, the city's emergency management office, and police headquarters had all been hit. He soon confirmed this from the TV and radio reports Baldelli streamed on his tablet.

"Gunny." Kosco lifted his head. "Up above."

Contrails criss-crossed the blue sky. Corcoran saw the sharp, gray shapes of F-22s twisting and turning. One vanished in a puff of orange and black. Another exploded seconds later. Streaks of white zipped away from the Raptors. Missiles. They were shooting back at their attackers.

Another F-22 exploded. Corcoran clenched his teeth as flaming wreckage tumbled toward the city. He scanned the sky for a parachute. There was none.

"Aw, dammit." Baldelli glared at his tablet.

"What is it?" Corcoran turned to him.

"I can't get any local TV or radio stations. They all just crapped out."

"The DPE's probably jamming 'em. Try Facebook and Twitter. People gotta be posting about this."

"More aircraft inbound," Kosco alerted them. "Fast movers."

Corcoran looked to the southwest. He counted a dozen gray shapes with pointy noses, delta wings, and a single tail. Rafales, top of the line French-built jets, and the DPE's primary multi-role fighter.

Contrails raced away from them. The remaining F-22s banked and weaved. A couple returned fire.

C'mon. C'mon. Corcoran balled a fist, rooting for the U.S. planes.

A flash of orange burst behind one Rafale. It shuddered, then rolled, trailing smoke.

"Yeah!" Gunny roared.

His excitement was short-lived. Two more F-22s went down. The sole surviving Raptor blasted another Rafale out of the sky before two missiles bore down on it. The American jet banked hard right, popping out little red dots and clouds of silver. Flares and chaff. Corcoran held his breath as the F-22 dodged one missile.

You got it, you got it. Dodge this last one, then go back and kick a—

Flames gushed from the F-22's right side. The wing spiraled away.

"Dammit," Corcoran growled as he watched the canopy fly off. Seconds later, a parachute sprouted in the sky.

He scanned the air over the city, now an enormous canvass of contrails and smoke. He only saw Rafales. Bitter cold wrapped around his spine.

The DPE had air supremacy over Anchorage.

"Twitter's blowing up with people sayin' there's been some explosions in Juneau," Baldelli reported.

"Not surprised," said Corcoran. "That is the state capital."

He gazed out at Anchorage. Clouds of smoke hung over the northern part of the city. Sirens wailed from one end of the city to the other. DPE Rafales circled overhead, aerial predators ready to pounce. Baldelli relayed more news he got off Twitter and Facebook. Explosions had been reported in Seward, Homer, and Kodiak Island, where the Navy and Coast Guard had bases.

"Aw man, now they're saying Washington's been hit." Baldelli's face stiffened as he stared at his tablet. "There's also some explosions in Norfolk and . . ." He slowly lifted his head. The veins in his neck twitched. "San Diego."

Corcoran swallowed. The DPE had to have hit Camp Pendleton. Worry slashed his stomach. All three of them had served at that base and still had friends there.

"More planes coming from the southwest," Kosco announced. "Big ones."

Dozens of aircraft approached Anchorage, all fat and oval-shaped with big wings. Transports, some with jet engines, others prop-driven. Corcoran identified particular types. Il-76s, An-12s, A400Ms, even a few American-built C-141 Starlifters the previous president had donated to the DPE. Anger lines dug into the skin around his nose. *Thanks, Prez. You give 'em our stuff and they use it against us. Hope you're happy.*

The ex-President probably was, given his political leanings.

The planes soared over the city. Rows of little dots fell out of their rears. Parachutes blossomed. Hundreds at first, then well over a thousand, stretching across the sky. Corcoran couldn't blink as the paratroopers floated toward the ground.

This is really happening. The United States was being invaded by a foreign army.

"Looks like a lot of them are coming down along Route One." Kosco cut his hand across the air going left to right. "I guess they want to make sure no one leaves Anchorage."

Corcoran's chest tightened. "Or enters."

SEVENTEEN

Ruud barreled down the Parks Highway in Krista's jeep when his satellite phone rang.

"Devil One," he answered, one hand on the wheel as the speedometer passed 80. "Go."

"Devil Two," replied Gunny Corcoran.

"What's the SITREP on your end?"

"It sucks. Anchorage is lousy with Blue Helmets." Even though UN troops no longer wore the famed blue helmets, the nickname still stuck. "They nailed JBER with cruise missiles before dropping airborne troops."

Ruud scowled. "That will make it tough to get to you."

"Forget about it, sir. Stay away from here."

"Like hell. I'm not going to sit on my ass up here while you're surrounded by the DPE."

"Those paratroopers are going to be in control of every access point into and out of Anchorage soon," Corcoran told him.

"Then I'll find another way in. That's our specialty, isn't it? Sneaking into places where we're not welcome."

"What if you're caught? Colonel, you're probably on the UN's ten most wanted list. Think about what a public relations victory it would be for them to frog-march you into The Hague and put you on trial."

Ruud shifted slowly in his seat, imagining himself in handcuffs being led into the ICC courtroom. He did not like that picture one bit.

That's still not going to keep me from my men.

"Think about The Corps, sir," said Corcoran.

Ruud grinded his teeth as the gunnery sergeant continued. "You know what kind of propaganda you being on trial will generate? You know all the crap they'll say about you, the Marine Corps? You get convicted, it will legitimize everything Saihi and his asshole buddies have been saying. You can't let them embarrass The Corps like that, sir."

He didn't respond, just let the words sink in. That crazy fucker Saihi would exploit the hell out of it if he got captured. How much would that damage the reputation, the morale, of the Marine Corps? Could it also result in Saihi gaining more followers?

A slow, frustrated breath flowed from Ruud's nostrils. Corcoran was right. He couldn't allow the DPE to capture him. He also didn't feel right abandoning his men.

"We'll be fine," said Corcoran. "You stay where you're at, do what you can to prepare in case the DPE advances north."

Ruud eased back on the gas. He had no doubt the Blue Helmets would move through the interior once they secured Anchorage. Their next objective would likely be Fairbanks, about 170 miles north. Right up the Parks Highway.

And right through Talkeetna.

Dark fear slithered through his stomach as he thought of Krista and the rest of the townspeople. *Gunny, Baldelli, and Kosco are trained to operate behind enemy lines. Krista and the others will need my help more.*

"All right, Gunny. I'm heading back. From now on we use the sat phones only for emergencies. Even if the UN can't listen in, they might be able to trace our signal."

"Copy. Watch your ass."

"You too."

Ruud tossed the sat phone onto the passenger seat. He threw the jeep into a sharp u-turn and headed north. Twenty minutes later, he pulled up to Millie's Café and went inside. None of the patrons had left. They all gazed at the TV, which showed a CNN reporter sitting in a studio. The sound had been turned up for all to hear.

"Alaska's governor is ordering all residents to stay off the roads and remain in their homes until further notice. This is to ensure clear travel for military, police, emergency services, and government personnel. In addition, all civilian aircraft within the State of Alaska are grounded until further notice."

Ruud took the announcement as a good sign. If the governor was still giving orders, then the DPE probably hadn't hit Juneau.

Yet.

"Jan-Erik!" Krista turned to him, eyes wide with shock and relief.

"I thought you were going to Anchorage," said Dempster.

"Change of plans."

"Thank God for that." Krista glanced back at the TV. "The UN's blowing the shit outta the place. Same with Washington."

Ruud nodded. "I heard from my men in Anchorage. The DPE's dropped airborne troops all over the city."

"Will they come here?" asked Ginny.

"Most likely, since this town's on the road to Fairbanks."

Ginny covered her mouth with both hands. More gasps went up from other patrons. A couple of them sobbed.

Dempster slammed his hand on the counter, causing many people to jump. "Let 'em come! The first Blue Helmet I see is gonna get a fucking hollow point through his head."

"Is that your solution to every disagreement?" Solstice snapped. "Shoot any person you don't like?"

"Disagreement? Have you been watching the news, hippie?" Dempster jabbed a hand at the TV. "The UN's invading us!"

"They're only doing this because they feel threatened by our militaristic culture."

"Lieutenant Colonel Ruud." Theresa O'Neill came up to him, her cameraman in tow. "Does this woman have a point? Is the United Nations invading America because you sank one of their ships?"

He narrowed his eyes at the reporter. "I can't speculate on the UN's motives."

"How can you say that, considering Secretary General Saihi's outrage over it, and all the protests and riots throughout the country?"

"Look, I don't have time to play guessing games. I can only deal in facts, and the fact is the United States has been invaded by a hostile foreign power."

"But the Army will stop them, won't they?" asked Millie.

"Not any units from Elmendorf-Richardson," Ruud answered. "The DPE's neutralized it. I know there's a Stryker Brigade at Fort Wainwright in Fairbanks. There are also some F-16s at Eielson Air Force Base, but they're mainly used for combat training. They may not have much in the way of actual munitions. If we want to defeat them, we need units from the Lower Forty-Eight."

"Good luck with that," Dempster snorted. "The DPE bombed the Pentagon, and from what you said they kidnapped President Moore and her cabinet. Who's left to give orders?"

"We still have plenty of generals and admirals out there. They'll take the initiative to organize a counter-attack."

"In the meantime," Krista said, "it sounds like we're on our own."

"Krista's right." Ruud looked around at everyone. "Most of the goods we get in Alaska come through Anchorage. With the UN controlling it, we can forget about resupply. Everyone needs to go home and take stock of food, clothing, batteries, and gasoline. Fill up every container you can with fresh water. If you have a generator, make sure it's topped off. The

DPE may knock out our utilities, whether intentionally or accidentally. We need to be prepared for that."

Ruud stepped over to Krista. "Talkeetna doesn't have a mayor. Who's the highest ranking civilian official here?"

"Paul Winn. He's our district representative on the Matanuska-Susitna Borough Assembly."

"Okay. I'll need to get in touch with him. Can you hitch a ride back to the house?"

"Yeah." Krista nodded. "What about you?"

"I need to meet with the state troopers," Ruud told her. "We have a lot of things to organize and probably not a lot of time to do it. When you get home, fill everything you can with water and inventory all our food and supplies . . . and your guns and ammo." He squeezed Krista's shoulders. "We're going to get through this."

To his surprise, she gave him a wry grin. "Remember that dive bar in Homer we played at back in college, the one the crazy drunks chased us out of? If we survived that, we can survive anything."

He couldn't help but smile. He knew he shouldn't have been surprised. Krista had never been a shrinking violet.

Ruud gave her a quick kiss before heading out to the jeep.

Minutes after leaving Millie's Café, he pulled up to the small State Trooper sub-station. He showed his ID to the receptionist and asked for Sergeant Harlow. An athletic-looking woman with short blond hair appeared. Definitely not Sergeant Harlow.

"Colonel Ruud. I'm Corporal Aubrey." She shook his hand. "I hope you brought more Marines with you."

"I wish I did. Is Sergeant Harlow available?"

"Yes, sir. He's back in his office. Follow me."

They walked past a pair of desks pushed together. Harlow's small office was just a couple feet away. The sergeant stood alongside his desk, a phone to his ear.

"Sarge, I've got Lieutenant Colonel Ruud here."

Harlow's brow furrowed. "Colonel Ruud? You're Krista Brandt's boyfriend. You said your name was John Erickson."

"I was under orders by my CO to use an alias. He thought it best if I keep a low profile." He showed Harlow his ID.

"I have a problem with people lying about their name."

"Sergeant, we have more important things to deal with than my name. The UN has invaded Alaska."

"I know. That's why I'm on the phone to Juneau."

"What have they told you?" asked Ruud.

"Nothing yet. I'm still on hold."

"How long have you been on hold?"

"About ten minutes."

"Hang up."

Harlow tilted his head. "Excuse me?"

"You don't have time to wait to talk with someone in Juneau. There are things here you need to start doing now."

Harlow straightened, lines of irritation digging into his face. "Look, we're dealing with a situation completely outside the norm. I need direction from Juneau."

"Juneau is six hundred miles away," said Ruud. "The DPE is just a two-hour drive from Talkeetna. If your bosses want to talk to you, they can call you. Meanwhile, you have to help the people here, starting with getting in touch with your district assemblyman and putting together a community meeting."

Harlow stared at the floor, then looked back at Ruud. "I think should check with Juneau first before we do anything."

Ruud fought off the urge to throw up his arms in frustration. He recalled the story Krista told him about Harlow, how he'd been exiled to Talkeetna after allowing a prisoner to escape. Now the trooper seemed afraid to make any sort of major decision without checking with his superiors first.

For better or worse, Harlow was in charge of this sub-station. Ruud needed him to do something other than fall asleep waiting for some bureaucrat in Juneau to remember he was on the phone.

"Do you have a civil emergency manual?"

Harlow nodded. "Yes."

"Get it and see what it says about a situation like this."

Harlow straightened, a look of renewed purpose in his eyes. He set down the phone and stepped over to a metal bookcase.

Ruud had hoped that would work. If Harlow couldn't get orders from an actual person, a manual written by someone in officialdom was the next best thing.

Harlow pulled out a book titled *Alaska Department of Public Safety Disaster Preparedness and Response Manual.* The date was seven years ago. He flipped through page after page.

"There's nothing in here about invasions."

Ruud bit his tongue to keep from going off on the trooper. Did the man not know how to improvise? "Look under terrorist attacks. That's what this is. A large-scale terrorist attack."

Harlow nodded and flipped through the book. "This should do. Man-caused disasters."

Agitation boiled in Ruud. *Man-caused disasters.* God, how he hated political correctness.

Harlow read quietly for a minute. "Okay, we'll need to call the volunteer fire department and have them stand by to assist with any injuries or fires. We've got a few doctors around, so they should probably be ready, too. We also need to plan for possible evacuation."

Ruud didn't know whether to be happy that Harlow had started dealing with the situation or infuriated that the man needed to consult a book written seven years ago before making a decision.

"I better call Assemblyman Winn," Harlow continued. "We're going to need to bring him in on this."

He told Aubrey to contact the Talkeetna Volunteer Fire Department and all the doctors in town. Harlow then phoned Assemblyman Winn and put it on speaker so Ruud could hear.

"Mornin', Paul."

"Ed. How's everything in Talkeetna?"

"Fine. All the action seems to be in Anchorage right now."

"Hopefully it'll stay that way," said Winn.

"Hopefully, but we need to be ready if it doesn't. I've got Lieutenant Colonel Ja-"

"I'm a member of the military," Ruud cut off Harlow before he could mention his full name. If the DPE knew he was in Talkeetna, they might rush troops up here to get him. "I'd rather not say any more than that. This is an open line. We don't know who might be eavesdropping. Understood?"

"Um, yeah," replied Winn. "So is the Army heading down to Anchorage?"

"Again, sir, I cannot answer that over an unsecured line. For right now, we need to concentrate on safeguarding the residents of Talkeetna. You have to come here and tell folks what they need to do during this crisis."

"Okay. Sounds like we should have a community meeting. We can have it at the --"

"Keep it to yourself, sir," Ruud interrupted Winn again. "Unsecured line, remember. We'll get a location prepped while you're en route."

Winn paused. "Um, okay. I can be there within the hour."

The assemblyman hung up.

"Where's the best place to hold a community meeting?" Ruud asked Harlow.

"Probably the high school."

"Good. Get in touch with the principal and tell him to get things set up for a big meeting at fourteen hundred hours."

"We'll have to get the word out to folks," Harlow told him. "We have a system where we can send texts and emails to people to alert them of an emergency. We can use that."

"No." Ruud cut his hand across the air. "Don't broadcast this in the open. A lot of people under one roof makes me think of one word, target."

"You really think the DPE would bomb us for having a community meeting?"

"I'd rather not risk finding out the hard way."

"Then how are we supposed to let everyone know about the meeting?"

The veins in Ruud's neck stuck out. How the hell could someone so incapable of thinking for himself become a sergeant in the State Troopers? "Your cars have loudspeakers. Use them. It shouldn't take too long to drive around town and tell folks about the meeting."

"Okay, we'll do that."

"Good. I'll see you at the meeting." Ruud shook the sergeant's hand and left.

When he returned to Krista's place, he found her in the living room cleaning one of her hunting rifles. Three more lay on the floor, along with four pistols.

"How are we looking?" he asked.

"I filled both the bathtub and my hot tub to the rim, along with every water bottle and thermos I have. We've got plenty of meat and a good amount of fresh fruit."

"Which will spoil if the DPE knocks out power. What about canned goods and other non-perishables?"

"We should be pretty good for a while. I did buy more than usual on my last grocery run since you're staying here. You know, you still eat like a horse and don't gain a single pound, just like when we were in college . . . bastard."

Ruud grinned. It was nice to see even in the face of an invasion, Krista kept her sense of humor. "How are we with our guns?"

"I counted up all our ammo. We've got three hundred-thirty rounds for the rifles and about a hundred fifty rounds for the pistols."

Ruud nodded. Not bad. He picked up a Winchester Model 70 hunting rifle and checked it out. Krista had done a good job cleaning it. Not that it surprised him. She'd been hunting since she was ten.

Something rumbled outside.

Krista stared at the ceiling. "Are those jets?"

Ruud didn't answer. He hurried to the front door, Krista following. They stepped onto the porch in time to see a dozen F-16s blast overhead, streaking south.

"They must be from Eielson Air Force Base," Ruud noted.

"Good," said Krista. "Maybe they can stop the DPE."

Ruud bit his lip. He knew it would take a hell of a lot more than twelve jet fighters to defeat the Directorate of Peace Enforcement.

EIGHTEEN

Ruud stared out the passenger window as he passed the general store, where a line of vehicles stretched down the street, waiting for their turn at the gas pumps. Horns honked. People screamed out their windows.

"Refugees." Ruud shook his head. He'd seen his fair share of them in war zones throughout the world. He never imagined he'd see that same sight in America.

Krista gripped the steering wheel, glancing over her shoulder as they left the store behind. "Well, they're lucky. How many others are trapped in Anchorage?"

Ruud shifted in the passenger's seat, a slow breath flowing from his nostrils. His thoughts turned to Gunny, Baldelli, and Kosco.

They're not helpless. They're as far from helpless as you can get. That still didn't completely ease his worries.

He scanned his tablet. Several news and political commentary sites were no longer available, mainly ones whose philosophies were opposite of Saihi's. *Probably victims of cyber attacks.*

All the sites belonging to the UN Friends of Peace were up and active. Very active, Ruud noticed. He scanned countless posts.

Finely free of white supremacist power structure!

Fuck USA! UN #1.

Racist president out UN in great day!!!

Ruud played some videos from the Friends of Peace, most showing Saihi supporters cheering and high-fiving DPE soldiers as they made their way through the streets of Anchorage and Washington. Another showed smoke and flames billowing from Joint Base Elmendorf-Richardson.

"Yeah!" shouted the man with the camera. "Burn, you fucking butchers! Burn!"

Ruud's face tightened in fury. He clicked on another video. Several Friends of Peace dragged a portly man out of his SUV. They threw him to the ground, beating and stomping him. The camera panned to the vehicle's bumper, focusing on an Emily Moore for President bumper sticker.

"All you cocksuckers who support this Nazi cum dumpster," said the woman holding the camera. "All you who support oppression and those ass-sucking military murderers, your days are numbered."

Ruud fought the urge to smash the tablet against the door. *You're wrong, bitch.* Your *days are numbered.* No way was he going to sit around while this shit was happening. As soon as the community meeting ended, he'd head north to Fairbanks and link up with the Stryker brigade at Fort Wainwright. He doubted they'd turn away a Marine with his experience with America under siege.

The parking lot of Susitna Valley Junior-Senior High School was filled by the time Ruud and Krista arrived. They parked on the side of the road, already lined with vehicles, and walked to the school. Clouds of gnats buzzed around them. They swatted at the annoying bugs, not that it did any good. The damn gnats stayed with them.

"Lieutenant Colonel Ruud."

He spotted Corporal Aubrey near the school's entrance, waving to him. "Yes, Corporal?"

"Sergeant Harlow wanted me to get you. He and Assemblyman Winn figured since you're with the military, you should address the crowd, too."

"All right." He nodded to Aubrey, told Krista he'd see her after the meeting, and followed the Alaska trooper inside. She led him to a locker room adjacent to the gymnasium. Harlow stood in the coach's office with two other men, one a stout Eskimo wearing a light blue shirt with a firefighter badge, the second bearded and overweight.

"Colonel." Harlow nodded to him. "This is Dennis Ugyuk, Chief of the Talkeetna Volunteer Fire Department, and our District Assemblyman, Paul Winn."

Ruud shook their hands.

"So is the rest of the Army on its way to Alaska?" A hopeful look formed on Winn's face.

"Sorry, Assemblyman Winn, but it's going to take a while before any forces arrive from the Lower Forty-Eight."

"Oh." A nervous tick developed under Winn's right eye.

"I can't imagine why the UN would even bother coming to Talkeetna," said Ugyuk. "We have barely nine hundred people in this town."

"They'll come here because we're sitting on the main road between Anchorage and Fairbanks," Ruud told him. "They'll need to secure all the towns along the Parks Highway."

"Are you sure about that?" asked Winn.

"That's what I'd do if I were the DPE commander."

Winn's Adam's apple bobbed. His chest rose and fell with quick breaths.

Ruud could tell from Winn's body language the man felt completely out of his depth. This was a politician used to dealing with budgets, road projects, and maybe a flood every once in a while. Not an invasion.

"We should evacuate the town," said Winn.

"No." Harlow shook his head. "The Governor wants all civilians to stay off the roads. Emergency and military traffic only."

"Did you see the line at the gas station?" Winn held out a hand for emphasis. "Those people got the hell out of Anchorage. Why should we have to stick around?"

"They should be arrested for violating the Governor's orders."

"Come on, Sergeant," said Ruud. "You only have two other troopers covering, what, a seventy-five to hundred mile radius. Do you really think you can enforce that order?"

Harlow chewed on his lower lip, as though trying to come up with a rebuttal. After several seconds, he groaned in resignation.

"We should call the Governor," Winn suggested, "see what he wants us to do."

"That might be difficult," Ruud told him. "I saw some posts that Juneau was hit by cruise missiles. The DPE likely took out all key state government instillations. Governor Powell might be dead for all we know."

Winn's mouth hung open, a lost look in his eyes. Harlow shifted his weight.

"Gentlemen, it's time to face reality." Ruud spoke in a forceful tone. "The Executive Branch has been neutralized, the state capital has been bombed and we won't see reinforcements any time soon. We are on our own."

He turned to Harlow. "Sergeant, I happen to agree with Governor Powell's declaration. But we don't have the resources to enforce it. If people want to leave, we can't stop them. All we can do is urge them to pull over to make way for any military or emergency traffic."

Harlow nodded, tacking on a dissatisfied grunt.

"Assemblyman Winn, get in touch with your counterparts in every town between here and Fairbanks and have them make preparations to receive large numbers of refugees. And we need to do that ourselves."

"We can use the school for an emergency shelter," Ugyuk pointed out. "Maybe the local hotels, too. If they get filled up, we can ask people to open their homes to refugees, or send them to campgrounds and RV parks. Thankfully, it's summer and not winter, otherwise that wouldn't be an option."

Ruud nodded, thanking God the fire chief didn't need any prodding to come up with a course of action.

After hammering out some final details, the four headed into the gymnasium. The bleachers had been pulled out and rows of folding chairs filled the court. Still it wasn't enough to accommodate all the attendees. Several sat on the floor or stood in the back. Ruud spotted Theresa O'Neill and her cameraman striding toward the front of the gym.

A microphone stand had been set up under the basket. Winn walked up to it. "Ladies and gentlemen, if I could have your attention, please."

Hundreds of separate conversations died down.

"Thank you. For anyone who doesn't know me, I'm Paul Winn, your district assemblyman. Joining me to address the, um, situation in Anchorage are Sergeant Ed Harlow of the Alaska State Troopers, Fire Chief Dennis Ugyuk, and Lieutenant Colonel Jan-Erik Ruud of the United States Marine Corps."

Gasps and stunned whispers filled the gymnasium. A man raised his hand. "Hey. Isn't that the guy who sank that UN ship?"

"Hell yeah, that's the guy." Ruud recognized Andy Dempster's voice. Several people cheered and clapped.

"Don't cheer him!" Solstice pointed at Ruud. "He's a murderer!"

"Bullshit!"

"Shut up, ya commie!"

"Hand him over to the UN. Maybe they'll leave."

"People, please." Winn waved his hands, urging the crowd to quiet down. "We have more important things to concentrate on, like making sure we have enough food and supplies to last us as long as possible." He told the audience to inventory all their necessities and fill up every container they could with fresh water.

"What if we run out of food and water?" someone asked. "What do we do then?"

"We live off the land." The answer came from Miles Koonooka, the man who did his own internet survival show. "We won't have much choice. Many of you hunt or fish. You'll just have to do it more. We have plenty of rivers and lakes here, so we have an ample supply of fresh water. Just remember to boil it. And if worse comes to worse, we can always eat insects and tree bark."

Several people scrunched their faces in disgust.

"I didn't say it would taste good," Koonooka added, "but when it comes down to a choice between living and starving, you will eat whatever you can get your hands on."

"It sounds like you want us to stay here," said a middle-aged woman. "Those UN soldiers are just a two-hour drive from here. We need to leave."

Dozens of voices responded, "Yeah!"

"We should head up to Fairbanks." One person jabbed his hand to the north.

"Forget Fairbanks," said someone else. "I say make for Fort Yukon, maybe even Arctic Village. No way the UN would go that far north."

"Or maybe head for Canada," a woman offered.

Harlow came to the mike. "First of all, the Governor issued a declaration of emergency ordering folks to stay off the road."

Many in the audience jeered the state trooper.

"I ran into a bunch of people who said they came up from Anchorage," a brunette in her mid-twenties stood, hands on her hips. "If they can leave, why can't we?"

"Yeah," chorused a few dozen people.

"Besides," barked a burly, bearded man. "I heard they bombed Juneau. Governor's probably dead. Why should we take orders from a dead man?"

"Even if the Governor is dead, and mind you, we don't know that for certain," said Harlow, "we should still abide by the emergency declaration. But the truth is, I don't have enough troopers to enforce it. If you want to leave Talkeetna, just make sure you have plenty of clothes, food, water, and gas with you. And if you see any military traffic, pull over and let them pass."

"Speaking of refugees," Chief Ugyuk spoke. "We've already had some come into town. You can bet more are coming."

"We should tell them to keep on going." The burly man jerked his thumb to the side. "More people here means less food for us."

"No." Krista stood. "We're not going to turn away anyone who needs help. I'm betting a lot of people got out of Anchorage with nothing but the clothes on their backs. If we can give them some food and water, we should."

"Easy for the rich rock star to say. You're probably sittin' on a shitload of caviar and champagne. You can afford to be generous."

Krista narrowed her eyes at the burly man. "Herk, you're as full of crap as ever. I don't have a bottomless pit of food. Rich or poor, we're all in the same boat. We can't start turning on each other and fighting over every little crumb. If we're gonna get through this, we're gonna do it by helping each other." She swung her head left to right, taking in the audience. "Dammit, we're Americans. Whenever there's a disaster anywhere in the world, we're always there to help. If we can give stuff to people halfway around the world, how can we not do the same for our fellow Americans, our fellow Alaskans?"

Pride surged through Ruud as he stared at Krista.

No one in the gymnasium spoke. A few people looked at one another with guilty expressions.

Chief Ugyuk returned to the mike, informing the audience what they can do to prepare for more refugees.

"Um, excuse me, Chief." A tall, blond man in his mid-thirties stood and held up his cell phone. "I don't mean to interrupt, but you may want to hear this."

"Sure, Curt. What is it?"

"My cousin in Fairbanks just texted me. He . . . He said there've been a bunch of explosions at Fort Wainwright and there're a bunch of parachutes falling all over the place."

Gasps and loud, nervous chatter rippled through the gymnasium.

Ruud maintained his stoic look. He should have expected this. The DPE couldn't wait for their ground forces to drive the 360 miles from Anchorage to Fairbanks, giving the troops at Fort Wainwright a chance to organize a counter-attack. They had to take out the base now.

"Folks." Winn raised his hands. "Folks, please. Please calm down."

"What the hell are you talking about calm down!" shouted a woman in the third row. "The UN's in Fairbanks."

The distressed voices grew louder. Winn, Harlow, and Ugyuk pleaded with the crowd to calm down. They were ignored. Several people got out of their seats, trying to leave, pushing others as they did. Angry shouts erupted. Shoving matches broke out. Ruud sensed they were seconds away from a full-scale riot.

"Everybody, please. Please calm down." Winn begged. "Please."

Ruud snatched the microphone away from Winn. "QUIET!"

Silence descended upon the gymnasium. People stood frozen, their eyes on him.

"Sit down, now!" Ruud stabbed a finger at the floor.

Everyone sat down.

Ruud dialed back his volume, but kept his tone firm. "Panicking accomplishes nothing. All it does is waste time, and we do not have time to waste."

He gazed around at the audience. Everyone gave him their undivided attention.

"Now, Fairbanks is obviously not an option for refugees any more. Even if you go to places like Gold Creek, Broad Pass, or Windy, sooner or later the DPE is going to show up. So we have to decide on other options. We can sit tight, or take all the supplies we can and hide in the forest, or make for the Denali Highway and head east to Canada. But the DPE may set up blocking forces along the highway."

Several people shifted in their seats or stared at their laps with nervous expressions.

A man hesitantly raised a hand.

"Yes?" Ruud pointed to him.

"Won't the military send more troops here to get rid of the UN?"

"I'm certain they will, but it may not be for a while."

"Excuse me, Colonel," Theresa O'Neill spoke up. "The military takes its orders from The President, or whoever's next in the line of succession. How can they act with no one in the Executive Branch available?"

"We're not automatons. We can think for ourselves, and with a foreign army occupying U.S. soil, my superiors will do everything in their power to repel them, with or without orders from The President."

"Won't that be illegal?"

Ruud fought to suppress his anger. Trust a reporter to talk about legal issues when the U.S. was being invaded.

"No it won't. Even with President Moore and everyone in the line of succession captured, we still have the authority to act. It's part of the oath every Marine, soldier, sailor and airman takes when they enlist. 'I do solemnly swear that I will support and defend the Constitution of the United States against all enemies foreign and domestic, so help me God.' The way things are right now, that's all the authority we need."

Ruud took a breath. "Now, what we should do is --"

"Excuse me, Colonel." Clyde Lasher stood, holding up his phone. "Sorry to interrupt, but the board op back at the station just texted me."

"What did he say?"

"Secretary General Saihi is about to make a speech he says will change the course of America forever."

NINETEEN

Lasher streamed the broadcast from KTNA on his phone, holding it up to the microphone. Ruud stared at it, biting his lip. Whatever Secretary General Saihi had to say would not be good for the U.S.

"We understand that UN Secretary General Ohmara Saihi is ready to make his statement regarding the invasion of America," said the newscaster. "We now go live to his temporary Headquarters at DPE Base Atar in Mauritania."

Ruud's face stiffened, trying not to reveal any of his growing anxiety.

"Greetings, my fellow global citizens." Saihi's smooth voice seemed to float through the gymnasium. "These past few weeks have been a trying time for those of us dedicated to the cause of peace. The United Nations has been the victim of not one, but two murderous and unprovoked attacks carried out by agents of the United States Government. This has resulted in the deaths of hundreds of men and women, with many more injured. Many Americans took to the streets, demanding their leaders be held accountable for their unconscionable actions. President Moore not only ignored their pleas, she ordered the police to murder her political opponents in cold-blood in Los Angeles. When citizens protested these barbaric killings, when they demanded justice, the police responded with brutality. Entire neighborhoods were burned to the ground, neighborhoods where the poorest, most vulnerable members of American society live."

A growl percolated in Ruud's throat. No surprise, the lying fuckstick failed to mention it was the protesters doing the brutalizing and burning, not the cops.

"Because of the chaos engulfing America's cities," Saihi continued, "because of the atrocities committed against the disenfranchised of American society, and because of the recent war crimes committed by

President Moore and her administration, the United Nations could no longer stand by. We had to act. To that end, I authorized the Directorate of Peace Enforcement to undertake an operation in the United States of America to restore calm to its cities and make its leaders answer for their crimes against humanity."

Ruud noticed Solstice in the middle row, eyes closed, a serene look on her face. He easily read her lips. "Yes. Oh thank you, yes."

Saihi went on. "I wish to make this clear. Our operation is *not* directed against the citizens of the United States. It is directed against President Moore, her administration, and the military and corporate power structure that supports her, and oppresses, abuses, and exploits the impoverished peoples of the world. DPE peace enforcers have already arrested President Moore and her cabinet. Very soon, other key supporters of hers will be apprehended, and rest assured, they will face justice."

Ruud scanned the crowd. Half looked angry, half looked terrified. Solstice, however, beamed with joy.

Be grateful I don't believe in hitting women.

"No doubt," said Saihi, "as a citizen of America, you are wondering what will become of you with your leaders imprisoned. I assure you, you have nothing to fear. All your needs will be seen to. With the approval of the responsible member states of the United Nations . . ."

Ruud wanted to laugh. "Responsible member states" likely meant countries who were enemies of the U.S.

". . . I have designated the United States and all lands under its jurisdiction as a special UN administered territory and have appointed one of your fellow citizens as its administrator. He is the Minority Party Leader in your House of Representatives, Mister Ismael Villarreal."

Gasps went up from the audience, along with more than a few grunts of, "Fucking traitor." Ruud waved everyone to be quiet.

"You will now hear from Territorial Administrator Villarreal, who has an important statement regarding the course of your territory's future." A pause. "The dawn of a new age is upon us, an age of peace and enlightenment, an age we will all be of one mind, one voice, one world. Now, I give you Administrator Villarreal."

Ruud glared at Lasher's phone, thinking back to the newscast where Villarreal ripped the U.S. and its military over the *Klaipeda* sinking. No wonder Saihi made him his puppet. Villarreal hated America as much as the Secretary General.

"I bring you greetings, citizens," said Villarreal. "First, I wish to thank Secretary General Saihi for giving me the honor of overseeing America during this time of transition. Thanks to the United Nations, we have the chance to make amends for the sins this country has committed throughout its history. The empire-builders are no longer in power. The people of the world who have lived in fear of America's power no longer have to do so.

We will demonstrate that we are truly part of a world community that seeks peace and enlightenment. Not with words, but with deeds."

Ruud tensed, wondering what the bastard had in mind.

"By the authority vested in me as Territorial Administrator, all citizens of the United States and the lands under its jurisdiction are ordered to take no violent action against any Directorate of Peace Enforcement personnel or any other members of the United Nations. All citizens will comply with the orders and directives of DPE and UN officials. They are not here as occupiers. They are here as liberators."

"Bullshit!" Dempster barked. Several in the audience voiced their agreement.

"Second, given the size of this country, and the scope of this peace enforcement operation, the DPE will need assistance. Therefore, I am granting full public safety powers to all chapters of the UN Friends of Peace within the American Territory."

Dread twisted Ruud's gut. With one decree, the United Nations created an instant army numbering in the millions.

"They will have full authority to undertake peace enforcement operations," said Villarreal, "including arrest powers. Third, in order to show the rest of the world we are no longer a threat, I hereby disband the United States Armed Forces, effective immediately."

Shocked gasps came from the audience.

"All members of the Army, Navy, Air Force, Marines, and Coast Guard are ordered to disable their weapons, aircraft, ships, computer systems, and satellites and abandon their bases."

"He can't do that," said a man in the front row. "Can he?"

"Furthermore," Villarreal continued, "the national intelligence agencies, such as the CIA and NSA, are also disbanded. I am also placing all local, state, and federal law enforcement agencies under the immediate control of this territory's UN administrative authorities. In conjunction with the DPE and UN Friends of Peace, they will execute arrest warrants on the following Americans who have been charged with violations of international and environmental laws, and war crimes, by the International Criminal Court."

Villarreal read off a long list of names. It included former presidents, vice presidents, cabinet secretaries, senior military officers, intelligence officials and operatives, corporate executives, even some current and former governors and mayors. He also mentioned the names of the Marines involved in the *Klaipeda* sinking, including Lieutenant Colonel Jan-Erik Ruud. Many eyes in the gymnasium fell on him. He ignored the stares and kept listening to the "Territorial Administrator."

"Some of these people will be easy to apprehend because of their fame. Others, however, will attempt to hide. If you have any information on their whereabouts, contact your local chapter of the UN Friends of Peace. You will be rewarded should your information lead to an arrest."

Ruud looked at Solstice. He half-expected her to get out her cell phone and tell someone about his location.

"Not only have we subjected others around the world to violence, we have also turned a blind eye to the countless murders of minority and disenfranchised citizens in our own country because of an archaic law written by slave owners and warmongers, that being the Second Amendment. This ends today." Villarreal emphasized all three words. "All citizens within this territory have forty-eight hours to surrender their firearms to UN authorities. After that forty-eight hour period expires, peace enforcers will have full authority to search your homes and seize any weapons found on the premises. The non-complying party or parties will be arrested and jailed for five years."

The gym exploded with shouts of panic and anger.

Ruud grabbed the mike. "QUIET!"

The racket died down. Several people sobbed or hugged one another.

"People," Ruud scanned the audience, "after what we just heard, now is not the time to panic."

"But what can we do?" a woman asked, her voice cracking. "That guy just did away with our military."

"Does he really have the authority to do that?" one man asked.

"The fucking UN's in control of Washington," said Dempster. "They've got all our leaders and put that asswipe Villarreal in charge, so I guess yeah, they do have the authority."

"So the Army's not coming to help us?" said a middle-age woman with tears in her eyes. "The UN's going to rule us?"

"Listen up," Ruud ordered. "I don't care what Secretary General Saihi says, and I don't care what Ismael Villarreal says. That man is not part of the recognized line of Presidential succession. He has no executive authority, and I will not follow any order he gives."

"So what?" blurted one man. "The UN arrested the President, they blew up all the Army bases in Alaska. There's nothing we can do."

"You're wrong," Ruud declared. "There is something we can do."

"What?"

"We can fight."

TWENTY

Shocked silence blanketed the gymnasium. Little by little, the audience found their voices.

"Is he serious?"

"We're not soldiers."

"Hell yeah!" Dempster pumped his fist. "Let's kill those fuckers."

"Colonel Ruud." Winn stepped over to him. "You can't seriously ask these people to fight. They're civilians. They'll be slaughtered."

"Don't speak for me, buddy," shouted a man from the audience.

"Yeah!" another spoke up. "I'd rather go down fighting than live in a country ruled by the damn UN."

Several people nodded.

"People, people," said Winn. "You need to think this through. What kind of chance would you have against real soldiers?"

"Hey, I was a real soldier," Dempster fired back. "Two tours in Iraq. I know what I'm doing."

"I did a four-year hitch in the National Guard," stated a dark-haired man in his late twenties.

A middle-age man with a sizable gut raised his hand. "I commanded an MLRS battery in the Gulf War. Dropped a lotta rockets on Saddam's boys. But I'll gladly pick up a rifle and fight for this country again."

"And why is this country worth fighting for?" Solstice looked from the Gulf War vet to Ruud. "You heard why the UN is doing this. America was built on war, oppression, and greed. What has this country ever done that was truly good?"

"What have we done?" Ruud fixed his gaze on her. "How about 600,000 dead to end slavery? How about 400,000 dead to rid the world of

Nazi and Japanese tyranny? Look at all the money and resources we dedicate to disaster relief around the world, the billions we donate to charities every year. We live in a country where you can criticize your government without fear of going to jail or being executed, a country that gives you an opportunity to change your lot in life if you're willing to work hard. Do you want me to go on?"

Solstice folded her arms, a sour look on her face.

Ruud continued. "We're not perfect. We've made our share of mistakes and done things we're not proud of. But that shouldn't negate all the good we've done. Every country has its warts, some bigger and more numerous than others. All we can do is learn from our past mistakes and try not to repeat them, to live up to the ideals our Founding Fathers put forth in the Constitution. We won't have that chance if the UN wins."

No one spoke, letting Ruud's words sink in.

Krista clapped. So did Dempster. Soon the vast majority of the audience applauded. Ruud squared his shoulders, the loud clapping and cheering sending a rush of energy and pride through him.

When the applause died down, he said, "I'm not going to force any of you to fight, but all of you have to ask yourself one thing. Do you want to live in freedom and control your own destinies, or do you want to be ruled by a dictator who can make whatever laws he wants on a whim?"

Krista got to her feet. "I'm with you, Jan-Erik."

"Yeah, me too." Dempster shot out of his chair.

In less than a minute, most of the people in the gym stood.

Solstice, no surprise, was not one of them.

"All right," Ruud began. "We have a lot to do. First, I need someone to get paper and pens and pass them around. I want everyone to write down your name, age, occupation, hobbies, special skills and any military or law enforcement history you might have. That will help me determine the best duty to assign you. While foot soldiers are a priority, any current or former doctors, nurses, and paramedics will go into our medical unit. Some of you won't be fit for the front line because, well, you've been around for a while."

"Oh, just say it," blurted Deke the gold panner. "Because we're old."

Ruud couldn't help but crack a smile. "All right, because you're old. But you can still help us in support roles. Logistics, transportation, communications."

The school's principal volunteered to get some paper and pens from her office.

"We should also form hunting parties," suggested Koonooka, "to make sure we have an ample supply of food."

Ruud nodded. "If you're going to hunt, use bows and arrows. Every bullet we have has to be reserved for a Blue Helmet."

"Got it," replied Koonooka. "Along with bows and arrows, I can also make spears and clubs. If our ancestors hunted like that, so can we."

"I refuse to take part in this repugnant meeting any more!" Solstice yelled. "You're talking about killing human beings like you're making a shopping list. The UN wants to help us, to eliminate the violence and greed that have corrupted our society."

"Yeah," Dempster snorted. "By taking away our freedom, our guns. And what are they gonna do if we don't go along with Saihi's enlightenment bullshit? Throw us in jail? Shoot us?"

Solstice's face reddened. "You people sicken me! I won't do anything to help you murder other living beings. Who'll join me?"

She pushed through the people in her row and stormed out of the gym. Ten others followed her.

Concern scratched the back of Ruud's mind. Solstice loved the UN too much for his taste. Maybe enough to . . .

"Sergeant." He turned to Harlow.

"Yeah?"

Ruud jerked his head for the state trooper to follow him. When he felt certain they were far enough away from the microphone, he spoke in a low voice. "I don't trust Solstice."

"That's a little harsh, isn't it?"

"You heard her opinions about this country and the UN. In times like this, people like her are the first to become collaborators."

Harlow tilted his head. "Don't you think you're overreacting?"

"My God, Sergeant. Did you not hear her?" Ruud jabbed a hand toward the door where Solstice had exited. "I wouldn't put it past her to send an email or tweet to the UN about what we're doing. We can't afford to have that kind of security risk."

"But what can we do about it?"

Ruud hesitated. "This is going to be very hard to accept. I need you and your troopers to relieve Solstice of her computer and cell phone, and disconnect her landline. Her and every person who followed her out of the gym."

Harlow gaped at him. "Are you kidding me? I can't do that without a warrant."

"And where are we supposed to get a warrant right now?"

"Colonel, what you are saying is blatantly unconstitutional, and that comes after you told everyone we need to fight for the Constitution."

Ruud looked away from the trooper. Harlow was right. He sounded like a hypocrite. Part of the oath he took when he entered the Marine Corps blared in his mind. *"I will support and defend the Constitution of the United States."* What he'd asked Harlow to do was contrary to that.

At least the support part of it. What about the part that says "defend?"

"It's just like in the Civil War and World War Two," said Ruud. "This is one of those times when in order to save the Constitution and the country, we have to temporarily break some rules."

Harlow shook his head. "I can't do this."

"Sergeant, look out there." Ruud pointed to the audience. "Those are the people who are going to war against the UN. If we let Solstice keep her phones and computer and feed the DPE intel on us, they will be able to attack us more effectively. Many of those people are going to die, people you and I took an oath to protect. Are their lives worth making sure someone who's ready to welcome the UN with open arms has the right to tell them everything we're doing?"

Harlow stared at the audience, then at Ruud. His shoulders sagged. "All right, Colonel. I'll do it, but I won't like it."

"That's good to know, because if you and I start liking that, we won't need the UN to turn this country into a dictatorship."

Ruud headed back to the microphone. "Sorry about that, everyone. Now, some other things to consider. When we fight the UN, we're going to have our share of wounded. I doubt any of the doctors' offices in town can accommodate a lot of casualties, so we're going to have to designate another building as a hospital, preferably a hotel, a place with lots of room. Whatever place becomes our hospital, paint a red cross on it, as big as you can. We may not like the UN, but even they won't bomb hospitals."

"You can use my hotel." The Gulf War vet raised his hand. "My wife and I run the Quiet Pines Inn. We've got thirty rooms, a restaurant, and a few other places that could accommodate wounded."

"Good. Thanks, Mister . . ."

"Plummer. Gene Plummer. Retired major, U.S. Army."

"Thank you, Mister Plummer." *He's a candidate for my XO.*

Ruud paused before talking, gazing out at the audience. His stomach knotted. How many people in this gym would end up in that hospital?

His gaze settled on Krista. His insides went cold.

He gathered himself and continued. "We'll also need scouts to keep watch on the Parks Highway. We'll have to come up with codes to describe any DPE activity. Cell phone calls and texts can be easily intercepted. Speaking of which, for the sake of operational security, don't contact anyone outside of this town, unless you receive authorization from me, Sergeant Harlow, or Assemblyman Winn."

"Excuse me, Colonel," Teresa O'Neill said in an indignant tone, "but I have reports to file with my network. I have to contact them."

"And what about my son?" asked a worried-looking redhead in her early thirties. "Teddy is very shy. Most of his friends are online. He's always on Facebook with them. How will he cope if he can't keep in touch with them?"

Ruud stared unblinking at her. "Ma'am, the United States is at war. Our leaders are prisoners. American cities are under enemy occupation. It's time to accept the fact there are bigger problems than your kid not being able to post on Facebook." He then looked at the reporter. "Miss O'Neill, we are putting together a resistance group. One thing you do not do in war is announce to the entire world what you are doing. There was a saying in World War Two. 'Loose lips sink ships.' If the UN learns where we are positioning our forces, where do you think they're going to drop their bombs? The people in this room, the people sitting next to you, will die. Is that worth a post on Facebook or a report on TV?"

Neither the mother nor O'Neill said anything. Ruud hoped they got the message.

The principal returned to the gym with a stack of copy paper and several pens. That's when another thought struck Ruud. "Also on the paper Principal Burgmeier is passing out, write down the types of guns you own and how much ammo you have."

"Most people around here have hunting rifles or pistols," Plummer noted. "Not exactly the best weapons against troops with semi-auto rifles, machine guns, and rocket launchers."

"Then get Andy Dempster to cough up some of his stash," Herk said. "He's got all kinds'a military-type weapons."

"Herk, dammit, shut up. That's no one's business." Dempster shifted in his seat. He locked his gaze on Harlow. It made Ruud wonder how many of the man's weapons were illegal.

"Andy," said Ruud. "If you're worried about having weapons you shouldn't have, I promise you, you won't be prosecuted for it. Right, Sergeant?"

Harlow frowned, but seemed to relent. He had to know they had more important things to deal with than Dempster possessing illegal firearms.

"Given what's happening," Harlow began, "I promise you, Andy, I won't arrest you or report you to any other law enforcement agency."

Dempster stared hard at Harlow, then turned in his seat to address the audience. "They're my guns, you know. I bought 'em, for my protection. I was the one who prepared for this day. No one else did."

"Okay, you're right," said Ruud. "We didn't listen to you and we should have. We're sorry. But you said you want to kill Blue Helmets. Think about what will happen if you loan your guns to other people. Imagine how many more Blue Helmets we can take out."

Dempster sat quietly, contemplating Ruud's proposal. "Yeah, I do want to see all those fuckers six feet under. All right, Colonel. I'll do it." He then looked at the others. "Just remember, I'm not giving you my guns, I'm loaning them to you. You better take good care of them and blow away all the Blue Helmets you can."

"Speaking of weapons," Ruud continued. "We'll need to make Molotov Cocktails and see what we can use to make IEDs. We also need to foul up the Parks Highway. Tear up asphalt, drop trees across the road. We have to do everything we can to disrupt DPE operations."

"You keep saying 'we' and 'our country'," Herk's eyes narrowed, "but that accent of yours doesn't sound like anything American. Just where the hell are you from?"

"My family and I emigrated here from Sweden."

"Sweden, huh? Quite a few Swedes in the DPE from what I hear. What's to say you won't go over to their side?"

"That's bullshit!" Krista spun around to face Herk. "I've known Jan-Erik since we were in college. He's as American as any of you, and if his fifteen years in the Marine Corps isn't enough to convince you, then you're a dumbass."

"Yeah," Dempster chimed in. "Besides, this is the guy who sank a DPE warship. That makes him a great American in my book." He threw Ruud a salute.

Ruud responded with a half-smile. "All right, everyone. Fill out those sheets and I'll start assigning your duties. We have a lot of work to do and not a lot of time to do it."

While most people scribbled on their paper, Krista walked up to him. "Hell of a speech, Jan-Erik. You got me ready to shout, 'Oo-rah'."

Ruud chuckled softly at her use of the Marines' battle cry.

"Still," Krista continued. "I hope you're wrong about us being on our own. I'm gonna pray that the rest of the Marine Corps shows up to blow the shit out of those UN fuckbags."

"Same here, but right now, if anyone's going to blow up UN fuckbags, it's us."

TWENTY-ONE

General McCullum jumped out the side door of the NH90 helicopter. He relished the jolt going through his feet when he hit the asphalt.

It's good to be back on solid ground. He'd been anxious as hell to get off that carrier. A soldier belonged on land, not at sea.

He doubled over and jogged away from the helicopter, its rotors pounding him with a hurricane-force downdraft. Four members of his protective detail surrounded him, their Ak5 rifles up and ready. Anchorage may have been declared secure, but there were still a few soldiers, police, and armed civilians on the loose taking potshots at DPE personnel.

The group hurried across the tarmac of the cargo area of Ted Stevens International Airport. He glanced behind him. His staff emerged from the helicopter and followed him to a pair of squat armored vehicles with eight wheels and sloped hoods. A DPE lieutenant standing by the lead Boxer directed them to the rear hatch. Once McCullum and his bodyguards were seated, the hatch closed and the Boxers rolled toward the street. A couple of minutes passed before McCullum climbed into the cupola.

"Sir, I wouldn't recommend that," urged the head of his security detail.

"Don't worry, Captain. I'll be fine."

McCullum threw open the hatch and stuck his head through the top of the Boxer. He leaned back as the wind blew into his face. They drove past Earthquake Park and some residential neighborhoods. He took a deep, satisfied breath as he gazed at houses and buildings along the way.

I did it. He was the first general to occupy American soil since World War II, and even then Japanese had only taken over two tiny islands in the Aleutians. His DPE controlled a major American city

Before long, they would be in control of *every* American city.

The Boxers pulled into the parking lot of the Alaska Division of Motor Vehicles office. McCullum got out, his bodyguards close by. A tall, lean man in green and brown fatigues greeted him near the front entrance.

"General." He saluted. "Captain Pinto. It is a pleasure to have you here." The man spoke with a Portuguese accent.

"Thank you, Captain. Is everything ready?"

"Yes, sir. Communications, command, control, and computer networks have all been set up. My people have also prepared a suitable office for you."

"Good." McCullum scanned the bland, white rectangular building. Rolls of barbed wire stretched around the perimeter. He spotted two machine gun nests along the sidewalk, and a third on the roof. Sentries and boxy GAZ 2975 utility vehicles with machine guns guarded the entrances to the parking lot. Security looked satisfactory. He also noticed the flagpole near the building. The American flag, a symbol of oppression and slavery, had been replaced by the flag of the United Nations.

"Good work, Captain," he added.

"Thank you, sir. This way." Pinto led him toward the front door.

Something cracked in the distance. A rifle shot.

McCullum ducked on instinct. His bodyguards hustled him through the front door. Once inside, he relaxed.

Pinto stared through the glass doors, pistol in hand. He lowered it and looked at McCullum. "I'm sorry, General. We are still trying to root out extremists."

"Then we need to step up those efforts. I want those fanatics eliminated as soon as possible."

"Yes, sir." Pinto nodded, then led him past rows of empty chairs. McCullum spotted a pair of vending machines along the wall, one with sodas, the other with candy and chips.

"Get rid of those." He pointed at the machines. "I will not have our men poisoning their bodies with that filth."

"Yes, sir." Pinto nodded.

The office reserved for McCullum had belonged to the DMV director and was set up in typical bureaucratic fashion with a desk, a swivel chair – not of ergonomic design, he noted – and filing cabinets. One of his aides entered with a case containing his laptop and other belongings, including his digital photo of him and Fawn.

After setting up his new desk, he checked his tablet, smiling at the latest updates on Operation: New Dawn. Along with Anchorage, Juneau, Seward, Homer, and Kenai were all under DPE control. Fighting continued in Fairbanks, but peace enforcers were gaining the upper hand. The latest casualty figures had 93 dead and 140 injured, not as high as he'd expected. They'd also lost seven Rafales and two SU-30 fighters, but all the American F-22s and F-16s sent against the DPE had been shot down.

In the Continental United States, fighting still raged between peace enforcers and rebellious U.S. military and law enforcement personnel in Washington. Major bases and command and control installations along the East, West, and Gulf Coasts had been hit by planes or cruise missiles. In the Caribbean, DPE submarines and carrier-based aircraft had sunk three American warships and crippled the carrier *George Washington.* Thousands of U.S. paratroopers and Marines were now trapped on Trinidad and Tobago, out of the fight.

McCullum checked his schedule. He had meetings with the general in charge of the Anchorage occupation and the new mayor, a former municipal attorney who shared many of Secretary General Saihi's beliefs, as well as a representative of the UN Friends of Peace.

At least there was time for a quick lunch. He moaned with delight as he devoured beans and rice, crackers, and flax bars from his ration pack. He wouldn't need regular meditation and crystal therapy to combat sea sickness like he did on the damn carrier.

Security issues dominated his meetings with the general and new mayor. Both expressed concerns about armed civilians and soldiers who'd escaped the assault on Joint Base Elmendorf-Richardson. The mayor didn't feel the vast majority of the Anchorage police department could be trusted to accept UN rule. That fact didn't worry McCullum. Between his peace enforcers and the UN Friends of Peace, they would maintain order.

Ten minutes after the mayor left, a stocky man in his early thirties with shaggy black hair entered McCullum's office. Hoop earrings stretched out his earlobes and a piercing hung from the corner of his right eyebrow.

"Mister Sudakis." McCullum nodded to him. "A pleasure to meet you."

"The pleasure's all mine." A smile stretched across the young man's face as they shook hands. "I'm so glad you're here. I mean, all you guys in the DPE. I've been hoping something like this would happen for a long time. You freed us from the warmongers and their corporate masters who ruled us for centuries."

Sudakis practically bowed, continuing to grasp McCullum's hand. Much as he appreciated the other man's gratefulness, McCullum had to pull out of Dillon Sudakis's grip when he felt the handshake went on too long.

"Please sit."

"Sure. Thanks." The younger man dropped into a red upholstered chair. He sat on the edge, eyes wide, an aura of exhilaration around him.

"So, you've been told why I want to see you?" asked McCullum.

"Yeah. Your DPE guys said you want me to be in charge of all the Friends of Peace in Anchorage. I can do that. I've organized a shitload of protests. I know how to lead people."

We shall see. The Security Information Department had done a background check and psychological profile on Sudakis and many other Friends of Peace to determine which ones would be suited for leadership positions. Along with organizing numerous protests, his podcasts, blogs, and twitter account had well over thirty thousand followers. His writings showed him to be passionate and committed to Saihi's vision of peace and enlightenment. That, however, did not qualify one to be a leader.

But for now, he is the best choice we have.

"Your organization will play a significant role during this time of transition," said McCullum. "Millions of Friends of Peace, added to our DPE forces, will give us the numbers needed to enforce UN rule over the entire United States."

"You bet we'll help." Sudakis's head bobbed up and down in an animated nod. "Actually . . ." He pulled out a thumb drive from his pants pocket. "We got Facebook posts, tweets, and blogs from people all over Alaska talking shit about the UN. We also took pictures of the flag-waving Nazi fucks who protested us a few days ago. Hopefully you can identify them and . . . shit, I don't know. Throw 'em in the river for all I care."

McCullum took the thumb drive and nodded in satisfaction. He gave the young man points for initiative and forethought. The more of these disruptive elements they could identify and detain, the better. "Good work, Mister Sudakis. I will pass this along to our Security Information people."

"Yeah. Glad to help, man."

McCullum winced. Sudakis did hold a position of power now. He should act accordingly.

Address it later. Sudikas could be an important ally. Best to start things off on the right foot.

"If you see any of these people," McCullum held up the thumb drive, "or know their whereabouts, you and all the other Friends of Peace have the authority to arrest them."

"I know. So cool." Sudakis grimaced. "Just one problem. A lot of people in this state have guns. They're just as bad as the redneck assholes in Texas."

"Don't worry. The DPE will make sure the Friends of Peace are well armed."

"Aw, hell yeah." Sudakis gave a fist pump. "I can't wait to see how those gun-loving shitbags look when *they* get a gun shoved in their faces."

"Along with weapons, these will be distributed to the Friends of Peace." McCullum took out a pack of playing cards and handed them to Sudakis.

The younger man shuffled through them, smiling. "Oh yeah. We'll be on the lookout for 'em."

"Good. You and your people will also receive a crash course in how to use your new weapons. We need the Friends of Peace in action right away."

"What do you want us to do?" asked Sudakis.

McCullum called up a map of Alaska on his tablet. "We couldn't afford to wait for all our units to land in Anchorage, then travel 360 miles overland to pacify Fort Wainwright and Eielson Air Force Base in Fairbanks. It had to be done on the first day of operations with our airborne forces. That means it's vital we secure the Parks Highway so we have a safe supply route between here and Fairbanks."

He traced his finger along the black line that represented the highway. "I don't believe that every American military unit will obey Administrator Villarreal's order to disband, so I need as many peace enforcers in Anchorage and along the Kenai peninsula as possible. But I also need to these towns along the Parks Highway secure. All of them are very small, maybe a few hundred people at most. We can take them with a handful of DPE mechanized platoons and two or three company-sized units of the Friends of Peace."

"Yeah. Cool." Sudakis nodded and smiled.

"We'll start here." McCullum tapped the map. "With Willow, then go to Caswell, then Talkeetna . . ."

TWENTY-TWO

Ruud bit his lip, sympathy welling up as he watched the middle-age woman sitting across from him. She trembled and sobbed, clutching tissues in her hands. It was a marked improvement from an hour ago when she'd sped into town in hysterics, fleeing the DPE advance.

"Just relax, ma'am." He reached across the table in the small conference room of the State Trooper sub-station and held the woman's shaky hands. "Everything's all right."

The woman, Sharon, nodded and sucked down a couple of breaths.

"I just need you to answer a few questions for me, then we'll find you a place to relax, okay?"

"O-Okay." Sharon's jaw trembled.

Ruud continued to hold her hands. "When did the DPE arrive in Caswell?"

"I-I guess around six. I was going to the inn for my shift when . . . I heard shooting down the street, then saw that . . . that tank, and . . . and . . ."

Ruud furrowed his brow, picked up his tablet, and went to Wikipedia. He pulled up the article on the Directorate of Peace Enforcement and clicked on the weapons and equipment section. "Which one was the vehicle you saw?"

"Th-That one." Sharon tapped the image of a Boxer armored personnel carrier.

Ruud nodded. He didn't think Sharon saw an actual tank. But to most civilians, any armored vehicle was a tank. "How many of these did you see?"

"T-Two."

Ruud lowered his eyes, thinking. Two Boxers, eight soldiers apiece, sixteen total. There had to be at least a couple more for a full mech platoon. The DPE probably didn't need more than that to take a small spot on the map like Caswell.

"It-It . . ." Sharon shivered. "It shot up this house. I got in my car and just drove. There were a couple of houses on fire. Then . . . Then those people."

"What people?"

"I don't know. They had guns and were beating up this old couple in their front yard."

"Were they soldiers?" asked Ruud.

"No." Sharon shook her head. "They were regular people. But they had guns and . . . and they just beat those poor people."

"Any idea why?"

"I don't know."

Ruud felt Sharon's hands quake under his. "Were any of them wearing blue armbands?"

"I think so."

A groan reverberated in Ruud's throat. Just as he thought. The Friends of Peace. The DPE didn't waste much time using them to augment their forces.

"I drove past and . . . and they shot at me. For no reason! I just drove until I got here." Sharon convulsed with a sob. She lowered her head and broke down.

Ruud rubbed her hands, reassured her she'd be okay, and left the conference room. A thin, raven-haired woman in a flowery dress stood in the hallway.

"You want me to take her back to my place?" asked Maggie Johnson, a member of Talkeetna's medical unit who was first on the scene to help Sharon. "I can whip up a herbal tonic to help calm her down."

He didn't answer right away. Maggie was a natural healer, and Ruud had always been dubious of that field. But since the town had only a few doctors and nurses, he had to take anyone with anything that resembled a medical background to help with the wounded, or the traumatized in Sharon's case.

"I'm sure it couldn't hurt," he said. "Do what you can to help her."

"You got it."

Ruud walked out of the sub-station and stared at the woods around him. *We don't have a lot of time.* Caswell was barely thirty miles from Talkeetna. The DPE would likely be here within the next twenty-four hours.

Maybe within the next four hours.

He ground his teeth, wishing he'd ordered his Talkeetna fighters to block the Parks Highway with trees and vehicles. But he wanted to keep it clear as long as possible to give any refugees a chance to flee the DPE.

Now your compassion's going to bite everyone in the ass.

Ruud couldn't afford to beat himself up. He had to get this town ready for battle.

He texted the order to start blocking the Parks Highway, then headed into the woods. Twenty fighters were hidden among the trees, every one of them in woodland camouflage.

Great thing about Alaska. A lot of people hunt.

When the DPE came, Ruud expected the sub-station to be one of their main objectives, along with the radio station and the small airport. He had other fighters concealed in the forests around those places, as well as the high school. More fighters had been positioned throughout the downtown.

Ruud let out a slow breath. *We can do this.* From what Sharon had told him, the resistance in Caswell probably amounted to a few people firing rifles from their windows. They'd be better prepared for the DPE here. Between the town's population and refugees, he had about thirteen hundred people. Thanks to Andy Dempster, several of them were armed with more than just hunting rifles and pistols. The Iraq War vet's basement had been stocked with all manner of weaponry. Pistols, rifles, and a few machine guns, some dating back to World War II. Dempster also had a Korean War-era 3.5-inch rocket launcher and a homemade mortar. The man appeared ready for World War III *and* World War IV.

To think, nearly everyone thought people like Dempster were crazy when they went on about the UN taking over America. Now the UN had taken over America. Dempster hadn't been so crazy after all.

Worry took hold of Ruud. The townsfolk might be well-armed, but how would they fare when the shooting started? The majority hadn't served in the military. He'd done his best to give them combat tips, but that was a poor substitute for actual experience. He had no idea which ones would rise to the occasion and which ones would piss their pants when bullets began flying.

Ruud's cell phone chirped. Krista texted him. *Get to a TV.*

He had told everyone to limit their phone calls and messaging. He figured it had to be important for Krista to text him.

He walked to Millie's Cafe, where a line of people stretched out the door. Millie had turned her place into a communal mess hall. The first thing he noticed upon entering was everyone staring up at the TV. Even Millie and Ginny stopped doling out food to watch.

"What's going on?" he asked Millie.

"It's the President. The UN has her in Anchorage. They're putting her on trial."

Ruud stood frozen for a moment. Anger and shock rose inside him. He suppressed it, concentrating on something more important. There was finally some news regarding President Moore.

He looked up at the TV, which showed a couple of reporters discussing the charges against Moore, all of them bullshit, as far as Ruud was concerned. The scene cut to the outside of a courthouse. Several people in the cafe gasped or shook their heads. Even Ruud blinked a couple of times to make sure what he saw was real.

President Emily Moore, shackled and clad in an orange prison jumpsuit, was being led out of the federal courthouse in Anchorage to a waiting convoy of APCs.

Ruud clenched a fist, staring at the screen through narrowed eyes. President Moore, who had sent U.S. forces to keep Albania from destabilizing and liberate the people of Trinidad and Tobago, was being treated like a common criminal.

"For those of you just joining us," one reporter spoke over the image of Moore and her guards, "President Moore was seen for the first time in two days, shackled and under UN guard, at the U.S. Federal Building and Courthouse in Anchorage. A spokesman for the United Nations says the President appeared for her initial hearing before a special three-judge panel of the International Criminal Court for war crimes and human rights violations. When asked to enter her plea, President Moore reportedly kept silent."

"What the hell's wrong with her?" blurted a bearded man near Ruud. "She should've told those UN dickheads to shove it up their asses."

Ruud thought about it. "The code of conduct."

"Huh?" Ginny scrunched her face in a puzzled look.

"The code of conduct for the Armed Forces. It covers how to act if any of us becomes a POW. That's how the President sees herself. She spent six years as an MP in the Army National Guard. She knows the code. Don't make any statements the enemy can use for propaganda purposes. If she entered a plea of not guilty, it would make this ICC trial look legitimate. It's probably the reason why they're holding this kangaroo court in Anchorage, to show the world they're in control of the United States and make Representative Villarreal's position as Territorial Administrator valid."

"Everyone's gonna know that's bullshit," said the bearded man.

Ruud frowned. *Some* people would think it's bullshit. Others, unfortunately, would buy into it, either because they support the UN or felt powerless against them.

He tuned out the TV, and everyone in Millie's Cafe. He needed to contact the other Iron Devils and have them gather intel on the courthouse and the security around it. Then they could –

Ruud received a text. *R1. 4 turtles. 3 raccoons. 2 otters. 10 mikes.*

His chest tightened. The message had come from Recon Team One. According to the code, they had spotted four APCs, three trucks, and two "other type of vehicles" ten miles south of Talkeetna.

The DPE was coming.

TWENTY-THREE

Ruud held his breath as he stared at his phone. The text had come from Gene Plummer. *Alpha. 1 turtle. 1 raccoon.*

"Alpha" was the designation for Susitna Valley High School. The DPE had an armored personnel carrier and a truck there.

Standing on the roof of Millie's Café, he stared past the trees and other buildings around him, thinking of the school less than fifteen miles away, and of the rest of the DPE mech platoon approaching Talkeetna.

"Moment of truth," Ruud whispered to himself, then looked over his shoulder at the three men kneeling by the parapet. "Get ready. The Blue Helmets are twenty to thirty minutes out."

The trio nodded. Ruud studied their faces. Zimmer, a skinny State Trooper barely six months out of the academy, looked pale to the point of sickly. Beads of sweat slid down the forehead of Fitzgerald, a pot-bellied, middle-aged man. The young, stout mountaineer named Tibbs kept his face tight, as though trying to hide whatever fear he felt.

How are they going to do when the shooting starts?

Ten minutes later, Ruud received a text from Dempster.

Bravo. 1 turtle. 1 otter.

The DPE had arrived at the airport.

Another text came two minutes later, this one from Corporal Aubrey. *Charlie. 1 otter.* The enemy was at KTNA.

Ruud removed the Browning Automatic Rifle, or BAR, from his shoulder. He gripped the big World War II-era rifle, which he'd retrieved from Dempster's sizeable arsenal, taking slow breaths to steady his heartbeat. The DPE was proceeding through Talkeetna as he expected. First the school, then the airport, then the radio station. If they continued according to plan, they'd seize the downtown next, then the State Trooper sub-station two blocks over. Instead of one main force, Ruud's fighters would have smaller enemy units to deal with in different parts of town. That gave them much better odds for success, so long as everyone held their fire or didn't reveal themselves until the DPE reached all five locations.

Ruud tried to beat down his worry and concentrate on the advantages they had over their foes. *We have numbers. We have the element of surprise. We know the terrain better.*

Doubt seeped into his mind as he considered their disadvantages. *The DPE are better trained. Some are probably veterans of the Central African Republic or Somali pirates campaigns. They also have four armored vehicles, and we have a grand total of zero.*

Ruud scanned down Main Street, his eyes settling on a green and brown wooden building with a slanted roof. Hidden among the trees around it was Krista, hunting rifle in hand. Dread engulfed his soul. He wished he didn't have to use her as a sniper. Hell, he wished Krista wasn't anywhere in Alaska right now. Ruud closed his eyes, throat constricting. He'd let her know earlier that he couldn't live with himself if anything happened to her.

"How do you think I'd feel if anything happened to you?" Krista had responded. "I'm not gonna sit on my ass while those UN piss drinkers take over my country, so I'm in this fight. End of discussion."

Krista was tough. She'd known how to shoot since she was ten, and she was a damn good shot. She'd be fine.

Please, God, let her be fine.

A low rumble drifted through the air. Ruud concentrated on the sound. It came from the south.

"Wh-What is it, Colonel?" Zimmer asked.

"Company's coming."

Fitzgerald shuddered and crossed himself. Ruud low-crawled to the eastern side of the roof. He pulled out his binoculars and scanned the southern part of town. Three vehicles made their way up D Street, a Boxer, a van, and a pickup truck with at least eight people in the bed. Not soldiers. Civilians. Probably Friends of Peace.

The vehicles reached the intersection with Main Street and halted. The rear ramp of the Boxer opened. Eight DPE soldiers emerged, seven armed with Ak5 rifles, the last carrying an FN Minimi light machine gun. They wore multicam fatigues made up of green and brown pixels. The helmets were also multicam, not the famous blue of the old UN Peacekeepers. In spite of that, most people still called them the "Blue Helmets."

Hold your fire, Ruud mentally urged the fighters, hoping none of them would jump the gun before he gave the word.

The soldiers stayed behind the Boxer, weapons up, scanning Main Street. It was a stark contrast to the Friends of Peace. They stood around their vehicles, some looking around, some staring at the Blue Helmets. Most either held their rifles by their sides or had the barrels pointed at the ground. A couple even stretched their legs.

No clue how to operate in a combat zone. They probably thought holding a gun and having the DPE close by made them invincible.

They're in for a rude awakening. Ruud chuckled softly. *No pun intended.*

One of the soldiers produced a loudspeaker. He spoke in English with a Spanish accent.

"Attention. Attention. By the authority of the United Nations, all citizens in the area of Main Street are ordered to assemble outside immediately. You and your dwellings will be searched for any weapons or other illegal contraband."

Long seconds passed. The only sounds came from the gentle breeze and a few birds chirping.

The soldier spoke again. "We know one of the Marines responsible for sinking the United Nations peace support vessel *Klaipeda* is in this village. Lieutenant Colonel Jan-Erik Ruud."

Ruud caught the others staring at him. He wondered if Solstice or one of her hippie friends got a message to the UN before their phones and computers were confiscated.

"He is wanted for war crimes and must be turned over to the DPE," announced the soldier. "Any citizen who harbors Lieutenant Colonel Ruud will be charged as an accessory in his war crimes."

Again, he was answered with silence.

The soldier repeated his demands. Main Street remained deserted. He swung his head left to right, looking at his subordinates. Even from up here, Ruud could tell the guy was pissed.

"This is your last chance," the soldier's voice blared through the bullhorn. "Comply with our orders or you will be removed from your dwellings by force."

No one complied.

The Boxer's engine rumbled to life. The squat armored vehicle slowly rolled down Main Street. The soldiers jogged behind it in two four-man stacks. The Friends of Peace followed, two dozen in all. No formation, just a big group of people. Some checked their surroundings, others watched the DPE soldiers. For a moment, their lack of discipline offended Ruud as a professional warrior. It quickly faded. The more untrained enemies they faced, the better.

He crawled back to the others and reached for a plastic crate. Inside were eight Molotov Cocktails. He grabbed one, pulled a lighter from his pocket and peeked over the parapet. The Boxer approached Millie's Café.

Ruud held the lighter close to the gas-soaked rag sticking out of the glass bottle.

Just a little closer . . .

"Wait! Wait!" A woman shouted.

"Who the hell is that?" Tibbs whispered.

Ruud watched a figure dash toward the intersection. The DPE soldiers swung around and brought up their weapons.

"Don't shoot! Don't shoot!" The woman waved her arms. "I'm on your side!"

The veins in Ruud's neck stuck out when he recognized her.

It was Solstice.

TWENTY-FOUR

Damn you. Ruud's eyes locked on Solstice. For a split second, he was tempted to blow the traitor bitch's head off.

The DPE soldiers held their fire as Solstice ran toward them. The Boxer stopped fifty feet from Millie's Café. At the intersection, the Friends of Peace stared at Solstice. Some cocked their heads or scrunched their faces, unsure what to do.

"The people here formed a resistance group!" Solstice screamed. "Colonel Jan-Erik Ruud is with them! They want to kill you!"

The soldiers swung their heads left to right, scanning for threats. Several dropped to a knee or edged closer to the Boxer.

"That fucking hippie sold us out," Tibbs growled.

Ruud buried his anger and brought up his BAR. He had wanted to wait until the last DPE unit reached the State Trooper sub-station before launching his attack. Thanks to Solstice, that option was no longer viable.

He put the BAR's sights on the DPE soldier at the rear of the left-hand squad. The man was down on one knee, rifle up, scanning a nearby building.

A short, deep chatter burst from Ruud's rifle. The soldier's head vanished in a cloud of red. Another soldier hurried over his fallen comrade. Ruud tracked him and fired. He jerked and collapsed.

The surviving Blue Helmets crowded behind the Boxer. Two of them fired. Ruud ducked as rounds cracked overhead and thumped against the parapet. More shots rang out. Single, sharp blasts from hunting rifles. Steady punches from semi-auto rifles. Talkeetna's defenders had joined the fight. Zimmer and Tibbs fired over the parapet. Fitzgerald hugged himself and trembled.

Ruud yanked out his phone and texted the team commanders at the high school, airport, radio station, and trooper sub-station.

Open fire!

The cracks and pops of gunfire echoed up and down Main Street. Ruud glanced over the parapet. Four Friends of Peace lay dead near their vehicles. Another crawled toward the pickup, leaving a trail a blood on the street. Solstice scrambled beneath the passenger van.

A Friend popped up from behind the hood of the pickup, spraying his AK-74 at the thicket of trees along the intersection. His entire upper body was exposed.

Ruud fired a short burst. The .30-06 rounds tore apart the Friend's chest. He dropped from view.

The Boxer cut to the left and stopped in the middle of the street. The DPE soldiers fired from behind it. Two Molotov cocktails sailed through the air. Both crashed on the street, forming small pools of fire near the armored vehicle. Orange flickers came from a window of the inn across the street. A Talkeetna fighter opened up with an M-60 machine gun from Dempster's arsenal. Rounds sparked off the Boxer's hull. Several soldiers ducked. Ruud also fired at them.

The armored vehicle's remote-controlled .50 caliber machine gun swung to the right. It opened fire with a deep chugging sound. Huge holes exploded across the wooden facade of the inn.

The machine gun then swung toward Ruud.

"Down!" He dropped to his stomach. So did Zimmer and Tibbs.

Fitzgerald continued to shake and hug himself.

"Get down, dammit!"

Part of the parapet disintegrated. Thick wooden splinters rained down on Ruud. Fitzgerald toppled over. Blood poured from the huge holes in his chest.

"Zimmer! Tibbs!" Ruud hollered over the gunfire. "Grab a couple of Molotovs and follow me. Stay low."

They each snatched two gasoline-filled bottles from the plastic crate, then slithered toward the access hatch. More .50 caliber rounds hammered the café, sending shudders through the roof.

Ruud lay on his side and flung open the hatch. The trio crawled down the ladder into the storeroom. He spotted Ginny and several children clustered behind a refrigerator.

"It's okay." Her voice quivered as she hugged a pair of sobbing girls. "It'll be okay."

More rounds thudded against the walls. Many of the children cried out, trembling as tears cascaded down their cheeks. The stale stench of urine hung in the air. One or more kids had wet themselves.

A .50 caliber shell snapped overhead and punched through the opposite wall. The children screamed.

Ruud crawled out of the storeroom and into the dining area. Someone moved to his right.

Millie faced him, a .38 revolver in her hand.

"Millie, it's me." Ruud held up a hand.

"Thank God." Her shoulders sagged in relief. "I was afraid you were one'a those UN bastards. They . . . They killed Burt and Willie."

Gunfire rattled nearby. Millie gasped, pointing her revolver toward the front of the café.

Ruud checked around the dining area. Shattered glass and wooden splinters littered the floor. Two men lay dead, pools of blood under them. Two others, a lanky teenage boy and a portly middle-aged man, sheltered behind an overturned table.

"Over here." Ruud waved for them.

The teen, Will Tracey, got to his feet.

"Down! Crawl!" Ruud ordered.

The pair got on their stomachs and slid across the floor toward him.

"You two are coming with me." Ruud pointed at them. "We're going to take out that APC."

"The what?" Tracey's face scrunched in confusion.

"Armored Personnel Carrier."

"What?" Tracey's eyes bulged. He shuddered.

"How are we going to do that?" asked the middle-aged man.

"With these." Ruud held up a Molotov.

The man's mouth hung open in silence for several moments. "Are you crazy? You want us to fight that thing with some bottles?"

"Unless you want everyone here to die, we have no choice." Ruud gave him a hard stare. "Now move out."

They crawled into the storeroom, with Ruud asking the middle-aged man for his name. It was Floyd Higgins.

They rejoined Tibbs and Trooper Zimmer and crawled out the back door, then slid along the wall to the edge of the café. Ruud checked around the corner. No sign of any DPE troops. The Boxer's big .50 caliber continued to chug. Ruud heard sporadic return fire from the Talkeetna fighters. Most were probably keeping their heads down.

Or lost them, literally.

The group sprinted to the next building, then the next, and the next. Beyond it was a thicket of trees at the corner of Main and D. They ran for them.

Ruud peered around one of the trees. Two Friends of Peace bolted down D Street, away from the fighting, their weapons abandoned. Other Friends hurried toward the battle. Once they were out of sight, he turned to the others.

"All right. We're going to use these trees for cover, come around, and hit the enemy from behind."

"What about that tank?" asked Tibbs. "What are we gonna do about it?"

APC. Ruud didn't bother correcting him. There were more important things to do. "Chuck those Molotovs at the tires and the machine gun. If we can immobilize it and knock out its weapon, then it's just a big, useless hunk of metal."

The four men looked at Ruud, each one showing fear and uncertainty in their faces.

"We don't do this, everyone in downtown, your friends, your neighbors, people you care about, they're all dead. This is your home. Fight for it."

Zimmer and Tibbs nodded, their faces stiffening with resolve. Will Tracey clenched his rifle, jaw quivering, looking determined to fight back the tears glistening in his eyes. Higgins blew out two loud breaths and crossed himself.

"Let's go." Ruud slid out from behind the tree. He stepped onto the asphalt, gazed down the street . . . and froze.

Another Boxer and a pickup truck packed with Friends of Peace rolled toward him.

TWENTY-FIVE

Ruud waved for the others to duck into the trees. He watched the Boxer and pickup rumble closer to the intersection. That had to be the unit assigned to take the Trooper sub-station. They probably got contacted by their buddies downtown before they reached their objective.

He crouched against the tree, pulled out his cell phone and texted Dempster. *Knock out turtle @ Bravo. Buster to Delta w/35.*

He pocketed the phone. He couldn't afford to wait for Dempster's response. Ruud just hoped the Army vet "busted his ass" to downtown with his 3.5 inch rocket launcher before the place turned into a bloodbath.

He checked around the tree. The Boxer made a sharp turn onto Main Street. The pickup with the Friends of Peace neared the intersection.

A *crack* reverberated through the air. Blood flew from the head of a Friend in the bed. He fell against the cab and slumped out of sight. The other Friends stared at the corpse in wide-eyed shock.

Another shot. A second man fell out of the pickup and onto the street.

Ruud smiled. *Krista.* He glanced at the trees around the museum across the street, where his girlfriend hid with her hunting rifle.

The pickup's driver looked over his shoulder, scanning the bed. The vehicle slowed.

Ruud dropped his BAR and grabbed a Molotov. He broke from cover, lighting the rag and racing toward the pick-up. The Friend in the passenger seat grabbed the driver's shoulder with one hand and pointed at Ruud.

He threw the flaming bottle and dove behind a tree. A crash and *whoosh* followed. Ruud peeked around the trunk.

Flames washed over the roof of the pick-up. One man tumbled out of the bed, his torso afire. Another Friend, a woman, shrieked and thrashed about as flames spread over her body. The remaining three people in the back jumped out.

Krista shot one in the chest.

"Take 'em out!" Ruud hollered.

Zimmer, Tracey, Tibbs, and Higgins opened fire. The pickup's windshield shattered. Both men in the cab jerked. The Friends who'd bailed out of the truck shed their weapons and ran away from downtown.

Ruud dashed along the trees, picking up his BAR. He slapped Zimmer on the shoulder. "With me! The rest of you, guard the intersection."

The state trooper followed him. Ruud glanced down D Street, hoping to see Dempster with his bazooka.

The street was deserted.

What if he's dead? Ruud thought about the phone in his pocket, but had no time to check it for a response.

He and Zimmer ran behind one building. Two deep thumps came from the Main Street. The sharp *crunch* of explosions followed. Grenade launchers.

Ruud slid up to the edge of the second building. He checked around the corner. The second Boxer sat in the middle of the road, parked at an angle. Its rear hatch was still down. He thought they would have buttoned up by now.

Then he saw a DPE soldier help a wounded comrade toward the vehicle.

Stroke of luck. Ruud lit his last Molotov, then did the same for Zimmer's bottle.

"Go!"

They ran along the side of the building. Both DPE soldiers went up the ramp.

Ruud skidded to a halt, reared back, and threw the Molotov. Zimmer hurled his a split-second later. Both bottles soared through the open hatch and exploded. Fire surrounded the two soldiers. They screamed, hands flailing at the flames that covered their bodies.

Ruud and Zimmer ran away from the burning Boxer. A few DPE soldiers and Friends of Peace by the other armored vehicle turned toward them.

"Move it!" Ruud shouted, pumping his legs harder.

They reached the edge of the building when gunfire erupted. A shower of wooden splinters jumped off the wall as they ducked behind cover.

"Shit," Zimmer said breathlessly. "Shit, shit."

Ruud swung around the corner and fired his BAR. A Friend pitched backwards and fell to the street. Ruud shoved a fresh twenty-round clip into the big rifle.

More grenade launchers thumped. Clouds of gray smoke rose along Main Street. Ruud held his breath. The DPE was about to push further into downtown.

Several soldiers and Friends rushed around the Boxer. Its .50 caliber blazed away. The soldier with the Minimi planted its biped on the Boxer's sloped hood and fired. Two Friends knelt, rifles pointed in Ruud's and Zimmer's direction.

Bullets thudded against the wall. Ruud and Zimmer dropped to their knees. Ruud risked a glance around the corner.

Two DPE soldiers and two Friends of Peace ran toward Millie's Café.

"Dammit." Ruud clenched his teeth, thinking about Millie, Ginny, and the children inside.

"Make for the café," he told Zimmer. "I'll lay down cover fire."

"What?" the trooper replied in a shaky voice.

"Just do it!" Ruud leaned out and fired.

One Friend crumpled to the ground. Ruud rushed out from behind cover, still firing. Zimmer paused, then jumped up and ran.

Ruud twisted his body as he sprinted between the two buildings, shooting from the hip. Blood gushed from the chest of another Friend. The DPE machine gunner swung toward them. His shoulder jerked. He stumbled and fell to his side, probably shot by another Talkeetna defender.

The Boxer's .50 caliber rotated toward him.

A jolt of fear shot through Ruud. He raced for the café. Zimmer was already through the back door.

The big machine gun pounded away.

Ruud reached the café as several rounds snapped past him. He dashed inside.

Ginny sat in front of the children, who were pressed against one another. Most of them cried. Ginny held a small semi-automatic pistol in her trembling hands.

Two sharp cracks came from the dining area. Ginny and the children yelped in fear. Ruud changed out the magazine of his BAR and hurried out of the storeroom.

Zimmer stood behind the counter to his left, AR-15 rifle pointed at the front of the café. To his right, Millie gripped a smoking .38.

"You fat, fucking bitch!" Someone yelled outside.

Beyond the shattered window, a Friend sat on the ground, clutching his bleeding shoulder.

"Nice shooting, Millie," Ruud called to her.

She turned to him, forcing a smile.

Another Friend appeared at the window, AK-74 at his hip.

"Down!" Ruud shouted.

He, Zimmer, and Millie ducked behind the counter a split second before the AK rattled. Bullets hammered the wall above them. A framed photo clattered on the floor next to Ruud.

The gunfire ceased. The Friend had fired full auto, burning through his entire 30-round magazine in about four seconds.

Ruud leaned around the entryway that split the counter. The Friend stood at the window, pulling out the empty mag. He looked up as Ruud raised his BAR. The Friend's eyes widened. He shifted to the right, trying to duck out of sight.

The BAR chattered. The Friend staggered backwards and fell.

The front door crashed open. Two DPE soldiers stood on either side of the frame. .

Ruud whirled around and threw himself flat on the floor. Rifle fire filled the café. A storm of 5.56mm rounds thudded against the counter between Ruud and the soldiers. Zimmer leaned around the entryway, firing his Glock.

Ruud crawled along the floor, then looked at Zimmer. The trooper slid back behind the counter to reload his pistol. Teeth clenched, Ruud got to one knee and stuck his BAR over the countertop. The two soldiers appeared at the edges of the doorframe.

A long burst erupted from the BAR. Wooden splinters leapt from the frame and the wall around it. The soldier on the left stumbled and fell, blood covering his torso. The surviving soldier dropped to his knees and lobbed a round object into the dining area. It skipped across the countertop.

"Grenade!" Ruud let go of his BAR and lunged for the grenade. He caught it just before it hit the floor. He lobbed it over his shoulder and fell to his stomach.

The grenade exploded in mid-air with a sharp *bang*. Shrapnel smacked against the counter and walls.

Zimmer fired his Glock around the entryway. Ruud peeked over the counter. The DPE soldier staggered, the 9mm rounds striking his chest. Zimmer did what all cops were taught, shoot at the center of mass.

The center of mass, however, was protected by body armor.

Ruud snatched up his BAR and fired. Two rounds blasted through the soldier's chest. His armor wasn't strong enough to stop high-powered 30.06 rounds.

"You two okay?" Ruud looked at Zimmer and Millie. The trooper nodded.

Millie clutched her chest, shaking. Ruud feared she might have a heart attack.

"I don't . . . ." She swallowed. "Can't remember ever being this scared."

"You're doing fine." He gripped the portly woman's shoulder. "Just imagine those people outside as every asshole that ever said your food sucked. I bet you always wanted to put a bullet in their asses. Now's your chance."

Millie responded with a half-cough, half-laugh. "Good thing is I won't get arrested for shooting 'em."

Ruud smiled and gave her shoulder another reassuring squeeze.

A rumble filtered into the café. He caught movement out the corner of his eye. He turned to the window.

The Boxer smashed through the wall.

TWENTY-SIX

Ruud threw himself to the floor. The groan from the Boxer's engine filled the dining area. His chest tightened, thinking of the machine gun on the vehicle's roof. He glanced at the wooden counter. Against .50 caliber rounds, he might as well have been using tissue paper for cover.

They needed to get back to the storeroom, get Ginny and the children out, before –

A horrific *crash* shook the café. A roar battered Ruud's eardrums. He crawled to the entryway and peeked around it.

Flames consumed the rear of the Boxer. The top hatch popped open. A DPE soldier tried to scramble out.

Ruud shot him in the head.

The smoke thickened, carrying the stench of burning metal and rubber.

"Come on! We gotta move!" He waved for Millie and Zimmer to head to the storeroom, then followed.

"Ginny!" Millie called to the waitress. "Get the kids out of here."

Ginny nodded. "C'mon, everybody. Run. Run."

Zimmer stood by the door, covering the children as Ginny led them outside. He then hurried out, Millie and Ruud behind him.

A thunderous blast rocked the building. The Boxer's fuel tank exploded.

A column of black smoke rose above Millie's Café. Ruud's jaw clenched. They couldn't use a burning building for cover. He checked around the corner. Smoke from the fire and the DPE grenades hovered along Main Street. He saw no Blue Helmets or Friends of Peace.

"Go! Go! Go!" He waved the others toward the building next door. Ruud stepped out from behind the café.

Someone ran out from behind the other building. Ruud brought up the BAR, but held his fire. The other man looked at him, holding a bazooka against his shoulder.

"I got here as soon as I could, sir," said Andy Dempster.

A smile spread over Ruud's face. He lowered his weapon and stared at the Iraq War vet. "Congratulations, Dempster, you just made my Christmas card list."

Dempster grinned, caught sight of Millie, then looked back at the burning café. "Um, sorry about your place."

"We're all alive, that's what matters."

"SITREP." Ruud asked for a situation report.

Dempster straightened before he answered. "Sir, most of the Blue Helmets are down, same with those Friends of Peace assholes. I took out the APC at the airport, to." He patted the bazooka. "My unit had the bad guys on the ropes when I left."

"Good work."

"Thank you, sir."

Ruud fired off texts to Aubrey at the radio station and Plummer at the high school. Hopefully, they had the upper hand over the DPE, too. He looked at Millie's. A pang of sympathy for the proprietor went through him as he watched the fire consume the front half of the café, along with the Boxer. Two other buildings along Main Street were also ablaze. He texted Chief Ugyuk. His volunteer fire department should be here in a few minutes, hopefully in time to save Millie's and the other buildings.

Bodies lay up and down the street, most of them DPE or Friends of Peace. Only a handful stirred. Smoke stung Ruud's eyes and scratched his throat and lungs. He coughed.

Someone nearby cried out for help. Ruud saw a woman, one of the Talkeetna fighters, kneeling over a bloody man. He took a step toward them when another woman ran out of a gift shop just down the street, towels in hand. She bent over the wounded man to administer first aid.

Ruud texted his two "medics" assigned to downtown. Maggie Johnson, the natural healer, and Danielle Hayes, a health and PE teacher at the high school. *Triage wounded. Prep serious ones for transport.*

Another text came in, this one from Aubrey. KTNA was secure. Most of the enemy force, made up entirely of Friends of Peace, either died or ran away after a five-minute firefight. Next he received a text from Plummer. Fighting continued at the high school. Ruud ordered Harlow's unit at the sub-station to reinforce the fighters there.

He scanned the downtown, his eyes lingering on the wounded. A cold ball formed in his stomach. How many other men and women had been injured throughout Talkeetna? He thought of the small number of doctors and nurses at Plummer's inn, now serving as the town's makeshift hospital. Were they ready to deal with a mass influx of casualties? How many of the wounded would die because they couldn't be sent to a proper hospital?

"You mother fuckers!" someone shouted. "I'm gonna fucking kill you!"

Ruud spun around. He saw Tibbs, Tracey, and Higgins guarding the enemy prisoners near the intersection. A burly, bearded man stomped over to them, a compact Bushmaster carbine in hand.

"Now hang on a sec, Herk." Tibbs held up a hand.

"Get outta my way, dickless."

Ruud ran toward them.

"Please, no kill." One DPE soldier, a short black man, held up his hands. "Please."

"Fuck you, darkie. You're first."

Herk brought up his rifle.

"Stand down!"

The big man looked at Ruud, anger lines marring his face. "What the hell for?"

"No one is shooting any prisoners."

"Go to hell," Herk blared. "How many Americans have these fuckers killed? I say we return the favor."

"Yeah, do it, Herk," urged a Talkeetna fighter. Two others behind him nodded in agreement.

"You can't shoot unarmed prisoners," Zimmer's voice cracked as he stepped forward.

"Stick your badge up your ass. I say we can." Herk swung his rifle toward the black soldier.

"Please." The young man trembled. "Please."

Ruud yanked the rifle from Herk's grasp and stepped between them.

"What the fuck? Gimmie that!" Herk reached out for him.

Ruud's knee shot into the bigger man's groin. He doubled over. Ruud kneed him in the face for good measure. Herk crumpled to the ground.

Taking a breath, Ruud looked at the others. "I know you people are pissed off at the DPE, and justifiably so. But these men are part of an internationally recognized military force. They surrendered and *we will* afford them all rights accorded to any POW under the Geneva Convention. That's what we do as Americans. If anyone has a problem with that, then you will have a problem with me." He jerked his head toward Herk. "You do not want a problem with me."

The three fighters who supported Herk cast their gazes away from Ruud.

He turned back to the prisoners, catching Tracey mutter, "Bad ass."

There were three DPE soldiers and two Friends of Peace. The latter weren't technically POWs according to the Geneva Convention.

Right. They're traitors. For now, he'd treat them the same as POWs, mainly because he had far more important things to worry about than the legal status of collaborators caught on the battlefield.

"Zimmer." He turned to the state trooper. "Take charge of the prisoners."

"Yes, sir. But where do we put 'em? The sub-station only has a little holding cell."

Ruud hadn't even thought of the possibility of POWs. Most of the available space in town was taken up by refugees. There had to be –

"You filthy fucking murderers!"

Everyone whipped their heads toward the middle of the intersection. Solstice stood there, teeth bared, shaking with rage.

Ruud's eyes narrowed. The woman's fury mirrored his. How many people died because she warned the DPE about their ambush?

He stomped toward her. "You love the UN so much? Fine. You can join the POWs."

"Don't you fucking touch me!" Solstice backpedaled. "You stay away from me!" She stopped near the body of a Friend of Peace, an AK-74 lying beside him. Her gaze locked on the rifle.

Ruud slowed, gripping his BAR tighter. She wouldn't, would she? Solstice hated guns.

She snapped her head toward Ruud. "I won't let you kill anyone else. I won't!"

She reached down for the AK. Ruud started to bring up his weapon. *Crack!*

A spray of blood flew from Solstice's throat. She staggered, eyes wide. Her hands pressed against her throat in a vain attempt to stem the river of blood. Ruud searched the area, trying to see who fired the shot.

Solstice fell to her knees, then on her side. Her body shuddered, then lay still.

Krista stood on the museum lawn beyond the intersection, decked out in green-brown-black splotched hunting clothes. Her face was smeared with mud to cover her pale features. She held her hunting rifle near her hip, then stomped over to the dead woman.

"Fucking traitor." Krista spat on Solstice's unmoving form.

She walked up to Ruud, who hugged her and kissed her forehead, not caring about the mud he got on his lips.

"Damn good shooting, babe."

"Thanks." Krista put a hand on Ruud's bearded face, then stared past him. "Well, we beat 'em."

He looked over his shoulder at the burning Boxers and dead enemy soldiers. Yes, they had won Round One with the DPE.

He feared Round Two would be much bloodier.

TWENTY-SEVEN

Twenty-four dead and thirty-seven wounded.

Ruud fought to maintain a stoic expression when Plummer gave him the casualty report for Talkeetna's defenders. Death and injury were inevitable in war. That didn't stop the pangs of guilt. He wondered if he had any right to ask these civilians to fight.

Would you rather tell them to sit on their asses and let the UN rule their lives?

The townspeople and the refugees knew what was at stake. They had volunteered for this. That still didn't make it easier for Ruud to accept their deaths.

He gritted his teeth, beating down those feelings of guilt. He didn't have time for it. The DPE would send more troops to Talkeetna. They had to be ready.

Ruud led Plummer over to a bullet-riddled SUV parked along Main Street. Beyond it, Chief Ugyuk's firefighters performed mop-up operations at Millie's after keeping it from burning to the ground. Koonooka, holding a camera, stood near the charred hulk of the Boxer that had crashed through the café. Ruud wanted the survival expert to put the images on YouTube to show people they can resist the UN. Hopefully, it would get a lot of views before the DPE's cyber unit removed it.

Ruud spread the map on the SUV's hood, grimacing. Several different odors hovered in the air. Blood. Sweat. Shit. Burnt metal and rubber. Burnt flesh. It was the smell of war. He couldn't count the number of times that stench filled his nostrils. Even after all these years, he still had to fight off the nausea it caused.

"It's time to shut down the Parks Highway," he told Plummer. "I want you to assemble squads and have them drop trees along the roadway or use vehicles to create roadblocks." He drew Xs on several areas of the highway. "Do the same to the highway north of town. I wouldn't be surprised if the DPE paratroopers in Fairbanks commandeer some vehicles and head here."

"You got it. What about the Susitna River Bridge? Do we blow it or hold it?"

Ruud bit his lower lip, pondering his options. They had several sticks of dynamite, courtesy of Andy Dempster and a local business that specialized in blast fishing. Dempster, helped by a few locals, also made IEDs with gasoline and fertilizer. But to significantly damage the bridge would require most, if not all, of their explosives. Ruud would rather use them against DPE vehicles or troop concentrations.

"We hold it for now, and blockade it with anything we can. We only blow it as a last resort."

"Gotcha." Plummer nodded. "We should also assign more patrols along the river in case the DPE try to use it to invade the town."

Ruud stared at the blue stripe of the Susitna River on the map. "I doubt they'd use the river as an invasion route, but they could use it to infiltrate special ops troops. Station sentries along it."

"Yes, sir."

Plummer set off to carry out his tasks. Ruud walked across the street to a pub that had been set up as a drop-off point for recovered enemy weapons. All the tables had been pushed to the side. Rifles, pistols, and a few light machine guns and rocket launchers lined half the floor. Hand grenades, magazines, and combat knives were piled on several tables. Dempster stood next to one, scribbling on a yellow notepad, probably listing all the weapons they captured.

"Looks like we made a nice haul." Ruud eyed the small arsenal.

"That we did, Colonel." Dempster grinned. "We even recovered the fifty cals from two of the Boxers."

"Good. This'll put us on even footing with the DPE next time they show up."

"Yes it will, until we run out of ammo."

Ruud's mouth curled in a half-grin. "You have to think positively, Dempster. If we need ammo, we kill more Blue Helmets and take it from them."

"Ha!" Dempster barked. "I like the way you think, sir."

"Good, because I'm giving you the chance to do that."

Dempster straightened, eyes ablaze with anxiousness. "What do you need me to do?"

"Assemble some squads and deploy them along the Parks Highway," said Ruud. "I want them in position to ambush any DPE convoys. We need to whittle down their numbers before they reach Talkeetna."

"Yes, sir." Dempster threw him a salute, nearly bouncing with enthusiasm. "I'll get right on it."

He dropped the notepad on a table and headed out of the pub.

Hands clasped behind his back, Ruud walked along the rows of rifles laid out on the floor. His eyes lingered on the weapons taken from the dead and captured Friends of Peace. It was a mix of G3s, AR-15s, and Kalashnikovs. A number of them looked brand new. Ruud figured they'd been taken from gun stores. Others, however . . .

He picked up an AK-47. It showed several scars and nicks on the wooden stock and grip. The metal parts were a very dull gray.

Looks like this weapon's been around the block a few times. Hell, it's probably older than me.

Most of the Kalashnikovs were in the same condition. He doubted these were taken from any gun store. They might have come from private collections. Or maybe the black market.

Why didn't the DPE just give them the same rifles they use? Maybe they didn't have enough to go around to all the Friends in the U.S. Or maybe they didn't want to give their best weapons to a bunch of untrained civilians/traitors.

"Colonel."

Ruud looked over his shoulder. Harlow stood in the doorway.

"What is it, Sergeant?"

"We put all the POWs in one of the hangars at the airport."

"How many are there?" asked Ruud.

"Six DPE and nine Friends of Peace." Harlow stepped inside and scanned the captured enemy weapons. "Damn."

"I know. We're putting together a nice little armory."

Harlow nodded. "We also have four DPE soldiers and seven Friends at the hospital being treated for injuries. I assigned a few people to guard them."

Ruud let out a harsh breath. Taking care of their own wounded would put a big enough dent in their medical supplies. How many more drugs, needles, and bandages would they have to use to take care of the enemy? Stuff that could be used to treat Talkeetna's defenders in future battles.

Ruud lowered his gaze. He couldn't bring himself to deny medical treatment to wounded enemy prisoners. Not only did it violate the Geneva Convention and the DoD Law of War, it also violated his own ethics.

"I also have some bad news," Harlow continued.

"What?"

"At least five Friends of Peace and one DPE soldier fled into the woods during the fighting. I had Aubrey put together a search party to find them."

Ruud snorted. He was tempted to tell the sergeant to forget about the fugitives. He needed every warm body available to help repel the next DPE assault. But there was no way he could have enemy personnel on the loose to either gather intel on them or commit acts of sabotage.

"Don't use too many people in the search," said Ruud. "Our first priority has to be preparing for the next DPE attack."

"I understand, Colonel." Harlow stuck his thumbs in his belt and looked away in thought for a second. "I could talk to Ollie Glanville. He runs one of the flightseeing businesses at the airport. He can do an aerial search. That might help us find 'em quicker."

"Do it." Ruud nodded. He hadn't given much thought to any of the aircraft in Talkeetna. They were all small, single-engine civilian planes. No weapons, no defensive counter-measures. Small arms fire could bring them down.

Still, there had to be some role they could play in the town's defense.

"I also wanted to show you this." Harlow pulled a deck of cards from his pocket and handed them to Ruud. "We found these on all the DPE soldiers, as well as the Friends of Peace."

Ruud looked at the cards. Each one had a photo of a person, along with their name. On the back, personal information about them was printed in English, French, and Spanish, three of the six official languages of the UN.

The first card showed Phillip Wiley, one of Alaska's U.S. Senators. The next was Seward Mayor Neil Martin. The third card featured Josh Olsen, President of the Independent Alaska Movement.

Ruud continued flipping through the cards. They displayed politicians, radio talk show hosts, members of conservative activist groups, bloggers, religious figures, authors . . .

He stopped when he got three quarters through the deck. He gazed at the photo, too shocked to blink. Slowly, he looked up at Harlow. "Take me to the airport. I need to talk to the POWs."

Ruud followed Harlow to his SUV. They drove down Main Street and turned onto the Talkeetna Spur.

"One other thing I found kind of curious," Harlow said as they passed a gift shop with a slanted, green roof. "All the MREs we collected from the DPE soldiers, they're vegetarian meals. Pasta, beans, and rice. Not a single one with any meat."

Ruud nodded, a stab of worry in his stomach as he though of that last card.

Minutes later, the SUV pulled into a small parking lot in front of a red wooden building that housed the offices of the flightseeing business. A stocky, unsmiling man with a sleek GSG-522 rifle stood on the porch.

"What's your name?" Ruud walked up to him.

"Milt Linzy."

"Where are you keeping the prisoners?"

"The hangar back there." Linzy pointed a thumb over his shoulder.

"Get me one of them for interrogation."

"You got it." Linzy strode off.

Ruud went inside as Harlow drove away. He spotted a small office past the reception desk. There wasn't much to it, just a desk, a few chairs, and a filing cabinet.

Good enough. Ruud stowed his BAR, pistol, and knife in a storage closet down the hall. He didn't want the POWs tempted to make a grab for his weapons.

When he entered the office, he gathered up a coffee mug, a letter opener, a few framed photos, and all the pens and pencils from the desk and threw them into a filing cabinet. He then removed the extra chairs from the room. Again, he didn't want anything within easy reach that the POWs could use as a weapon.

Ruud found some company stationary in a desk drawer and took a pen from the filing cabinet. He placed the notepad on the desk when Linzy appeared with a lean, dark-haired soldier.

"Name and rank?" asked Ruud.

"Peter Jensen, Sergeant, United Nations Directorate of Peace Enforcement. Nation of origin, Denmark."

Ruud wrote it down on the notepad. "Why did your unit come to Talkeetna?"

"Under the Geneva Convention, I am not obligated to answer any more questions."

"Why has the United Nations invaded the United States?"

Jensen remained silent.

The questions continued. How many troops did the DPE have in Alaska? Were any reinforcements coming? What was the purpose of the cards?

Jensen didn't utter a word.

Ruud ordered Linzy to take away Jensen and bring him another prisoner. He returned with the young African soldier Herk had threatened to kill.

"Name and rank?"

"Private Bakaye Diabate. I come from Mali. Family is poor. I join UN for money to help family. Is truth."

Ruud tilted his head, regarding Diabate. POWs weren't supposed to give their life's story to their captors, but this young man did so without any prodding. This was exactly the kind of prisoner he wanted.

"What unit are you with?"

"Fifty-Second Armored Reconnaissance Battalion."

"How old are you?"

"Nineteen."

Ruud wrote it all down. "Why did you come to Talkeetna?"

"They tell us to go here."

"Are there other DPE units heading this way?"

"Not know. That is truth. I am sorry." Diabate lowered his head and hunched his shoulders. Ruud wondered if the young African thought he would yell at him or hurt him for not being able to answer the question.

"I believe you," Ruud responded in a calm voice. He didn't see the need to scream like a DI. Diabate was just a scared young man thousands of miles from home who'd probably been fed all sorts of stories about how the U.S. military loved to torture prisoners. He probably hoped being helpful would spare him any pain, even though Ruud had no intention of laying a hand on him. He wanted Diabate to see him as a friend, a protector. Sometimes, the nice guy approach loosened tongues better than "enhanced" methods.

"Are you hungry, Private?"

"Yes."

"Do you have enough MREs?"

Diabate's face scrunched in confusion.

"Food," said Ruud. "Do you have food?"

"Yes. I had six ration packs. They took when I caught."

"Well, I can have your ration packs returned to you and the other prisoners."

"Thank you, sir," Diabate said in a low tone, his shoulders sagging.

"You don't sound happy about that. Well, I guess no matter what army you serve in, all field rations are horrible, huh?"

A small smile came and went on Diabate's face.

"What do you have in your ration packs?" asked Ruud.

"Noodles, rice, beans, crackers, dried fruit, crispbread."

"No chicken, no beef?"

Diabate shook his head. "No. Our general say no to it."

"Who's your general?"

"General McCullum. He commands everything."

Ruud assumed "everything" meant the UN's Alaska invasion force. "What can you tell me about him?"

"He from Australia, maybe New Zealand. He not like us eating meat."

"Why?"

"He think not good kill animals and eat them. He say it make people bad."

Diabate's answer gave Ruud a little insight into McCullum. It didn't matter to him if someone wanted to be a vegetarian. That was their choice. But when someone forced that belief on everyone, he had a problem. It sounded like McCullum was as much the aspiring social engineer as Secretary General Saihi.

Ruud asked where McCullum's headquarters was, but Diabate didn't know.

"Do you feel what you're doing here in Alaska is right?"

Diabate shifted in his seat. "I-I not know. I do what officers say do."

"Mm. We all have to follow orders. Even me, and I'm a Lieutenant Colonel."

Diabate responded with a soft chuckle.

"Are you scared, Private?" asked Ruud.

"No." Diabate shook his head emphatically. "No, I am not."

"Well that's a lie."

Diabate froze, his eyes bulging. Now he looked scared.

"Relax, Private." Ruud held up a hand. "There's no shame in being scared. I've been in the Marine Corps for fifteen years. I've seen my share of combat. But if I were in your shoes, sitting across from a man I'd been shooting at just a couple of hours ago, I'd be pretty scared myself."

"I-I just follow orders."

"I know. We're both warriors. That's what we do. We fight the enemy until one of us is dead or surrenders. You chose to surrender, and one warrior to another, I promise so long as you do not cause trouble, you and your fellow POWs will be treated according to the Geneva Convention. You will not be abused. You will be sheltered and fed." Ruud shrugged. "Granted, an airplane hangar isn't the greatest of accommodations, but we have to make due with what's available. As for your food, once your ration packs run out, we will feed you. You can even have meat if you want."

Diabate sat up straighter. Ruud expected the young man to salivate. He wondered how many other DPE soldiers were like Diabate when it came to their desire for meat.

"Thank you, sir."

Ruud asked a few more questions. How many DPE troops were in Alaska? Where was their headquarters? Where was President Moore being held? Diabate didn't know.

"These cards." Ruud pulled them out of his pocket. "You and the other men in your unit were all found with them. Why are you so interested in these people?"

"My sergeant gave them to me. He say DPE want them found."

"Why?"

Diabate shook his head. "Sergeant not say. Just tell us DPE want them found."

Ruud summoned Linzy to escort Diabate back to the hangar. He'd gotten some good intel from the private. Not as much as he'd like.

He hoped for better luck with the next POW.

TWENTY-EIGHT

Ruud finished jotting down notes from his last interrogation when Linzy returned. He brought one of the Friends of Peace, a short, squat woman in her mid-twenties with dark hair.

"Siddown." Linzy told her.

The woman sat. She lifted her chin, jaw stiff. She also clenched the ends of the armrests. Her eyes shifted constantly, never looking directly at Ruud. He could tell the woman was trying to look defiant, but had a hard time hiding her fear.

"What's your name?"

The woman sneered. "Fuck you."

Ruud shrugged. "Okay, Ms. Fuck You." He wrote her name with a flourish.

The woman's eyes narrowed.

"Where are you from?"

"Blow it out your ass, baby killer."

"Are you an American citizen?"

Ms. Fuck You drew a loud breath. "I'm a subjugated person living under the racist, corporate tyrants that rule this country."

"Uh-huh." Ruud noticed the woman's muscles relax a bit. It appeared she was getting braver with each response. "How many Friends of Peace are in Alaska?"

"None of your fucking business, you Nazi."

"Who is your leader?"

"Eat shit."

"Why have you taken up arms against the United States?" asked Ruud.

Ms. Fuck You squared her shoulders. "To bring President Moore to justice and free all those she and the white supremacist power structure are oppressing."

Ruud managed not to roll his eyes. It sounded like she was parroting talking points instead of giving her own opinion. "How many Friends of Peace are in Alaska?"

The woman didn't answer.

Ruud slammed a fist on the desk. Ms. Fuck You jumped and gasped. "How many Friends of Peace are in Alaska?" he yelled.

The woman shivered. "I-I want a lawyer."

"Excuse me?"

She tensed, stopping herself from quaking. "I want a lawyer. The Constitution says I'm entitled to legal defense."

"Yes it does." Ruud leaned forward. "But your UN buddies are in control of the federal government, and they've pretty much suspended the Constitution. That means any rights you have are the ones I feel like giving you."

"Bullshit. The Geneva Convention --"

"Nice try. Since the UN has overthrown our government, that means all treaties signed by the United States are null and void, including the Geneva Convention. So, let's try this again. How many Friends of Peace are in Alaska?"

"I-I-I want a lawyer." The woman tightened her face muscles, attempting to conceal her fear.

Ruud, however, could still see it in her eyes. All he needed was a little push to make her crack.

Or maybe a big push. He stomped to the door. "Linzy!"

The man jerked in surprise. "Yeah?"

"Assemble a firing squad."

"What?" Linzy gaped.

"You heard me. Tie this woman to a tree and put a firing squad in front of her. And I want it done in five minutes, otherwise you and every person guarding this airport are on half-rations for a week."

Linzy blinked, as if trying to process what he'd heard. "Um, um, okay."

Ruud turned back to the woman. Her eyes bulged, legs trembling. "Y-You can't."

"You are not wearing the uniform of an international army. You've taken up arms against your country on behalf of a foreign power that has overthrown the lawful government of the United States. You've committed hostile acts against your fellow citizens. That makes you a traitor, and treason is punishable by death."

The woman's mouth hung open in silence. She blinked slowly.

Ruud checked his watch. "Linzy. You've got four minutes and thirty seconds."

Linzy grunted. "Fuck it. I ain't goin' hungry because of a traitor. Let's go, bitch."

He marched over to her.

"No! No! Please!" She screamed. "I'll tell you whatever you want to know."

"Linzy." Ruud held up a hand.

The other man halted, then backed out of the office. Ruud stared hard at Ms. Fuck You, who had tears streaming down her cheeks. "Now let's try this again. What's your name?"

"A-Ally Cotto."

"How many Friends of Peace are in Alaska?"

"A-A lot."

"Be specific."

Ally shuddered. "I don't know. A thousand, maybe two."

Ruud grunted. He doubted Ally was very high on the FOP totem pole. She probably wouldn't have specific numbers.

A guesstimate is better than nothing. "Who's in charge of the Friends of Peace in Alaska?"

"Dillon Sudakis."

"Never heard of him."

"I'm telling the truth. He's big into podcasts and blogging."

Ruud almost wanted to laugh. The world was truly fucked up when a blogger who posted videos on the internet could lead a guerilla army. "Where did you get your guns?"

"The DPE gave them to us," Ally answered.

"And where did they get them from?"

"I-I don't know."

Lines creased Ruud's face. He locked eyes with Ally.

"I swear, I don't know." Her voice cracked. "They told us to come to the Army base and they gave them to us."

"You mean Joint Base Elmendorf-Richardson in Anchorage."

"Yeah. Yeah."

Ruud dug into his pocket for the deck of cards and shoved them inches from Ally's face. "What about these? Why is the DPE so interested in these people?"

"They told us they're against Secretary General Saihi's vision for America. They called them, 'enemies of enlightenment'."

"Why? Because they have the nerve to think differently from your glorious leader?" Ruud shoved the cards back in his pocket.

Ally's jaw trembled. "They . . . They spread hate. They steal from the poor and destroy the environment. They start wars to make their corporate masters rich. They --"

"Oh, cut the socialist bullshit. What are you supposed to do with these people if you find them?"

"Take them to a school in Anchorage."

"Which one?" demanded Ruud.

"I-I don't know the name of it. It's that school where the riot started last week."

Ruud knew exactly where Ally was talking about. "What happens to them when they're there?"

"I don't know. Seriously, I don't know. They just told us to bring them there."

Hot blades of nausea dug into his stomach as he thought about the card near the bottom. He folded his arms, keeping his hard gaze on Ally. She turned away. He doubted he was going to get much more out of a mere follower like her.

Ruud ordered Linzy to take Ally back to the hangar. He spent the next hour questioning the rest of the POWs, but did not get any new information from them. He sent what intel he did have to General Dobson via secure text on his sat phone. Hopefully his CO could make use of it.

After grabbing his weapons out of the closet, Ruud hiked back to downtown. Millie and Ginny set up a cooking fire in the café's parking lot, doling out bowls of stew to people. His stomach grumbled, reminding him he hadn't eaten anything since this morning.

Millie was stirring the big pot with a soupspoon as Ruud approached.

"Looks like even a war can't keep you from cooking." He nodded to the scorched facade of the café.

"Someone's gotta feed you all." Millie poured the thick, brown stew into a bowl and handed it to him.

"Thanks. Have you seen Krista?"

"I saw her go into the Roadhouse a while ago." Millie nodded to the brown and red wooden building down the street.

"Thanks." Ruud headed off, shoving a spoonful of stew in his mouth as he walked. A hot, tangy flavor enveloped his tongue. Seasoned beef broth with chunks of fish and vegetables. Delicious.

He wondered how much longer he, and everyone else in Talkeetna, would have food that tasted this good.

Ruud found Krista sitting at one of the tables inside the Roadhouse.

"Hey." She smiled as he walked in.

"Hi." He kissed her on the lips. "You doing okay?"

"Fine. It took a while for me to quit shaking. I mean, after all that . . ." Krista's jaw stiffened.

"I know." Ruud sat beside her and gently rubbed her back. "I went through the same thing after my first time in combat."

"Just . . . all those people, dead. Some of them I knew. And . . ." Krista bit her lip, then leaned into him.

Ruud wrapped an arm around her shoulder, resting a cheek on her matted hair. "You did good out there." He kissed the top of Krista's head. "You saved a lot of people, including me. Remember that."

"Mm-hmm." Krista slid out of his hold. She pressed her palms against the edge of the table and drew a couple of deep breaths. Her shoulders lowered. "I'm good. I'm good."

"Krista. There's something I have to show you."

"What?"

He took out the cards. "Sergeant Harlow found these on the DPE soldiers and Friends of Peace."

Her brow furrowed as she took the cards. "What are they for?"

"I think they're similar to the cards our troops were given during the Iraq War, the ones that had pictures of Iraqi officials wanted for crimes against humanity."

Krista looked through them, reading off the names. "Senator Wiley . . . Mayor Martin . . . Josh Olsen. What, the DPE wants to arrest them?"

"Yes," Ruud answered.

"Well, I know Senator Wiley is one of the biggest advocates of getting us out of the UN. Mayor Martin opposed having Kenai Fjords National Park named a UN World Heritage Site. And Olsen, he's never been shy about expressing his hatred for the UN and the Federal Government. I can see why the DPE would want them."

"Look about three-quarters down."

Krista thumbed through the cards, getting closer to the bottom. She froze, eyes wide. "Oh my God."

Ruud slipped an arm around her shoulders. He, too, stared at the card.

The card with Krista Brandt's face on it.

TWENTY-NINE

"One minute to air, Mister Secretary General."

Saihi nodded to the director, a thin, blond Swede, and adjusted himself in the cushioned chair. He glanced around the studio in the basement of the admin building at the DPE's Mauritania base. A carpeted floor lay beneath him, with an accent table next to the chair and a bookshelf and a picture window behind him. He wore a gray casual suit without a tie, and folded both hands over his left knee. It all helped create a relaxed atmosphere. Formal speeches were fine for rallying the masses. Keeping them engaged in the cause, however, sometimes required a different approach.

"Thirty seconds."

Saihi settled back in his chair, loosening his shoulders while waiting for the live webcast. He wanted the feel of chatting one-on-one with the person on the other side of the camera, to come across as relatable to them. That always proved a challenge. The common citizens of this world did not possess his sort of intellect.

Then again, who does?

The director held up his hand. "Five, four, three, two . . ." He held up his index finger without saying, "One," then pointed at Saihi.

"Good day, global citizens. I am pleased to tell you that much progress has been made since the start of our peace enforcement operation in America. We are ridding the territory of the guns that have brought death and misery to the most vulnerable of society. Witnesses are being gathered from all over the world to testify against former President Emily Moore in her upcoming trial. Preparations are also being made to put other politicians, corporate officials, and members of law enforcement and the military on trial for crimes against their own citizens, and citizens all over the world."

Saihi wished that Moore's trial had already happened and the arrogant bitch was rotting in jail. But he needed as many victims as possible to expose her administration's brutality, further legitimizing his takeover of the U.S.

He leaned a little closer to the camera. "More and more of you are turning away from a lifestyle centered around selfishness and giving yourselves fully to the only cause that matters . . . the well-being of our planet and everything that inhabits it."

The smile vanished from Saihi's face. "Unfortunately, there remain those unable to move beyond the life they know and embrace a new, more beneficial way of thinking. It is understandable. There is comfort in what is familiar. Many of these people have been raised to think they earned all the money and material possessions they have. In reality, they have lived under a lie perpetuated by America's former rulers."

He leaned back, eyes focused directly on the camera. "The success they achieved came at the expense of the disenfranchised, those who are prevented from joining society's privileged because of their skin color or their economic circumstances. The more wealth and resources the privileged few horde, the less is available to help those truly in need. But the successful class are unaware of the harm they cause. Their rulers have convinced them there is equal opportunity for all in America. In truth, their system is designed to benefit those who have what they believe is an acceptable skin color and who espouse certain beliefs."

Saihi tilted his head and closed his eyes halfway, trying to look sympathetic. "Yet, these people cannot be blamed for their refusal to change. They are the victims of years of manipulation and propaganda. It is not easy to abandon such deeply held beliefs. But they can be shown the truth, with your help. Should you know people like this, who are unable to admit the harm their lifestyle does to the less fortunate, please contact us."

Saihi paused to give the viewers a chance to read the phone numbers and email addresses the graphics operator in the control room put on the screen.

"Let us know their names and where they live," he continued. "We will send a United Nations representative to their home to talk with them, give them information on how they negatively impact society and our planet, and guide them on a path to enlightenment. With your help, we will all be of one mind, one voice, one world."

Saihi smiled to the camera. "Thank you for time, and good day to you."

After a few seconds of silence, the director announced, "Clear."

Saihi rose and thanked the director, who told him a recording of the broadcast would be posted on the UN's website and YouTube channel within two hours.

He headed upstairs, two bodyguards in front of him and two behind. Confidence and anticipation soared with each step. His previous two webcasts had resulted in an increase in membership to the Friends of Peace and visits to DPE recruiting offices. He expected the same following this cast.

With the added benefit of compiling a list of those who refuse to accept enlightenment.

Saihi strode toward the lobby of his office, where a thin African woman sat at a desk, typing on her keyboard. Zaffeka, his assistant. Three men sat on the couch across from her; DPE head Agustin Palacio, Security Information Chief Emre Irtegun, and Cyber Security Chief Claude Dupray.

Zaffeka looked up from her computer. "Good morning, Mister Secretary General." She stood to greet him, as did the three DPE officials.

"Good morning." He nodded to them before entering his office. Palacio, Irtegun, and Dupray followed. Sunlight made the curtain over the bulletproof window glow yellow.

Saihi walked around the boomerang-shaped ergonomic desk and sat. The DPE officials seated themselves on a sofa in front of the desk.

Palacio began the briefing. "I can report that DPE forces are in control of Southern Alaska and Washington D.C. While we have damaged the runways of several major military airfields, other air bases remain intact. U.S. warplanes have launched a number of air strikes on Washington. Thankfully, our air defense network shot down many American aircraft, and our forces suffered limited damage."

"Excellent." Saihi clasped his hands. "Convey my regards to all our peace enforcers in North America."

"I will, Mister Secretary General. There are still reports of sporadic resistance in Alaska and the American capital, but it is only a matter of time before all opposition is pacified."

Saihi nodded, his lips tightening. He knew some of the American populace would try to fight the DPE. Still, it infuriated him. Did they believe their guns and sense of freedom was more important than the planet as a whole? How could their government – *former government* – allow people with such limited perspective and intelligence to own an instrument of death?

"How goes our efforts to disarm the American population?"

"The forty-eight hour period for civilians to turn in their firearms has expired," said Irtegun. "From what we can gather, less than fifteen percent of gun owners have turned over their weapons to authorities."

Saihi felt the veins in his neck stick out. He had to fight to keep from pounding his desk. This defiance, this arrogance, was unacceptable. "We gave them a chance to surrender their guns without consequence. Now let them suffer the consequences."

Palacio grimaced. "It may not be that easy."

"Explain." Saihi's eyes narrowed.

"Many governors, mayors, and police chiefs throughout America have publicly stated they will not obey Territorial Administrator Villarreal's orders."

"That is why we have the Friends of Peace. They will enforce Villarreal's orders if local police and government officials won't."

"Therein lies the problem," said Palacio. "There are regions in America where the Friends of Peace do not have large numbers, mainly in the central and southern parts of the country. They could be overwhelmed by local police, even armed civilians."

Saihi intertwined his fingers. This was unacceptable. No matter the odds against them, the Friends of Peace had to disarm the population if the local authorities refused to do it. "Tell the Friends of Peace if they have to, take local police and government officials hostage. Better yet, take their families hostage to get them to comply with Administrator Villarreal's orders."

"Yes, Mister Secretary General."

"What of the American military? Are they still refusing to disband?" Saihi's gaze fell on Irtegun.

"So far, only the commanders of Kitsap Naval Base and Fort Indiantown Gap have ordered their bases closed. A few others have been occupied by Friends of Peace chapters, mainly small National Guard armories and bases that do not have combat units."

"Unfortunately," Palacio stepped in, "The bases that host large combat units show no signs of disbanding, even the ones attacked in the opening phase of Operation: New Dawn. They may be trying to organize a counter-offensive. I recommend follow-up strikes until they surrender or their forces are severely degraded."

"Approved." The thought of an American counter-attack made Saihi tense. "What of the facility north of Washington? Is it well protected?"

"Yes, Mister Secretary General." Palacio spoke in a firm, assured tone. "We have two companies of peace enforcers and forty SAU personnel on site, backed up by armored vehicles, anti-aircraft batteries, and aerial support. As you ordered, we made security a top priority."

Saihi took a slow breath, his anxiety lessening.

"There is also the issue of U.S. forces outside of North America," said Irtegun. "None of their overseas bases have closed. They also have two carrier strike groups at sea, the *Nimitz* in the Indian Ocean and the *Truman* in the Pacific, along with a Marine Expeditionary Unit in the Atlantic with more than two thousand naval infantry."

"Those ships have to be neutralized." Palacio spoke in an urgent tone. "Just one American carrier could severely disrupt our peace enforcement operation."

"Do whatever you must to sink those ships." Saihi looked away for a moment. "Continue to monitor the Americans' overseas bases. If it appears like they will take action against us, pacify them."

"Yes, Mister Secretary General."

Dupray raised a finger. "We are also having trouble shutting down websites and social media pages opposed to us. New anti-United Nations sites are going up every few minutes. Our opponents are also posting on Facebook, Twitter, and Instagram, and putting up propaganda videos on YouTube."

"But you are deleting them as soon as you see them, correct?" asked Palacio.

Dupray slouched, frowning. "It is not that simple. We are talking about millions and millions of posts and web pages and videos. The Cyber Security Section is stretched beyond its limit trying to find and shut down anything that criticizes our peace enforcement operation. Even sites we do shut down sometimes return. Their cyber experts are not only countering our efforts, but have even tried hacking into our systems."

Irtegun groaned. "We should just shut it all down. Social media, web providers. Everything."

"No." Saihi sliced his hand over his desk. "We need the internet to maintain our connection to our supporters. The Friends of Peace are also using social media and other sites to let us know about anyone who opposes enlightenment." He looked to Dupray, spreading out his hands. "You know what is at stake, my friend."

"Of course I do."

"Then you and your cyber experts must do everything you can to defeat these . . . deviants. If your people are exhausted, remind them that what we do, we do for the welfare of the planet, for all those forced to live in squalor and despair by the rich and powerful. If we win, they will have fulfilling lives, and the planet will heal and become vibrant again. But if we fail, we condemn everything on Earth to death. Let that knowledge strengthen them."

Dupray raised his head and stuck out his chest. "Yes, I will tell them, Mister Secretary General. We will not fail."

The cyber chief ran down the names of American politicians who expressed their desire to cooperate with Administrator Villarreal when Saihi's intercom buzzed.

"Yes, Zaffeka?"

"General McCullum is on secure Skype for you."

"Put him through to the main monitor."

The three DPE officials twisted their bodies around to view the monitor attached to the wall. Saihi leaned back in his seat as McCullum's hawkish face appeared.

"Good morning, General." Saihi did a quick calculation in his head. There was a nine-hour time difference between Mauritania and Alaska. "Excuse me. I should say good evening instead."

"Mister Secretary General." McCullum nodded.

Saihi studied his friend's face. He didn't smile. His eyes drooped. He thought McCullum was tired, but dismissed the thought. The general seemed . . . morose.

"Something troubles you. What is it?"

McCullum's gaze shifted away from the camera for a moment. "We've had a setback in our advance up the Parks Highway."

"What sort of setback?"

"The reconnaissance company assigned to secure Talkeetna was attacked."

Saihi straightened. "Who did this?"

"The townspeople, in all likelihood," replied McCullum. "We discovered this video on YouTube a couple of hours ago."

McCullum's face vanished, replaced by the image of a burnt out armored vehicle.

"This proves we are not helpless against the UN," a man's voice said off-camera. "They're not invincible. You can fight them. You *must* fight them, unless you want to live in a country ruled by a dictator telling you what to do and how to think."

A twitch started on Saihi's left cheek. Fury burned within him. *How dare they?*

"Delete that video immediately." Saihi had to concentrate to keep from yelling.

"My cyber unit did when they first saw it," McCullum told him. "But the video appeared again shortly afterward. We deleted it again, but it will probably get re-posted."

Saihi's chest rose and fell rapidly. *Damn these Americans. Damn their defiance.*

He closed his eyes, trying to quell his anger. Slowly, his muscles uncoiled. Saihi opened his eyes. McCullum's face was back on the screen.

"Did any of our forces escape Talkeetna?"

"No." McCullum shook his head. "All attempts to contact them have failed. We can only assume the entire company was killed or taken prisoner."

"This is Lieutenant Colonel Ruud's doing," Saihi said in a sharp tone. "He must have encouraged the villagers to attack our peace enforcers." He'd been surprised and pleased when the Security Information Department informed him Ruud was in Talkeetna. Not only had his order to sink the *Klaipeda* been the catalyst for Operation: New Dawn, but it gave a face to the evil that was the American military. Putting him on trial along with former President Moore would further demonstrate the UN's power.

"Not only is Colonel Ruud still free," said McCullum, "but Talkeetna is also the location of another one of our most wanted subversives. Krista Brandt, the singer."

"I do not care about a singer." Saihi waved a dismissive hand. "I want Ruud."

"According to intelligence, Colonel Ruud and Krista Brandt had a relationship while in college. That's likely the reason he's in Talkeetna. If we find her, chances are we find him. At the very least, we can use her as a bargaining chip to draw him out."

Saihi eased back in his chair. Again, he closed his eyes. *This is not a defeat. Lieutenant Colonel Ruud only bought himself a reprieve. We will capture him.*

He re-opened his eyes and released a slow, cleansing breath. "Do whatever it takes to capture Lieutenant Colonel Ruud. In addition, show the people of Talkeetna what happens to those who defy our will."

THIRTY

Ruud's eyes snapped open when his cell phone's alarm went off. He reached out from his sleeping bag and silenced it. Beside him, Krista moaned and stirred.

"Go back to sleep." He gently kissed her on the head.

Krista moaned again and pushed her head deeper into the integrated pillow.

He stared at her, thinking about her reaction yesterday after finding her card in the DPE's most wanted deck. After her initial shock faded, Krista barked out a laugh and said, "The DPE must be the biggest pussies in the world if they think a little ol' rock singer like me is such a threat. But if they want a piece of me, they're getting a bullet between the eyes."

Ruud couldn't help but feel pride. Krista's take-no-shit attitude had been one of the things that attracted him to her back at UA-Anchorage. But with that pride came worry. At first, he couldn't understand why the UN would be so interested in Krista. How could a singer in a heavy metal band possibly threaten them?

He then took into account Secretary General Saihi's beliefs. The man despised individuality and freedom, and felt everyone must conform to his beliefs for the greater good.

Heavy metal was the antithesis of that. Bands like Krista's railed against conformity and authority, and preached of not being afraid to stand out from the crowd.

To a man like Saihi, Krista Brandt and Icefire were a threat to his power and had to be silenced.

The only way that's going to happen is over my dead body.

Ruud slid out of the sleeping bag, grimacing at the stiff knots in his shoulders and back. He took a minute to stretch. Damn, he missed Krista's queen-sized bed. But an elderly couple who escaped Anchorage now slept in it. Two young children had the bed in the guest room, while four other refugees sacked out on sofas and futons in the living room. After everything they'd been through, Ruud and Krista agreed the least they could do was offer them the most comfortable places to sleep.

After all the times I've slept on the ground, I'm not gonna complain about using a sleeping bag.

Ruud went to the bathroom, did some push-ups and sit-ups in the hallway, then crept quietly through the living room, careful not to wake the sleeping refugees. When he entered the kitchen, he checked the microwave. The glowing blue numbers on the display told him two things. It was 0410, and Talkeetna still had power. He wondered how much longer that would last.

He ate a peanut butter and jelly sandwich and washed it down with a glass of water. Next he went to the basement to field strip his BAR and Ruger SR9. Both were in perfect working order.

It was still dark when Ruud went outside. Or rather, dark-*ish.* Instead of pitch black, the sky was more dark blue. Even without a flashlight, he could see fairly well.

Not the best environment to fight in. Special ops owned the night. But here in Alaska at this time of year, there was little to no night to own.

Ruud hopped on a mountain bike he'd borrowed from one of the townspeople and pedaled toward Talkeetna proper. He had ordered motorized vehicles limited to essential travel in order to conserve gas. Like any good officer, he believed in leading by example.

The sky brightened a little by the time he reached the Alaska Troopers sub-station. He entered the small conference room to find most of his "command staff" had already arrived; Gene Plummer, Sergeant Harlow, Chief Ugyuk, Miles Koonooka, Assemblyman Winn, and Bruce Brinkman, a local family doctor who Ruud tapped to command the town's medical unit. Several Styrofoam cups were laid out on the table. A warm, bitter smell hung in the air.

I wonder how much longer our coffee supply will hold out. When they finally ran out, Ruud half-expected a riot to ensue. Some people didn't know how to function without two or three cups to start their day.

Clyde Lasher entered the room a few minutes later, as did a short, fit man with gray-black hair. Ollie Glanville, who ran a flightseeing business out of Talkeetna Airport. With the help of his planes, two of the enemy combatants who escaped the battle had been found. Ruud had some other ideas on how to use the airplanes and tabbed Glanville, a former cargo pilot for Flight Alaska, as his air group commander.

Once everyone took their seats, Ruud began the meeting. "Any problems overnight?"

Everyone replied, "No."

He turned to Brinkman. "What's the status of the wounded?"

The portly, gray-haired man sighed. "We lost three more of our people during the night. That brings our death toll to twenty-seven."

Several people around the table hung their heads. Ruud gritted his teeth. Each death felt like a punch to the gut. It had to be worse for the command staff. They'd probably known most, if not all, of the dead for years.

Brinkman tried to force a stoic look on his face. "Also, two of the wounded POWs died. Three others are in critical condition, and need better care than we can give them here."

"Do what you can for them."

"I will, but we used up a lot of supplies after yesterday's fight. We did have a lot of people donate blood, so we're good in that area."

Ruud felt a pang of guilt. He'd forgotten to give blood yesterday. There'd been too many things to do. Still, that was no excuse. As soon as the meeting ended, he'd make his contribution to the blood bank.

"Much as I don't like doing it," Brinkman continued, "we can sterilize our needles and re-use them, but antibiotics, alcohol, gauze . . ." He bit his lower lip. "If we have another battle like yesterday's, it could deplete our stocks."

A slow, frustrated breath flowed from Ruud's nose. He thought of the Civil War, where inadequate medical care resulted in more deaths than combat. Would the same happen here in Talkeetna?

"We should go door-to-door and ask the residents to give whatever medical supplies they have," said Ugyuk.

Brinkman frowned. "I doubt they'll have anything other than band-aids and aspirin, but given our situation, I'll take whatever I can get."

"See to it, Chief," Ruud told Ugyuk, then turned to Koonooka. "What's been the reaction to your video of the burned out Boxers?"

"I've counted well over a million views and forty thousand likes, along a few hundred dislikes. But that's after reposting it about four times under different accounts."

"That's probably the UN's cyber guys." Lasher took a gulp of coffee. "I checked with some of my old contacts in the lower forty-eight. They say a lot of websites are down, mainly news and political sites that don't kiss Saihi's ass. But they're fighting back with their own computer experts, trying to stay online."

Plummer snorted. "Welcome to warfare in the Twenty-First Century, where taking down a webpage can be just as important as taking out a bridge."

"That's the MO of all dictators," said Ruud. "Controlling what people can see and hear."

He glanced at Lasher. "Any other info from your contacts?"

"Well, it looks like most of our military isn't going along with Ismael Villarreal's order to disband."

"Good." Ruud gave a sharp nod. "Hopefully they're planning a counter-attack against the DPE."

"They may have to get through those crackpots from the Friends of Peace to do it." Lasher scowled. "Those idiots are blocking the roads around several military bases. They've even overrun a handful."

Ruud's eyes stayed on Lasher, trying to process what the retired reporter just said. United States military bases were actually in the hands of a bunch of batshit crazy traitors. What else would they do to disrupt the armed forces? Plant IEDs along roadways? What if the DPE gave them heavy weapons like rocket launchers or surface-to-air missiles?

His worry mounted. If the Friends killed enough soldiers and destroyed enough vehicles and aircraft, they could delay any U.S. response long enough for the UN to secure the entire country.

That'll make what we do here more important. It may come down to a resistance movement to defeat the United Nations.

"What about the cops disarming civilians?" Plummer asked Lasher. "Villarreal's deadline for folks to turn in their guns has come and gone."

"In most places, the police refusing to enforce Villarreal's order."

"'Most places'?" Plummer's eyes widened in surprise. "Don't tell me there are cops actually going along with this?"

Lasher's shoulders slumped. "They are, in places like San Francisco, Oakland, New York, Seattle, Chicago, and a few cities in Massachusetts and Vermont."

Plummer threw up his hands. "I don't believe this. How can our own police go along with that shithead Villarreal?"

Ruud answered, "They probably feel with President Moore and her cabinet prisoners, Villarreal is the only legitimate authority we have in the United States. Hell, some of them might even agree with the son-of-a-bitch."

"Well, there are some folks who aren't giving up their guns without a fight," Lasher said. "There've been a handful of incidents of people shooting it out with police. I have a bad feeling that's going to happen a lot more."

Ruud pressed his hands on the table. They did not need American citizens getting into shootouts with police, and they sure as hell didn't need the cops ignoring the Constitution and being lackeys for a puppet ruler.

You'd think an invasion would unite us. Instead, it seems to be dividing us more.

He took a slow breath and looked at Koonooka. "How does our food supply look?"

"Pretty good. Most of the residents had begun stockpiling deer and moose meat for winter. We should have a few thousand pounds. With over eleven hundred people in town, we can stretch that out for a few weeks, and add to it whatever we catch. We have nets, baskets, and bottle traps set up in the river and the creeks. We've already caught plenty of fish. So long as we have electricity, we can refrigerate them."

"And what if the DPE shuts off the power?" asked Winn, his voice a touch higher than normal. "Then what?"

Koonooka answered in a calm voice. "We can dry or smoke the fish to keep them from going bad. Any rabbits or moose we catch, we can salt the meat or dehydrate it."

"And if all else fails, we go with Plan B." Ruud grinned briefly. "Eat tree bark."

Winn made a face and emitted a disgusted groan.

"I've done it on training exercises. It's . . . well, it's edible. Somewhat."

Lasher grunted. "Maybe it'll be all right if we put some ketchup on it. Of course, when we run out of ketchup, we're screwed."

Chuckles went up around the table.

"Mister Glanville." Ruud turned to the pilot. "Do you think the plan we talked about is doable?"

"It is. I talked with Andy Dempster and a couple of mechanical engineers in town. They assured me they can --"

The ringing of Ruud's phone interrupted the conversation.

"Yes?" he answered.

"It's R6," replied the leader of Recon Team Six. "The DPE sent a Boxer to our first roadblock."

"Just one?"

"Yes, sir, but here's the thing. They came waving a white flag."

That was not a report Ruud expected to hear. "Something tells me they didn't come to surrender."

"Far from it," said R6's leader. "I talked to this DPE colonel. He says he won't launch another attack on Talkeetna."

Ruud scoffed. "I doubt he's doing it out of the goodness of his heart. What does he want in return?"

"You."

THIRTY-ONE

Ruud held his breath as he stared out the windshield. A DPE Boxer sat in the middle of the Parks Highway, a few feet from where his people dropped a tree across the roadway. The white flag attached to its antenna fluttered in the breeze. Three soldiers stood beside the squat vehicle, two with their rifles slung over their shoulders. The Boxer's machine gun was turned to the rear. The four members of Recon Team Six stood along the side of the road. They, too, had their rifles slung over their shoulders. Under a white flag, neither side was supposed to shoot at one another. Usually the rule was respected . . . *usually.* It wasn't unheard of for soldiers to use a white flag to ambush their opponents.

Ruud could have just blown off the jackass. White flag or not, under the rules of war he was under no obligation to meet with the enemy. But he had a deal of his own he wanted to negotiate.

The Alaska Trooper SUV, driven by Zimmer, halted about forty feet from the Boxer. The two pickups following them also stopped. Ruud turned to the trooper, all the color drained from the young man's face. "It'll be fine. There's no shooting allowed under a white flag."

"Yes, sir." Zimmer slowly nodded, hands flexing on the steering wheel.

"But be ready in case things go south."

The trooper's head snapped toward him, eyes bulging. He swallowed and stiffened his face, trying to hide his fear. "Yes, sir."

Ruud removed his pistol and combat knife, laying them on the dashboard. Taking a deep breath, he got out of the SUV. Arms out to the side, he approached the Boxer. My God, he felt exposed. What if a sniper had a bead on him? What if that machine gun whipped around and opened up?

Then I'm dead, that's what.

He suppressed his fears as he neared the colonel, a tall, tan-skinned man with sharp features. "You are Lieutenant Colonel Jan-Erik Ruud?"

"I am." Ruud recognized the accent. He'd operated in that part of the world little over a year ago.

The man was Albanian.

Ruud stopped walking a couple of feet from the downed tree. The DPE officer stood on the other side of it.

"I am Colonel Dallku." He made no attempt to shake hands. "I am here to deliver an ultimatum on behalf of General McCullum, commander of all DPE forces in Alaska."

"Let me guess. He wants us to put down our weapons and embrace enlightenment."

Dallku's face twisted in aggravation. "The citizens of Talkeetna have defied the orders of Territorial Administrator Villarreal and committed acts of violence against United Nations personnel. That makes them subject to arrest. You are also wanted for the deaths of two-hundred eighty sailors on the *Klaipeda.* But General McCullum has a proposal for you. If you surrender, we will make no attempts to pacify Talkeetna, and its citizens will be granted immunity from prosecution for the deaths of any United Nations personnel in yesterday's confrontation."

"Okay." Ruud nodded. "Before I commit to anything, I have a deal of my own."

Lines etched into Dallku's forehead. He tilted his head. Ruud couldn't tell if he looked shocked or offended.

"You are in no position to make a deal," said the Albanian.

"It's not for me. See those pickups?" He pointed behind him. "We have nine of your people in them. They were wounded in yesterday's fighting and need better medical attention than we can provide. I'm willing to return them to you."

Dallku leaned to his left, peering around Ruud. "I wish to see them myself."

Ruud nodded and waved for him to follow. "Enemy representative coming through," he announced to the recon team members. "Do not fire."

He led Dallku over to one pickup. The Albanian scanned the wounded lying in the bed, a nurse from Talkeetna's medical unit tending to them. One DPE soldier, his face, shoulder, and chest bandaged, struggled to rise. "Sir? Sir?"

"Easy." Dallku raised a hand. "You will be fine."

The soldier gave a brief nod, grimaced in pain, then lay back down.

The two colonels walked back to the Boxer. "Thank you for caring for our wounded," Dallku said in a forced tone.

"You're welcome."

Dallku stepped over the fallen tree, then turned back to Ruud. "I assume you want something in return for our wounded."

"Yes. Ten ration packs and two first aid kits, for each wounded POW."

The DPE officer grunted. "Five ration packs and one first aid kit for each."

"Seven ration packs and one first aid kit each."

Dallku stood in silence for a few seconds. "I agree." He turned to one of his soldiers by the Boxers and ordered him to make the necessary arrangements.

"Now, back to my original proposal. You agree to surrender yourself to us and Talkeetna will be spared from any retribution. In addition, we have learned that the singer Krista Brandt lives in Talkeetna."

"Never heard of her." Ruud shook his head.

Dallku gave him a half-smile devoid of warmth. "I know that is a lie. You had a relationship with her while attending the University of Alaska. I am certain that is the reason you are in Talkeetna."

The admission didn't shock Ruud. If a network news reporter had learned about him and Krista, the DPE's spooks would also know about it. "There are a lot of female metal singers in the world. Why do you care about Krista?"

"The Directorate of Peace Enforcement has declared her a potential disruptive influence."

"Meaning she has a different opinion from your glorious leader Saihi."

Dallku scowled. "You and Krista Brandt are to turn yourselves over to our custody. If you do that, we will not pacify Talkeetna."

"What if I surrender and the townspeople still decide to resist?"

"Convince them otherwise."

Ruud shrugged. "What if they don't listen to me?"

A frustrated growl rose from Dallku's throat. "How many people are there in Talkeetna?"

Ruud cracked his mouth open, but held his tongue. There was no way he'd give this shithead any intel he could use against them. "Somewhere between one and one billion. Pick a number."

The skin around Dallku's mouth and nose scrunched in irritation. "I do not believe there are very many people in your village, certainly not many who are trained soldiers. They will not stand a chance against us."

"We did pretty well in our first go-round."

"Next time your people will face more than one recon company. Spare them any suffering and surrender."

Ruud rocked back on his heels and grinned. "I think I'll pass on the whole surrender thing."

"You would put the people of Talkeetna at risk because of your selfishness?"

"This has nothing to do with me." Ruud locked eyes with Dallku. "It has to do with fighting for this country."

"You have no country to fight for. This is a specially administered territory of the United Nations. The United States of America, as you know it, does not exist."

"So long as there are people who honor the Constitution and freedom, there will always be a United States of America."

Dallku glared at him. "You are delusional, and the citizens of Talkeetna will pay for your delusions."

"We'll see about that," Ruud said in a low, ominous tone.

The DPE colonel exhaled a slow, frustrated breath. He checked his watch. "The Boxers transporting your supplies should be here in an hour. You have until that time to change your mind."

Dallku spun on his heel and stalked off.

"Don't hold your breath," Ruud muttered before heading back to Zimmer's SUV.

He spent the next hour by the vehicle, his attention split between Dallku and his men and the road beyond them, waiting for any sign of the Boxers. Concern clawed at him. Now that he refused to surrender, he wondered if those armored vehicles would carry a platoon of soldiers intent on capturing him instead of food and medical supplies.

Will Dallku continue to honor the white flag? He will if he wants his wounded back.

What if he cared more about getting him than the welfare of his men?

Ruud went over to the pickup drivers and told them to be ready to get the hell out of Dodge if the DPE violated the truce. He stood beside the SUV, motioning to Zimmer to lower the passenger side window. Ruud wanted to be within reach of his weapons if the worst happened.

The drone of multiple engines put all of his senses on alert. He gazed down the Parks Highway, heart pounding.

Three Boxers appeared. Two had red crosses emblazoned on the hood. The third had its machine gun turned to the rear.

Good sign . . . so far.

He glanced at Zimmer. The young trooper's hand hovered over his holster, just in case.

The Boxers stopped behind Dallku's vehicle. Their ramps lowered.

Ruud held his breath. *Moment of truth.*

Several people exited the rear of the Boxers. Most wore red cross patches on their sleeves and carried stretchers and first aid kits. Others hauled crates. Nobody pointed guns his way.

"Enemy personnel coming through." Ruud held up a hand, walking toward the DPE. "Hold your fire."

The medics hurried over to the pickups. They checked the wounded and loaded them on stretchers while Ruud inspected the crates. Sixty-three ration packs and nine first aid kits, just as Dallku promised.

At least he's a man of his word.

When the medics loaded the DPE wounded into the Boxers, Dallku approached Ruud. "Have you changed your mind?"

"No. If you want me, come get me."

Dallku scowled. "Very well. Any deaths from this point are on your head."

The DPE colonel took a few steps toward his Boxer, stopped, and turned. "Don't expect our next meeting to be as pleasant as this one, Colonel Ruud."

Ruud shot him a wry grin. "If that's the case, I'll be looking forward to it."

THIRTY-TWO

Kosco's heart thudded against his chest. He slowed his pace as the pine trees that lined either side of Abbott Road gave way to a slew of businesses, restaurants, and homes. Just beyond was the Seward Highway and Anchorage proper. Anxiety slithered through him.

Suck it up, Marine. You're the only one who can do this. For three past days, he, Gunny, and Baldelli had limited their intelligence gathering to online recon. Trying to get useful information that way proved difficult. Most news and social media sites for Anchorage couldn't be accessed, and most TV and radio stations were off the air. The ones that remained had been taken over by the DPE. Their broadcasts and posts extolled the virtues of living under United Nations rule. The three Marines couldn't find out about enemy defenses, the condition of the populace, or the security around the federal courthouse where the President's trial would take place. They could only do that with boots on the ground.

Specifically, his boots. Gunny, a big, muscular black man, and Baldelli, a short Italian who gave off that New Yorker vibe, would stick out too much. But Kosco was of average height with a round, average-looking face covered by a beard. With a plain black ballcap covering his Marine regulation buzzcut, he didn't look the sort to draw undo attention.

At least, he hoped so.

Kosco checked his watch. 0710. The road should be packed with rush hour traffic. Instead, only a few cars passed by. The DPE had prohibited all non-essential traffic. The exceptions were first responders, hospital workers, sanitation engineers, and anyone who worked for utility companies. Even during an occupation, someone had to take care of sick people, pick up trash, and keep the lights on.

Kosco came to a bend in the road when he saw a boxy vehicle driving toward him. A GAZ 2975 utility car. Directorate of Peace Enforcement.

Just act casual. Kosco clamped down on his worries and let the canvas bag he carried dangle from his hand. He didn't break stride or walk faster, didn't turn away from the approaching DPE vehicle, didn't do anything that might look suspicious.

The GAZ drew closer.

Kosco held his breath, nervous ripples shooting through his stomach. *Please keep going. Please keep going.*

The vehicle passed him without stopping. He exhaled in relief and glanced down at the bag. That had been Gunny's idea. The DPE-controlled media outlets announced that food for Anchorage residents would be distributed at supermarkets, as well as certain restaurants and convenience stores, by UN personnel. People also had to bring their own bags, provided they were not paper or plastic. Carrying around a canvass bag would make Kosco look like a resident going to get some food.

He hoped he could keep up that ruse for the rest of the day.

Kosco saw more people on the streets as he moved beyond the Seward Highway. Most headed for a collection of box stores, many of which already had long lines.

At least they're not letting the population starve. That made him wonder if the UN might use food as leverage against people. "Do what we tell you or you get nothing to eat." A lot of people might find it hard to be defiant when they're hungry.

He walked through a residential neighborhood, noticing a few homes with doors and windows smashed in. Checking to make sure no one was observing him, he ducked into one of those houses.

Kosco checked the living room. DVDs and Blue-Rays lay scattered on the floor. In the home office wires and plugs lay on a desk where a computer should be. Drawers and papers littered the floor. He sifted through some of the papers, hoping to find some evidence why the DPE would storm through this house.

He found it in a bill for an online purchase of a DVD titled *The Climate Scam.*

I guess in Saihi's world, doubting climate change equals a crime.

He left out the back door and headed west, eating a piece of jerky and a handful of peanuts he'd stuffed inside his jacket before leaving the cabin. He washed it down with a couple of slugs of water and kept walking.

A few more UN patrols drove by, paying him no mind. It was mid-morning by the time he reached his first objective, Ted Stevens International Airport.

There wasn't much in the way of high ground around it, and Kosco didn't want to risk getting too close. He hiked around the residential neighborhoods near the airport, hoping to see as much as he could.

A few planes took off and landed, transports mainly. Kosco noted the type and their directions. Some flew west, probably toward the DPE base in the Kurils, while others headed north, likely to occupied Fairbanks. Both foot and vehicle patrols guarded the perimeter, with two sentries using K9s. He also spotted a pair of Buk M1-2 mobile SAM launchers on some grassy strips by the seaplane base across from the airport.

Kosco wished he could photograph it all on his cell phone, or at the very least draw some sketches. That, however, would look suspicious, and God help him if some UN patrol caught him with those photos or drawings. All he could do was commit it to memory.

He headed north, cutting through more residential neighborhoods. He wanted to check out Merrill Field, as well as the Sullivan Arena and the university. The DPE could use those last two as command and control centers, troop barracks, or detention centers. After that he –

A passenger van whipped around the corner. Tension knotted Kosco's chest as it veered left and screeched to a stop.

Oh shit. He balled his fists.

Six people jumped out. None looked over thirty. All of them carried semi-automatic rifles and wore Friends of Peace armbands.

Kosco braced himself. Maybe he could take out a couple before they got him.

The group rushed past him, heading toward a nearby house. The Friend bringing up the rear, a lean black woman with a nose ring, stopped and stared at him, her face twisted in a harsh look. "Keep walkin', whitey."

Kosco wanted to tell her to stick it. Instead, he silently nodded and moved along. He glanced over his shoulder as the Friends broke down the door and charged inside.

When he reached the corner, a feminine scream cut through the air. He turned to find the Friends dragging a slender brunette in her mid-thirties out of the house.

"Please! Please!" she begged.

"Shut up!" One Friend threw her to the ground and kicked her.

Fury coursed through Kosco. His muscles coiled. More than anything he wanted to run over and help the woman.

But he couldn't.

Focus on the mission.

"You think you can throw anyone you want in jail?" The Friend kicked the brunette again. "Racist bitch! It's your turn to rot in jail!"

Teeth clenched, Kosco forced himself to turn away. He shut his eyes, consumed with self-loathing.

What can you do? You have no weapons. They have six rifles. You'd just get killed.

That logic did nothing to sooth his anger, his guilt. He kept thinking about the woman. A cop, maybe? Or a prosecutor? Her screams still rang in his head. He was supposed to protect Americans. Instead, he just walked away while some innocent woman got assaulted by a bunch of slimebags.

Gather intel. That's all you can do to help the country.

Kosco walked by the Sullivan Arena, which looked deserted. Down the block, he passed a fast food restaurant. A rotting, rank smell hung in the air. He grimaced and looked at the dumpster. Kosco walked over and peeked inside, the stench scorching his nostrils.

Swarms of flies buzzed around piles of discarded beef and chicken patties, French fries, and cartons of melted ice cream. He shook his head. *Why would they throw all this stuff away?*

He continued east, passing Merrill Field. Among the small civilian prop planes he spotted several DPE helicopters and anti-aircraft weapons. Kosco filed it away in his mind and headed farther down the road to the University of Alaska-Anchorage.

He couldn't get within two blocks of the place. DPE sentries and roadblocks had been set up along all roads into and out of the school.

At least I know they're using it for something.

Kosco walked north, then cut west toward downtown. He came across a few more restaurants with the rank smell of rotting meat emanating from their dumpsters. He had a hard time believing the meat at so many different places had gone bad. So why had the owners thrown it out?

Another thought stuck him. What if it wasn't the owners? What if the DPE made them throw it out? He knew Secretary General Saihi was a big-time vegan. Would he try and force that belief on everyone in Anchorage?

His forces control the city, so what's to stop him? Judging from the man's past speeches, Saihi was not a believer in letting people decide for themselves whether or not they wanted to eat meat.

Kosco passed a large bookstore, slowing when he noticed a metal garbage can spouting flames by the front entrance. A Friend of Peace exited the store with an armful of books and DVDs. She dumped them all in the fire, smiled, and headed back inside.

Farther down the block, he passed two churches gutted by fire. He had a feeling both fires had been deliberate.

Book burning. Torching churches. Throwing out meat. Arresting people because of their politics. Saihi's in full-in dictator mode.

The thumping of rotors drew Kosco's attention skyward. He spotted a small helicopter with an oval-shaped fuselage circling downtown. An Alouette III. No doubt it was providing aerial coverage for his primary objective, the Federal Building and Courthouse.

He neared a large cemetery. One block past it, he would turn right, go up another block, then turn left on 8th Street. Then he could walk past the courthouse.

The plan fell apart before he got to the intersection.

Concrete barriers blocked the road ahead. Kosco counted six DPE soldiers behind them, along with a Boxer. The next intersection over also had a roadblock.

He crossed over to 10th Street, hoping to go east, then try to access the courthouse from A Street. His jaw stiffened as he passed a pair of ballfields. He had a bad feeling it wouldn't be that easy.

Kosco stopped at the intersection and looked right. Just as he feared, the DPE blocked the road with sentries and concrete barriers, along with a Panhard VBL armored car.

He made a circuit around the downtown area. Every intersection within two blocks of the federal courthouse was guarded by the DPE.

Damn. Kosco kept walking, trying not to stare at the roadblocks for too long. Anger welled up inside him. So did a feeling of failure. Gunny was counting on him to gather intel on the courthouse. Hell, all of Marine Special Operations Command was counting on him.

But he couldn't get within spitting distance of the building.

Kosco tried to recon Joint Base Elmendorf-Richardson and the Port of Anchorage, but the DPE blocked all access points within a two-block radius. His soul drowned in defeat. That pissed him off more. He was a Marine. Not just *a* Marine, but a special ops Marine. Defeat was unacceptable.

And what's one unarmed special ops Marine supposed to do against a company's worth of soldiers and armored vehicles?

Scowling, Kosco headed east, back to the cabin.

He stepped onto the front porch at 1910 hours, more than hour after the DPE's curfew. Luckily, he hadn't encountered any DPE patrols. Both Gunny Corcoran and Baldelli were in the living room looking at their tablets when he entered.

"Good thing you're home, young man." Baldelli shot him a faux glare. "Your mother and I were worried sick about you."

Kosco grinned.

"How did the recon go?" Gunny got out of his seat.

Kosco tried to meet the older man's gaze, but failed. "Good and bad."

"What was the bad?"

"I couldn't get near the federal courthouse. The DPE had roadblocks set up at every intersection within two blocks of it. Sentries, armored vehicles, concrete barriers. Sorry, Gunny."

"Don't be. No way you coulda got through all that solo and unarmed. Just tell us everything you got."

They gathered at the kitchen table. Baldelli spread out a street map of Anchorage. Kosco took a red pen and marked down the positions of all the DPE units, defenses, and aircraft he'd seen.

"This is great." Gunny nodded. "Good job, Kosco."

"Thanks, Gunny. I just wish I could've gotten closer to the courthouse."

"Don't sweat it. At least we know what their perimeter security's like, and that they've got eyes in the sky."

"I couldn't tell from my vantage point," said Kosco, "but I'd bet that Alouette was carrying a machine gun or two. Maybe even rocket launchers."

"And I'm sure they got snipers on some of these rooftops." Baldelli swept a finger over downtown. "Maybe one or two guys with MANPADS." He used the acronym for Man-Portable Air Defense Systems.

Gunny regarded the map for a few seconds, then looked up at Kosco. "All right. Snap some pics of this map, write up a report, then transmit it all to General Dobson."

"Yes, Gunny. But there are some other things I should tell you about."

Kosco paused to take a breath. That's when he heard a low, droning noise from outside.

Engines.

Gunny and Baldelli lifted their heads and stared at the window.

"I don't know about any of you, but I'm not expecting company," said Baldelli.

"Get your weapons," ordered Gunny. "Kill the lights."

They snatched the rifles leaning against the far wall of the kitchen, then rushed about the cabin turning off lights. Kosco and Baldelli took up positions at the window to the left of the front door. Gunny covered the window on the right side. Kosco peered through the glass.

A GAZ utility car rolled onto the dirt driveway. Two helmeted figures sat in the front seat. DPE soldiers.

Two more vehicles appeared, a pickup and a passenger van. They stopped behind the GAZ. People in civilian clothes spilled out of both vehicles.

Every one of them wore a Friends of Peace armband.

THIRTY-THREE

Ruud stood back, arms folded, and gazed at the map of Talkeetna taped to the wall of Sergeant Harlow's office. Various red marks noted the locations of recon units, roadblocks, ambush sites, sentry positions, and supply depots. Much of his attention focused on the Parks Highway. Worry scratched the back of his mind. Did he have enough fighters along the highway? How much could they slow down the next DPE assault? Could they turn them back?

We could blow the living shit out of them if I had eleven hundred Marines instead of eleven hundred civilians.

He grunted. Wishing for what he couldn't have was a waste of mental energy. Besides, many of the townspeople, Krista included, proved they could handle themselves in a fight.

Against a small company that wasn't expecting any resistance. He knew they wouldn't be so lucky again. The next time the DPE came here, they'd be ready for a fight.

Well so are we. That was his hope, anyway. Ruud was determined to hold Talkeetna for as long as possible. The DPE couldn't move supplies from Anchorage to Fairbanks by ground unless they secured all the towns along the Parks Highway. Sure, they could use transport planes, but trucks were more numerous, more convenient, and less expensive. Anything he could do to inconvenience the enemy gave the U.S. military one more advantage when they arrived.

Whenever that'll be.

Ruud lowered his head, wondering how many men and women it would cost to keep Talkeetna out of DPE hands.

A cold, sick feeling swept through his stomach. Would it cost him Krista?

Someone knocked on the doorway. Ruud looked up.

Krista stood there, holding a plastic container.

"Hey." She smiled at him.

"Hi." Ruud fought to erase a horrible image from his mind of Krista's body ripped apart by bullets. He walked up to her, hugged her tight, and gave her a deep kiss.

"Wow," she stammered. "Imagine if I'd brought you a filet mignon instead of this."

"Huh?" Ruud scrunched his face in puzzlement.

Krista pulled off the lid of the container. Inside was a small meat patty, some celery sticks, and a fruit bar. Ruud salivated. He hadn't eaten since late this morning when he got a blow of stew and some saltines from Millie.

He grabbed the meat and took a bite. It had a gamey taste and was barely warm. "Deer?"

Krista nodded. "I still have plenty of it in the freezer. Though you did get the last fruit bar."

Ruud looked at the container as he chewed. Between what the townsfolk had stockpiled for the winter and what Koonooka's hunting and fishing parties had gathered, they should have enough food for the foreseeable future, so long as they rationed it. The supply of other items worried him more. How many DPE attacks could they fend off before they ran low on ammo? With bigger battles certainly ahead, the medical unit would soon find itself hard pressed to scrape up a band-aid.

"So I heard you told that DPE ass-hat to go fuck himself," said Krista.

"I did, though in a less colorful way." Ruud took another bite of his patty. Even though he hadn't seen Krista since he left their cabin this morning, he did tell Zimmer and others to spread the word through Talkeetna about his meeting with Dallku, since it likely meant a second attack was imminent.

But the day had passed quietly . . . so far.

Krista snorted and shook her head. "Did that shithead really think you'd just give yourself up like that?"

"Hey, he wanted you, too."

"Aww." Krista put a hand over her heart. "That makes me feel so special. You told him no, of course."

"Of course. Unless you burn dinner, then I told him I'd gladly hand you over."

"Asshole." She slapped his arm. "Seriously, I can't believe those dipshits really thought you'd just hold out your hands and say, 'put the cuffs on, please.'"

"Neither do I," said Ruud. "But I think they had to give it a try."

"Why?"

"Not to sound egotistical, but the UN has to have me on its most wanted list. I checked with Ginny and her friends earlier today." Ruud had given the teens the job of monitoring the internet for news beyond Talkeetna, at least on those sites not shut down by the DPE. "I saw the coverage surrounding President Moore's upcoming trial, especially on the sites under UN control. They're interviewing legal scholars, UN ambassadors who back Saihi, former Gitmo prisoners. They're also criticizing our anti-terror operations, and our interventions in Albania and Trinidad and Tobago, calling them illegal. Saihi wants the President's trial to be a show, to point out everything he thinks is wrong with this country."

"And you think he'd do the same with you?" asked Krista.

"Absolutely. He puts me on trial, then trots out a bunch of so-called witnesses who'll claim how evil and out of control the Marines are in general, and me in particular. All of it will help legitimize the UN's invasion in the eyes of the world."

"You said the DPE will come here eventually. Why not wait till then to try and get you?"

"Because in any battle, there's always the chance I won't come out alive." Ruud noticed Krista swallow. A slight shiver went through her. He paused a couple of seconds before speaking. "You can't put a dead man on trial. They need me alive."

"Then why didn't they try and take you when you told them no?"

"Because they were under a white flag." Ruud shrugged. "Okay, it's not as though no one has ever violated the rules regarding the white flag. Still, maybe the UN doesn't want to risk a Geneva Convention violation getting out, not when they're trying to paint themselves as the saviors of the world. Or maybe that Colonel Dallku has some sense of honor. Whatever the case, I'm still here and not in a jail cell."

"And for that, I'm grateful." Krista smiled. "Actually, I think everyone in town is grateful."

"I didn't realize I was so popular."

"I'm serious." Krista took a step closer to Ruud. "I've talked to a lot of people. They trust you, they believe in you. Look at everything you've done in the past four days. Who else could have done it?"

"It's been a team effort."

"Every team needs a leader, and the people in this town have no problem following you."

Ruud nodded, rubbing his thumb over his deer patty. He wondered if the residents of Talkeetna would still follow him if the bodies piled up.

"Well, so long as --"

The lights snapped off.

***

Colonel Dallku stared at the overhead images of the Parks Highway on his laptop when the radio buzzed. He turned to see the R/T operator pick up the receiver.

"Jaguar Zero One . . . Yes . . . Understood. I will inform him." The young peace enforcer put down the receiver and turned to Dallku. "Sir, power has been cut to Talkeetna."

"Good." He swiveled in his chair, staring out the open rear of the Boxer. The parking lot of the small RV park in Caswell was crowded with Jeeps, trucks, vans, a tour bus, and the centerpiece of his motorized battalion, eight other Boxers, each one armed with a heavy machine gun or grenade launcher.

He strode out of his command Boxer, barking orders to his platoon leaders. They, in turn, barked orders to their men. More than 150 peace enforcers and 90 Friends of Peace sprinted around the parking lot. They hurried inside Boxers or jumped into civilian vehicles. The groan of engines saturated the RV park.

Dallku stood through his Boxer's cupola. He watched one vehicle after another roll onto the Parks Highway and head north.

"Let's go," he called down to the driver.

The Boxer lurched forward. Dallku pressed his hands on the cool metal surface, standing straight, chest sticking out. Exhilaration rushed through him. By this time tomorrow, Talkeetna would be nothing but smoking rubble, and Lieutenant Colonel Jan-Erik Ruud would be his prisoner.

TO BE CONTINUED IN *LIBERTY'S BLOOD*, BOOK TWO OF THE FALLEN EAGLE TRILOGY.
COMING SOON

More action/adventure from John J. Rust

SEA RAPTOR

From terrorist hunter to monster hunter! Jack Rastun was a decorated U.S. Army Ranger, until an unfortunate incident forced him out of the service. He is soon hired by the Foundation for Undocumented Biological Investigation and given a new mission, to search for cryptids, creatures whose existence has not been proven by mainstream science. Teaming up with the daring and beautiful wildlife photographer Karen Thatcher, they must stop a sea monster's deadly rampage along the Jersey Shore. But that's not the only danger Rastun faces. A group of murderous animal smugglers also want the creature. Rastun must utilize every skill learned from years of fighting, otherwise, his first mission for the FUBI might very well be his last.

DARK WINGS

Mothman and the Jersey Devil. For years they have been regarded as legends. Now humanity has learned the terrifying truth. These "cryptids" are actually beings from another world, and they have invaded Earth. Delta Force Major Jim Rhyne fights to survive in occupied Kentucky. Along the way, he is joined by mysterious allies. But can he trust them, and can they defeat the invaders?

Follow John J. Rust on Facebook at www.facebook.com/johnjrustauthor and on Twitter @JohnJRust

57754938R00100

Made in the USA
Columbia, SC
15 May 2019